LOSING MYSELF

The Sequel to Holding Myself

BY

VICTORIA J. BROWN

Copyright © 2017 Victoria J Brown

The right of Victoria J Brown to be identified as the Author of the Work has been asserted by her in accordance Copyright, Designs and Patents Act 1988.

First published in 2017 by Bombshell Books

Apart from any use permitted under UK copyright law, this publication may only be reproduced, stored, or transmitted, in any form, or by any means, with prior permission in writing of the publisher or, in the case of reprographic production, in accordance with the terms of licences issued by the Copyright Licensing Agency.

All characters in this publication are fictitious and any resemblance to real persons, living or dead, is purely coincidental.

www.bombshellbooks.com

Print ISBN: 978-1-912175-63-5

Also By Victoria J Brown

Holding Myself

See where it all began for Kat in Holding Myself, the prequel to Losing Myself.

COMING SOON:

Find out what the future holds for Kat in the final book.

Bombshell Books brings you;
Finding Myself coming December 2017

Praise For Holding Myself

A wonderfully captivating story of life and struggles, with some extremely heart rendering moments. with charming and engaging characters, and I am pleased to see there is a follow on and I am so looking forward to catching up with the next chapter of Kat and Max's life and what decisions they will make next.... – Bookstormer

Holding Myself was a great choice of read, and one I highly recommend to those of you who like to kick back and relax, and become lost inside a fictional world. One thing I will end on is … please don't pick this up thinking it's chick lit because it is not, it is something altogether much deeper and meaningful. – Pageturnersnook

Having really enjoyed this book I find it hard to believe that this is Victoria J Brown's first novel as the writing just flows and the style is very accomplished. It's an easy to read novel and although I've seen it described as chick-lit, the topics it deals with are very serious and sympathetically treated. – All things bookie

This is an easy read that I read one just one session. Victoria J Brown has a wonderfully enchanting writing style and the narrative just flows so perfectly, enveloping you in Kats life right from the first page, that it's impossible to put down. She has created an extremely likeable character that we can all empathise with and recognise, bringing Kat to life so vividly that the reader feels as though they are reading about a real life friend. And that ending!! – My Chestnut Reading Tree

Can I just start by saying what a beautiful cover this book has? This is certainly an emotional, inspirational and uplifting summer read for 2017. I enjoyed reading this book, very different from what I usually read but I found it very refreshing. Kat, now what an amazing character she is. She has gone through so much in this story but somehow comes through it successfully the other side. Holding Myself is easy to read, written well and contains short chapters. I would highly recommend this story to you all if you want something a little different from thrillers. A well deserved five stars from me and I will be looking out for future books by Victoria Brown. A very 21st century book! – Gemma's book reviews

If you're looking for that short, quick read about every day life's struggles, this is the perfect summer read for you. Take yourself out of your own world for a few hours and let Kat take over for you. – Where the reader grows

I was surprised by how involved I became in both the story and the characters lives and it was a deeper read than I was expecting to find. There are lots of themes that feature in Holding Myself including grief, trust issues, love and family. They are all packaged into a fantastic rollercoaster ride of emotions not only for Kat but the reader too. – Rae Reads

To my gorgeous girls, Alexia and Gabriella
Be who you want to be.

Prologue

Twins ... as in two babies ... as in not one ... but two mini people I'd be responsible for! These were the only thoughts that had fogged my mind since I'd driven away from the hospital. Max and I had hardly spoken as we left. Before we went our separate ways, he'd kissed my forehead and said, 'We'll chat later.'

What was there to chat about? This was happening; it wasn't as if we could say, 'Oh, two babies, yeah ... about that ... any chance we can just keep one?' The alternative option no longer seemed viable after we'd seen the two fuzzy bean shapes floating around. As I'd left the car park, I'd passed Max's car. He was sitting staring into the distance. I'd pressed my horn lightly, hoping it would encourage him to start his engine.

The drive back to the salon was robotic. My senses, which had programmed in the journey, led the way. The mechanics of my brain must have prevented me from crashing: worryingly, as I reached the Great Ayton signpost I had no memory of how I'd got there.

As I was driving through the village, my wits seemed to return and I noticed the new, refurbished shop. The shop had been out of use for a few months, with old sheets and a white substance covering the windows, shielding the inside from public view. The 'To Let' sign had been removed; to be honest I wasn't sure how long it hadn't been there. I'd not really taken any notice of the shop before, but today, as two men stood on ladders applying the new signage, my body felt another weight fall upon it. The silver, glimmering words 'Lush Lucia Salon' glared back at me.

Prologue

'You're not going to believe this,' I said, as I dashed into my own salon. 'There's a new salon opening around the corner.'

'How do you know it's a beauty salon?' Mandy didn't even glance up from her lady's nails.

'Lush Lucia Salon. It can only be a beauty salon. It doesn't sound like a hair salon.'

'It's a nice name.' Mandy still didn't look at me. Her unconcerned approach caught me off guard. I'd thought they would have been in uproar, like me. Melanie, who was performing a pedicure, sat on a cushion as she painted her customer's toes. Her cheeks coloured slightly; my indignant outburst in front of the customers seemed to embarrass her.

I wish I'd known then that it had nothing to do with her embarrassment about me, but about herself.

1

11 WEEKS LATER
15 WEEKS TO GO!

'I'm sorry, Kat, but I'm going to work for myself.'

'What?' I obviously hadn't heard Melanie right.

'I feel awful, I really do, but it's the right thing for me to do.'

'I don't understand.' I was glad I was sitting down as I could feel my legs starting to weaken, my stomach twisting into a thousand knots, as she explained that she would no longer be working for me. She'd no longer be working for me when I needed her most.

'I was always going to go on my own at some point.'

'Were you?'

'I can't work here for ever.'

'But … I thought you were happy here.'

'I am … but I've got to move on.'

'But why now?'

'I wanted to wait until the babies were here, but our salon has come along really fast and we don't really have a choice.'

'You have a salon? You're not going mobile? "*We*"?'

'I'm sorry, Kat, really I am.' Sitting down on the sofa that was designed to make our customers relax before their treatments, she clasped her hands together, staring at them, as my mind searched rapidly for a way I could make her stay.

'But we could have talked about you becoming a partner here.'

'I probably would have eventually … but Mandy has given me an opportunity—'

'Mandy?'

'The thing is, I didn't realise that Mandy's dad had already invested in her.'

'Invested in her?' I was confused. Our eyes met as I searched for an explanation, but hers seemed full of remorse. Suddenly this person standing in front of me, this woman who'd been my friend, was a stranger. She twiddled with the pocket on her pink uniform, her fingers caressing the cotton material. 'But we hired Mandy to help us out.'

'Well, she was already mobile when she came here. I think she wanted to expand. But I promise, I didn't know about the salon until she offered that we go into business together. The opportunity is too good for me to turn down. I own half the business, which I would never have asked from you—'

'But we could have talked about it.'

'Her father is also going to invest in training us in other treatments.'

'But we could have done that.' I knew I was fighting a losing battle. I'd always been on top form when it came to new treatments, ahead of the game when it came to new innovations in the beauty industry. But my babies had become my focus, building a life with Max and the future we were both heading towards with trepidation.

But still … she could have asked, she could have come to me.

'He's offered for us to train in permanent make-up. You know how much money can be made from that.'

'We could have done that here.' I was repeating myself, desperate for her to change her mind. I swallowed back the tears, my chest tight as I struggled to get air into my lungs.

'I'm sorry, Kat.' Melanie's hands pressed together, tears brimmed as her lip quivered. 'She's a friend and—'

'So, what am I?'

'I can't let her down.'

'But you can let me down?' I shook my head in disbelief. 'After everything we've been through …'

'Her father has already put the money in, I can't walk away now.'

'I could have made you a partner here. I'll send you on any course you want to go on. Please, Mel, don't do this.' I hated begging, but I had no choice. I needed her.

'It's too late, the legalities have already gone through.'

'Why didn't you tell me? We could have talked about this.'

'I didn't think you'd want to give up any shares in your business.'

'I can't believe you didn't ask me.'

'Let's be honest, Kat, your head has been elsewhere for the last few months.'

A silence knotted between us, hanging in the air. My heart was racing, pounding loudly, vibrating through the fear that was enveloping.

'Where's the salon?' I looked down, not wanting to meet her eye.

'Around the corner.' Her reply was barely a whisper.

'You're not serious?'

'I can't believe this …' I spoke to myself rather than to her. 'Oh my God, you're Lush Lucia …' These past few months had been a lie … had she and Mandy been laughing at me behind my back? They'd been working beside me, and deceiving me. Anger raced through my body at top speed, swelling rapidly to fury. 'Why would you do this?'

'I'm sorry. I feel—'

'I can't believe you would do this to me.' I couldn't breathe.

'Please—'

'Please leave, Mel.'

'Please, let me explain some more and maybe we can work something out together. Perhaps we could offer certain treatments and you could offer others, help each other out.'

'Just go!'

'Kat—'

'GET OUT!' My scream was so loud my babies must have felt the force of my rage. Melanie hastily grabbed her bag and coat. She stopped to look at me, but I turned away. Blood raced furiously through my veins. I needed her to leave before I committed a crime I would later regret. The bell chimed her exit. Chimed in the harmonious way I was so used to hearing. A chime that now sounded insincere and hollow as it echoed across the empty salon.

The silence in the salon was piercing. I looked around the sanctuary that was my safe place, wretchedness searing through me as I ran to the toilet to empty my insides.

2

We sat around the kitchen table, our usual monthly takeaway displayed in front of us. It had been Lawrence's choice; as always, he'd chosen Chinese. Lawrence had become a significant figure in Suzy's life since Melanie's wedding. They'd connected instantly and not really spent a day apart since. I'd wanted to cancel tonight, having had the most horrendous day, but it was the only time Lawrence and Max seemed to catch up.

The display of Chinese roast duck, chicken in cashew nuts, mounds of rice and other delectable dishes would usually have had me more than satisfied, but I couldn't eat a thing.

'She never said anything when you were training her?' I asked Suzy, who stopped dishing up her food and stared at me.

'Honestly, don't you think I would have told you if I'd known?' She sounded slightly offended.

'She must have been planning it then, though.' I shook my head, hoping that Suzy didn't think I was blaming her. I was just searching for answers.

'It sounds like this Mandy's had a lot to do with it,' Max said as he filled a prawn cracker with egg-fried rice, dipping it into the sweet and sour sauce, the runny, sticky dressing dripping across his plate, before he forced the full cracker into his mouth.

'Mandy has a lot to answer for.' My anger was still brimming.

'Maybe she had been planning it since then, but I promise I had no idea. She stopped her fitness sessions after the wedding,' Suzy said.

'I can tell,' I said cattily.

'Ooohhhhh!' Max and Lawrence mocked me.

'I know, but she's put on more than a stone since the wedding.'

'As I've said plenty of times before, that's what happens when you suddenly stop.' Suzy spooned a few tablespoons of boiled rice onto her plate; even when having a take-away she went for the healthier option. 'She'll probably end up putting more on than her original weight.'

'Good.'

'Kat …' Her authoritative tone scolded me as if I was a small child.

'I'm just so sick. I can't believe it. I really don't know what to do.' At that, the tears came. A huge sob erupted. Guilt for being so spiteful about Melanie's weight when I was hardly one to talk, were mixed with anger that I needed to vent.

'Oh, come here.' Suzy was up from her chair, her arms surrounding me. Max and Lawrence had fallen silent.

'I'm sorry.' I tried to hold back the emotion. Embarrassment taking over, I told them I was fine and excused myself to go to the bathroom.

As I stared into the small mirror, black streaks that had formed tracks down my puffy cheeks stared back at me. I wiped away the smudges that had made dirty patterns, fought away the suffocation that had grasped my lungs. I was strong. Since Mum had died I could handle anything.

At that thought I started to cry again.

Finally, I composed myself and headed back to the dining room.

I could hear the mutters from behind the door, an exchange of words that I'd clearly missed as I heard Lawrence say, 'Hormones, mate.' They all fell silent. I'd obviously missed a crucial part of their conversation.

'I should go and check on her,' Suzy suggested.

'No need, I'm here. Sorry I'm an emotional wreck.' I tried to laugh, but a funny croaking sound escaped; maybe laughter was too much.

'You okay?' Max asked.

'Yes, I'm fine.' I nodded, catching his eye. He looked away as I sat back in my seat, drinking my cold water, hoping it would take away the fear that was running through me.

Hormones, mate. What did that mean?

Of course, I was hormonal, I'd never felt anything like the rollercoaster of emotions I'd experienced since falling pregnant. One minute I was laughing and the next I would burst into tears. I think it freaked Max out a little. It freaked me out a lot. The worst thing to set me off was TV adverts – have you ever heard anything so silly? Most would have me sobbing, because they had sad or romantic music. It's true; it was something I'd never noticed before I fell pregnant. Now, I couldn't even watch an advert about pizzas without crying ... so don't get me started on the RSPCA.

Had Max complained about my dramatics to Lawrence and Suzy? It wouldn't surprise me. We did seem to bicker quite a lot lately, but we were just trying to get used to living together. I was also petrified about this next chapter in my life: I had no idea where to start when it came to taking care of babies, while Max seemed to have forgotten they were coming.

The evening seemed to pass by slowly, not like the typical nights we would spend together. A strained ambience was upon us. Suzy and I tried to help the conversation flow, but it was so difficult when the lump that had caught in the back of my throat felt as if it was choking me. Lawrence seemed to pussy-foot around me, seemingly worried I'd dart off in tears again. And Max stayed quiet for most of the night. Which again, wasn't unusual: he had a lot on at work, so his mind was generally doing the same amount of ticking over as mine.

Suzy and Lawrence made their excuses early, leaving us by nine-thirty. Before Lawrence, Suzy would have stayed to dissect 'the Melanie situation' with me. She hugged me close before leaving, telling me she was there for me and she'd call me tomorrow. I didn't want her to go. But, at the same time, I wanted to be alone.

We watched them pull away, the gravel that layered the driveway flicking against Lawrence's wheels. My body shivered in the cool night air. Max stood close to me. I wanted him to shield me from the chill, but his arms were folded. Our bodies were only millimetres apart but I felt an utter awareness that we weren't touching.

He left me at the door, leaving me to wave off our friends.

As I shut the front door, I could hear the football commentary filling the lounge.

'I'm going to go up.' I peered round the door into the homely living room, where his masculine physique was stretched across the sofa, the remote wedged in his hand.

'You okay?' He glanced at me.

'Really tired. It's been a harsh day.'

'Hopefully, things won't seem so bad in the morning.'

'Hopefully.' I couldn't see how things wouldn't be so bad. I assumed he was being somewhat flippant because he didn't know what else to say. We seemed to have fallen into a trap and lost the ability to have natural conversation. 'Are you coming up?' I offered, hoping he would say yes.

'Not yet, just watching the footy.' He shook his head, waving the remote at the television.

'Night, then.' I closed the door, letting the tears slowly escape.

I'd had the most dreadful day. I felt as if I'd been beaten up. Melanie leaving me not only left me angry, but the hurt that was raking through me, digging into every part of my body, was so painful.

I climbed into the cold sheets, which sent an icy chill through me, but I was pleased that my inbuilt thermometer was working quite well. My temperature was playing havoc at the moment. Mainly, I was boiling; I was the one wafting my arms around for cool air while everyone else was piling on scarves, hats and mitts.

I lay in the coolness, replaying the day's events. Melanie had seemed remorseful, as if she hadn't really wanted to go. Maybe I'd imagined her sorrow. What I hadn't imagined, though, was Max's inability to comfort me, treating the whole situation as if an employee was simply going to work for someone else. Melanie had been more than an employee. She'd been my friend. She'd been the person I relied on. I couldn't get my head around how she could not only leave me, but set up in competition practically next door.

It was so frustrating to think I'd always treated her with the utmost respect. I never felt like her boss, and I certainly didn't think I behaved like one. We were more like partners, except I had the bills to pay, the taxman to worry about, the complaining customers, the marketing, the networking; but she'd benefited with big bonuses at the end of the year. I'd allowed her to build her own clientele, giving her the same scope as if the salon had been her own. I'd listened to her. I'd discussed new ideas with her. I'd given her opportunities. She could have talked to me about becoming partners; I would have been open to the idea. I would have listened if I'd known that was what she'd wanted.

I was always going to go on my own at some point. Those words tormented me as I lay in bed, trying endlessly to get myself comfy.

Was she? Was she really? She'd always talked about the salon as if it was her second home; it was where we both belonged.

For all these reasons, Max's apathy was confusing. I'd rung him after I'd closed the salon, sobbing into the handset as I drove home in a daze, nausea and panic coursing through me, tears obscuring my view. But he'd abruptly stopped me, told me he would have to call me back because he was about to go into a meeting. He didn't call me back. When he arrived home, he told me he'd had the busiest day ever, and asked me casually to put the kettle on.

Tears had threatened as I did as he asked. He was searching through his phone, his fingers skimming across the buttons, as I handed him the steaming liquid. He briefly scanned my face, and asked me what was wrong. I explained again about Melanie, expressing my concerns, telling him I didn't know what to do.

He'd told me casually, 'It will be fine, we'll sit down and work out a plan.' He'd briefly hugged me before he quickly left me alone so he could go and get changed. I could hear him chatting on the phone upstairs, and by the time he came back down, Suzy and Lawrence had arrived.

His cool approach made me feel as if I was creating a fuss over nothing. But Melanie had been with me since the beginning, and I'd trusted her and Mandy to practically run the salon while I concentrated on my babies. Pregnancy hadn't suited me in the way I'd have liked it to. Nausea seemed to bother me constantly. If I ate, I felt sick. If I didn't eat, I felt sick. My back throbbed, my ribs hurt and indigestion caused me endless sleepless nights.

I'd needed Melanie and Mandy to keep the salon going. If they weren't there to help, I'd have to find the strength to do it on my own.

I couldn't lose my salon. It was all I knew.

Nine years ago, I'd started my first 'official' job as a beauty therapist, in the salon that I now own. I say 'official' as it was the first 'proper' wage I'd received. I was qualified but I still had areas to train and perfect; still, my bank balance looked pretty good, considering what I was used to.

As soon as I'd walked through the salon door for my interview I fell in love with the place. It was exactly where I wanted to work. I loved the cosiness of the village; I'd never wanted to work for a big corporation in a town or a city. It had been the perfect place to start my career.

The flat upstairs had been empty. I spoke to the landlord who owned the whole building, and he told me it was fine for me to rent it out. Libby lived me with me, catching the bus to school, as she was adamant there was no way she was changing schools – she only had a year or so to go. You'll probably remember me telling you, I'd not really enjoyed working for my boss: she wasn't the nicest of people. But it had been ideal. I was learning the trade, in a lovely location, and living directly above my work. Perfect.

When she announced three years ago that her husband had a new job in Bristol and that she would be closing the salon, I pounced on the opportunity. There had been two other girls who worked there at the time. One of them didn't stay. She'd worked there a long time before me, explaining as she left, 'I couldn't possibly work for someone under me.'

The other therapist stayed with me for a few months before falling pregnant; in fact, she helped when it came to interviewing for a new therapist, which turned out to be Melanie, but as her bump grew bigger she decided that once the baby was born she'd become a mobile therapist.

I loved the salon with its traditional small-paned windows, reminding me of an old sweet shop. The room was big enough not to feel cramped, but not so large that we lost each other. We were all still connected as we worked, we still shared fun moments, laughter and stories. We still embraced each other's company. We still felt as if we were part of something.

When had all that changed?

When did the bond break? At which point had our relationship turned from friendship to business? When did Melanie suddenly see me as her boss, not her friend? Had she always seen me that way?

Maybe it was Mandy with her powerful influences. But I refused to blame Mandy. Yes, she'd planted the seed, then she'd watered it, growing it until it was a fully-fledged flower; a beautiful future that Melanie couldn't resist.

I wished I'd not given her so much responsibility in the salon. Maybe she was upset that I was taking a bit of a back seat; perhaps Mandy had encouraged these thoughts. I never thought for a moment Mandy was working a weave. Not for a second. She'd been an amazing actress.

***

As I knew he would be, Max was wrong. Things *did* feel as bad, if not worse, when I woke. I'd hardly slept. I'd been struggling anyway, with our babies bashing their tiny bodies together, but with the added emotional torture I must have had two hours' sleep, if that.

'Might as well get used to that,' Suzy had joked.

She'd called before she'd left for a run with Lawrence. She was in her element, meeting a fitness fanatic who would run around the world with her if she asked. A run on a Sunday morning, or any other morning, filled me with panic.

I often wondered if Max was jealous of their relationship. He'd never said, but I knew he missed the training he used to do with Lawrence and Joe. He'd found it difficult with being away in the week; the week after our first scan he'd won a huge contract in London. I'd tried to encourage him to go on a weekend, but Lawrence and Suzy seemed to be doing their own thing. I didn't want him to blame or resent me, so I'd tell him to join them as I found he lacked the motivation to do it on his own. But he always made an excuse, even when Lawrence asked him. Joe could no longer train with him as he'd moved to London when he and Gina had split up. Apparently, an amazing job offer had come along. I think he was heartbroken and had taken any old opportunity, amazing or not. But I didn't tell Max this.

I didn't really like talking about his relationship with Gina. It felt strange that she'd lived in the house before me. It was easier to block it out than scrutinise every aspect of the decor, furniture, ornaments and cutlery; analysing which parts of her were still in the house.

Had she chosen the sparkly silver toilet seat, which gleamed in the downstairs loo? An odd thing to think about, I realise, but it wasn't really something she would have taken with her. I imagined the argument, 'yes Maxwell, I'll have the loo seat!' So instead of torturing myself about the parts of Gina that were still apparent in the house, I chose to ignore them. I tried not to dissect whether Max thought about Gina every time he went for a pee.

'I'll probably only do a night or so in London. I think the Leeds office has some projects backing up, so I'll probably be home mid-week,' Max said distractedly, as he packed his suitcase later that Sunday afternoon.

'Great.' I handed him some shirts. He meticulously folded them so they would be perfect when he got them out at the other end.

'How're you feeling?' He continued to pack, but his eyes met mine cautiously. It was the first time he'd asked me all day.

'I'm worried about going in tomorrow.' I admitted, sitting on the edge of the bed, letting the wave of nausea pass over me.

'You'll be fine. Why don't you contact the college tomorrow and put an advert in the paper for a new therapist?'

'Sophie's been great over the last few months. She'll probably be able to do a few more treatments.'

'You're still going to need some more help, Kat: you've already given yourself a ridiculous time frame.' He was referring to my non-existent maternity leave. He opened one of the drawers and took out numerous pairs of underpants and socks. His back was towards me. I studied his masculine shoulders. His broad physique held such presence and his magnetism had an innocent quality I'd always found endearing.

'You need to do something, Kat,' he told me when I didn't answer him.

'I know.' I spoke more into the air than to Max as I lay back on the bed, feeling the cosiness of the cushions.

'Christmas is coming, it's your busiest time …'

Staring at the ceiling, I didn't answer him.

'So, you need to sort this now, or you'll be popping into hospital to have the babies and then popping back to work.'

'I'll sort something.' What? I didn't know.

'You need that time off, Kat,' he said sternly, pressing down the lid of the suitcase. 'I don't want you having our babies in one of your treatment rooms and then—'

'Okay … I'll sort things tomorrow.' I needed him to stop lecturing me.

'If you need anything my mum's only down the road,' Max said, as he zipped the suitcase.

I nodded, biting my lip wanting to tell him to stay: it wasn't his mum I needed, it was him.

As I watched him pack it felt strange to be in the same room as him, but feel miles apart.

I wondered if he could have left his departure a little longer. Did he really need to leave this evening?

As he pulled away, the chippings spattering against his wheels, the headlights stretching to full beam as he flashed his goodbye, I knew he had no choice. He was so busy, it was unfair to ask him to stay.

But I'd wanted to ask him to hold me all night. I didn't want to face the morning alone. But I also wasn't sure if he would have stayed if I'd asked him to.

Over the past few months we'd drifted apart. I knew he was busy at work, but his mind was always elsewhere. I sometimes felt as if I was an inconvenience in his life. I worried that he'd stayed with me only for the babies. Suzy would tell me I was hormonal (the word was used a lot to excuse my behaviour and what she called 'irrational thoughts'). But I did wonder if he was having doubts: about us. Although these thoughts tormented me, I didn't dare ask.

I was scared of the answer.

Before we'd decided to go ahead with the pregnancy he'd had his own life and our six months together had been such fun. We'd had no real commitment, whereas now the honeymoon period was well and truly over.

I'd moved in two months ago, and all we seemed to do was bicker, not full-blown arguments, but bitty, insignificant disputes. I'd put it down to hormones, but I often wondered if that was an excuse.

Our first anniversary of being together was looming and I did sometimes wonder if we actually knew each other. But I would push these thoughts away, telling myself it was definitely the hormones. It was stupid things that wound me up, like how he didn't put the toothpaste cap back on, put the toilet seat down or pick up his towels after a shower. And he hated that I nagged him about these things, and that I was stuffing my face now that I had no waistline to worry about (although if Suzy could hear that argument she'd soon put Max right and tell him I wasn't that bothered beforehand). Plus, I told him, 'I need to eat or I feel sick,' not mentioning that I felt just as sick after eating.

After Max had left I ran the bath, something I'd routinely done every night for the past few weeks. I lay in the hot water, aware I shouldn't really have it at such a high temperature, wrapping the bubbles around my large body, rubbing the soft soapiness into my arms, loving the sensation of my body feeling weightless in the heated water. I would lift my backside off the bottom of the bath and feel my body lightly float back down as I concentrated on the warmth rather than my unrested thoughts.

After settling into Max's bed (I was still trying to get used to calling it 'our'), my dressing gown fully wrapped around me and my bump – well, nearly – and the television blaring out some bizarre comedy act, I tried to convince myself that Max was right: everything would be fine.

Not only with the salon, but with me and him.

He was always preoccupied but he had lots on at work. I told myself this every time he dismissed me. I told myself this even though Melanie leaving was so devastating, and he'd not offered me any kind of consolation or advice, except to find new staff before I popped the babies out at work, mid-facial. But then, I'd learned this about Max: business was business.

He could probably see the opportunity Melanie had been given. He could probably understand why she'd done it. Not that he would say this to me, of course.

I, however, only knew I would never have done it to her.

So, as these thoughts wrestled I convinced myself this was the case with Max. It was business. I had to fight any doubts I was having about him wanting me, because although I knew we were a little unsettled, it was all new; we'd been thrown in at the deep end, we were bound to be apprehensive. But we would get through it.

I told myself this, over and over, as I wrapped the covers around my body, folding the feathered duvet around my bump, loneliness smothering me.

3

I could have thrown up when I pulled up outside the salon. The place I'd made my home was desolate, although nothing but sentiment had changed. The morning skies were darkened by the heavy rain.

I stared aimlessly at the drops that hit my windscreen, bashing together as they slid slowly down the glass. I'd purposely driven past their salon: I couldn't help it. Shiny new lights bordered their windows, the 'Lush Lucia Salon' sign gleamed and a customer – I recognised her instantly as a regular of Melanie's – was already entering their new abode. I'd been watching my new competition for nearly three months, waiting for their big reveal, a launch, maybe, but there had been nothing.

Obviously now I could see why.

I was annoyed at myself for not noticing. How could I have been so stupid? They were doing it right under my nose and I'd not suspected a thing.

If Melanie hadn't told me herself, I'd have argued in court: 'She would never do that to me.' I would have shouted from the witness box. My instinct about others, I'd always thought, was a great talent I possessed; but maybe not.

I pressed the button that automatically lifted the shutters before I left the warmth my car heaters had created, then walked briskly into the windy downpour. My flat pumps tried to avoid the small puddles, but dirty water splashed against my legs, soaking my tights. My stockinged toes uncomfortably dampened, I mumbled expletives to myself and wished I'd put my boots on.

I entered the coldness of the salon. The hollow space held a feeling of solitude; the amity of the place I loved so much was absent. I was pleased when Sophie came in two minutes later, taking away the emptiness. I was even happier when she told me she'd known nothing about Melanie and Mandy's scheme.

'They never spoke to any customers in front of me about their salon,' she said. I wondered if she was lying, but didn't probe her; what good would it have done any of us if she'd told me she *did* know?

The October weather was proving to be dismal; it matched my mood. The rain bounced from the panes, dripping as if crying out its pain to the world. I sat watching each drop as if they were my own tears of misery and hurt. Usually I'd feel protected and cosy in my safe haven, but today I felt vulnerable and stripped; bare and naked for all to see. My customers would be watching to see how I dealt with this. Should I air my grievances to them, so they could see my emotional side? Would they trust me if I let rip on how angry and hurt I was? Would they think me unstable, a little unbalanced? Or did I show my professional side? If I didn't betray any emotion, if I said things like, 'Everyone has to have a start in life; I wish Melanie well,' would they think me cold?

A few customers had called this morning to cancel but I tried not to take it as a bad sign; many customers did rearrange their appointments when the weather was bad. However, Melanie and Mandy's diaries were full; they had the most appointments, and even Sophie had more than me. I'd backed off doing massages, facials and any other treatments that required me to stand for long periods of time, as requested by the midwife. I'd sat at the nail table for the past few months, but even then, that didn't help my back.

I'd depended on Melanie to keep everything running as smoothly as possible until I could focus again, and my own role had become more of an admin assistant than a salon owner – greeting customers, answering the telephone – but I thought we were supposed to be a team. I'd told her endlessly, especially over the last few months, how much I appreciated her help. I'd said on numerous occasions, 'What would I do without you?'

Those words haunted me now.

How could I have been so stupid to miss something so vital? Remember how I was always determined not to take my eye off the ball? Laughable now.

I wasn't so angry at Mandy. She'd only worked for me for a short time so I hadn't built such a friendship with her. It was Melanie with her bare-faced lies and shrewd antics who'd hurt me. I did wonder if Mandy had forced her arm, but it didn't matter: she'd still betrayed me.

It was done.

I usually had the ability to mentally shut off, but unfortunately this was one of those times when I couldn't bury my head.

I had to face this full-on.

With that in mind, I enquired at the college for qualified therapists, in hope that some newly trained girls were searching for work. They had a few girls so I asked if they could pass on my contact details.

Sophie, who'd been amazing, had placed a cup of steaming coffee in front of me. I didn't have the heart to tell her I wasn't drinking coffee at the moment. Melanie had known this.

I suddenly felt a renewed sense of loss.

While I was waiting for another customer to arrive, Clare practically flew through the door, holding onto the frame as the wind forcefully pushed her in. 'Oh, my Lord, how windy is it?' Her dramatic entrance made me smile, as she hugged me close. Our relationship had gone from strength to strength since I'd fallen pregnant. Max had been surprised at how well we got along since we'd accepted each other for who we were.

'Max told me, and I was passing by so I had to call in. I can't believe it, Kathryn. I should go and tell that girl she shouldn't bite the hand that feeds her.'

'I doubt it will do any good.' I smiled, touched by her motherly support.

'Well, Kathryn, you have the most precious things arriving soon, they can't take that joy away from you. So, try not to worry about them too much.' She smiled as she delved into a carrier bag that was wrapped around her wrist. 'This should cheer you up. I couldn't resist.'

She pulled out two miniature outfits, white trouser sets with bunnies bouncing across the bottom. They were adorable, but Clare had bought so much stuff it was starting to become annoying. I don't mean to sound ungrateful, but I was hoping to buy things with colour once the babies were here. At the moment, they had enough outfits in white to last a year. Plus, if the babies were different sexes I didn't want them dressed the same.

'They're lovely, Clare, but you really must stop buying things,' I said, hoping she would finally get the hint.

'I can't help it. These are simply adorable.' She held them up again, as if showing off a piece of art, a proudly crafted sculpture that needed admiring from all angles.

'They *are* lovely but honestly I don't think I can fit anything else into the wardrobe.'

'I'll have to buy you a new wardrobe, then.' She laughed. She wasn't joking!

The phone rang, making me jump a little. As always, I answered professionally. 'Soothing Salon, how can I help you?'

'Do you want me to come down there and sort her out?' Libby's words seethed through the handset.

'If you think you can take her on.' I joked with my sister, knowing full well Libby would eat Melanie for breakfast, but as for Mandy … maybe not!

'Marianne told me last night. I can't believe that silly bitch. What a complete arse!'

'I know,' I sighed loudly.

'I never liked that Mandy either.' She'd only met her a few times, but still I appreciated my sister's support. 'All that make-up and her hair always bloody perfect.'

'Kat,' Clare whispered, her hand signalling for my attention, 'I'll call you later.' She gave me a little wave. I nodded and mimed, 'Okay,' as she left into the blustery winds.

'I just can't believe I didn't see it coming,' I ranted at Libby, although quietly so Sophie and her customer couldn't hear too much.

'I didn't see it either.' This was no comfort, as Libby was generally wrapped in her own world, and never saw anything coming.

'Anyway, it's happened now. I've just got to figure out how on earth I'm going to keep the place running and give birth to two babies.'

'We're all here for you, any help you need, just shout.'

'Thanks, Lib.' I was being polite. Libby wasn't a beauty therapist and I wouldn't be leaving the babies with her: leaving them with an assassin would have felt safer. But still I appreciated her offer.

'Anyway, I was ringing to say what a bitch!' I shook my head at her ability to be crass but lovable. 'I've got to go, Calvin is taking me to uni; but you know I'm here.'

She was gone before I had a chance to ask about Calvin. I'd thought she didn't see him as much since they were no longer housemates. Admittedly, I hadn't seen her much since she'd enrolled on the teacher training course a few weeks ago, but she seemed to have settled down. When I called at Marianne's she was usually out at the library or with her new 'uni friends'. I think living with Marianne had helped her, although Marianne did spoil her and Libby wasn't complaining. Since Dad died, which was only a few months ago, Marianne had turned her focus onto Libby. I knew Marianne was the maternal type. She needed to feel she was taking care of someone; she needed to feel she had a purpose.

Mrs D came in, shifting my thoughts abruptly from Libby. I wasn't sure if she had an appointment: I couldn't see her name in the diary.

Oh God, don't tell me I'd double-booked; that was all I needed.

She closed the door against the ghastly weather, moving confidently in her extremely high heels.

'Hello, Mrs Donnelly, how are you this morning?' My false smile played its part.

'I'm not good actually, Kathryn. That's why I've come to see you.'

'Would you like to come through for a coffee?'

'No, it's only a flying visit.' She took off her black leather gloves, her perfectly manicured fingers grasping them in one hand. 'Look, I've come to tell you face to face because I don't like gossip.' Of course you don't! 'I'll no longer be using your services.'

'Oh!'

'I came to you in the beginning because you were my therapist but over the past few months you've passed me over to Melanie.'

'That's because I've had so much going on, but I'm back now.' I was struggling to get air into my lungs as I forced myself to speak.

'Now, come on, Kathryn, we know that's not going to happen when these babies are born.'

'I'm sorry I've let you down.' I could feel my lip beginning to quiver. I bit it hard, in hope to keep back the tears, trying to keep my dignity.

'You can't take this personally. That's why I wanted to tell you to your face. I'm not going to be like your other clients who will ring you up with their phoney excuses. I thought I owed you an explanation.'

'You don't owe me anything.' I tried to smile. She didn't owe me a thing: she paid for a service and I delivered. It was an exchange, a monetary trade in the exact way that it was for products in a supermarket. Admittedly though, I *did* hope for customer loyalty in the way people bought Heinz ketchup, but then I'd not been delivering in the way Heinz do. If I had, then I would have continued to do Mrs D's treatments and not passed her to Melanie. The list of customers I'd passed to Mandy suddenly sprang to my mind.

'I also wanted you to know that I won't be spreading the word amongst my friends; they will make their own decisions. If they do decide to join Melanie that has nothing to do with me.'

'Thank you.'

'Well, I best be off.' She walked towards the door, holding the handle tight as she turned to face me. 'If you can cancel all my—'

'Yes, I understand.'

'Good luck with everything.' She attempted to smile, but her eyes displayed sadness. I hoped it was regret and she would change her mind. 'I'm sorry it has come to this. You're a very good therapist, one of the best. One day when things are sorted for you, I will come back.'

I nodded and smiled, unable to speak as she left. It was regret. It was regret that I hadn't taken care of her properly. My service to people like Mrs D was all they lived for. Her three or four weekly treatments were her saviour, gave her a reason for living; and I'd let her down. But as I watched her walk towards her car in the pouring rain, her heels elegantly clicking against the wet pavement, the puddles splashing around her expensive, sleek feet, I knew she had the power to ruin me.

She may not tell her friends, but it didn't matter because I knew they would already know. That's how her clique worked: whispers, rumours, hearsay.

So, as I watched one of the most influential people walk away, I knew the war had just begun.

4

8 WEEKS LATER
7 WEEKS TO GO!

'I'd just like to say it has been a wonderful thirty-five years married to this amazing woman.' Henry was gazing longingly at Clare, his arm around her shoulder, as she shook her head in mock embarrassment. 'Clare has always been my rock, she's always been there, she's the reason this marriage works.'

'You're not wrong there,' a woman shouted from the back of the crowd. Laughter rumbled across the room like a wave. Friends they had known for years raised their eyebrows, and drinks were guzzled back quickly as an uncomfortable atmosphere clouded the party.

I studied their friends; maybe I was imagining the discomfort that seemed to hang uneasily in the air. It seemed unnoticeable to Henry. Clare, however, was blushing slightly, her fingers curling through her hair. Something was underlying, I'd never noticed anything before, but then I'd not really been introduced to many of their friends.

'So, please raise your glasses, everyone, to my wonderful wife.' Henry jerked his crystal glass out in front of him. Champagne sailed into the air, dripping from his fingers, as he gracelessly tried to lick off the remnants. Clare elbowed him. Henry had not been reserved in his drinking, whereas I knew there was no way Clare would allow anyone to see her less than sober. I'd never even seen Clare tipsy. A glass of wine, two at a push. But her cool reserved self would always be maintained. I had to admire her in some ways; I'd love to have that willpower. I already had bottles stacking up for when the babies arrived.

The quartet that Clare had hired started to play their soft, subtle tunes in the background as the thirty-odd guests chatted to each other. Loud voices rose higher as they tried to talk above one another, drunken laughter rang out, candles burned brightly, flickering as if in rhythm with the delicate music. I searched for Max through the mixture of happy faces. He was deep in conversation with an older man, holding his glass of wine and nodding as the man spoke intensely at him. It seemed far too serious to interrupt.

I needed to sit down; my back was throbbing from the heels. Yes, I'd managed some, only two and a half inches, but still, it was progress. I'd been so tempted to search for the killer four-inch, pink lace pair that would have lightened my black outfit, but knew I'd suffer far too much later. I'd not really thought about buying 'party clothes' as I'd not done much 'partying'. I'd pushed Clare and Henry's celebration to the back of my mind, so when the day arrived, I had nothing to wear but black.

I had, however, put a pink scarf with the tight, figure-hugging maternity dress, in hope that Max would notice my efforts.

But he didn't.

Since I'd fallen pregnant all compliments had diminished. If anything, he'd tell me constantly how tired I looked. Or that eating for two was simply an excuse and that I'd struggle to lose the weight when the babies were born.

As I scanned the room, not knowing who to talk to, as I said I didn't know many of their friends. But I'd thought Clare may have talked *of* me to them. So, I found it slightly bizarre that only a few of her friends had welcomed me. I thought most of their guests would have noticed the huge addition to my body that protruded below my breasts, as they stopped and said, 'You must be Kathryn.' But no-one did.

I wondered if she'd only told her close friends about me and Max. Did she not want the village community knowing 'her

Maxwell' was living in sin, let alone knowing his girlfriend was pregnant?

Clare had asked us about marriage, but Max had told her to move out of the dark ages. If she was embarrassed I was fine with this, as it felt nice to blend into the background; to be unknown.

'Kat, dear, how are you?' Jack Haslow was in front of me. One of Henry's good friends, plus the 'family accountant': Henry's, Max's, and because of them, mine.

'Hello, Jack, lovely to see you,' I said, as he leaned towards me, kissing both my cheeks.

'Henry says things are not good with your business …'

'Did he?'

'Come and talk to me … we need to talk.' His eyebrows raised, a serious expression covering his handsome face.

'Yes,' I said. 'I will.'

'Look forward to it,' he said, before he was diverted by another gentleman.

Henry had told Jack things were not good; did everyone know my personal business?

I left the noisy kitchen, heading down the hallway to the lounge, where I hoped to sit quietly. The door was slightly ajar. Opening it a little I peered into the room to ensure I wasn't interrupting anyone.

A couple were enfolded into each other on Clare's classic 'untouchable' leather sofa. Kissing passionately, her arms were wrapped around his neck, her dark curls bounced as he vigorously ran his hand up her back. I tried to step back quietly but the door creaked, the couple quickly ceased caressing. Gina met my eye.

'Kat,' she called out in alarm, as if she was surprised to see me at the party. 'Excuse us, don't go … come in.'

'Oh, I don't want to interrupt,' I said, mortified I'd just walked in on their bedroom antics.

'Don't be silly, it's good to see you.' She rose from the seat, walking towards me. I felt my back stiffen. Her hands were upon mine, pulling me gently into the room, leading me to the sofa that was opposite the one she was about to practically fornicate on. 'This is Dave.'

'Hi.' He lifted his hand briefly.

'Hi,' I replied, really wanting to leave.

'So, look at you. How have you been?'

'I'm great, thanks,' I lied.

'You look fantastic,' she lied.

'I didn't realise you were seeing someone else.' I smiled at Dave who hadn't spoken, but was drinking, what looked like a Jack Daniels, from a small glass.

'It's only been a few weeks …' She grinned at Dave, who winked at her. 'Joe just happened to be a bit full-on.' I nodded, unsure what to say. She was obviously drunk, and my sober-self found it hard to join in her gossip.

'I'm not full-on, am I babe?' Dave teased. Gina giggled as he winked at her, then grossly licked his lips.

'Such a tease.' Gina laughed. I forced a smile.

'What are you guys doing in here?' Paula appeared. I wanted to hug her for stepping in at the right time. 'Hello, Kat, how are you feeling?'

'I'm good, thanks.' I smiled, turning to her, hoping she would sit down and stay with us.

'Clare said you've been so tired and quite sickly,' she said sympathetically.

'Part and parcel, I suppose.'

'Would it be rude, Mum, if Dave and I leave?' Gina asked permission as if she was a teenager accompanying her mum to a 'grown-up' celebration.

'Now?' Paula's eyes widened.

'In half an hour?'

'Gina, seriously …?'

'An hour?' Gina said bleakly. Paula raised her eyes, shaking her head. I noticed she'd not acknowledged Dave. 'I'll fake an illness.'

'You're an adult, Gina, you know what's right and wrong.' Paula, tight-lipped, stared at her daughter.

A silence fell on the room. Dave pushed his hand through his long dark hair as he watched Gina intently. Gina bit her lip like a chastised child. While Paula, who seemed to be strangling the stem of the wine glass, continued a glare of disappointment. In fact, if it was at all possible, I would have expected Gina to have burst into flames from her mother's glower.

I didn't know where to look. Or what to say. Gina was about to use my excuse: I was going with the feigned illness. (I thought mine more plausible than hers.)

'Anyway, I best get back to the party,' Paula said stiffly.

'Me too.' I stood, desperate to leave. 'Better find out where Max is.'

'I'm here,' Max announced, entering the sitting room. Damn. 'Hey, so this is where the party is.'

'Hiya, Max.' Gina stood unsteadily, lurching towards him. He caught her as she spilled into his arms.

'Hang on, girl, had a bit too many, have we?' he laughed, as he held her upright.

'I had to drink before I came,' she whispered, her finger to her lips. She turned to Dave, and pointed, quite rudely I thought, but it was best I stayed quiet. 'This is Dave. Dave, this is Max.'

'Max ...' Dave nodded, his eyes narrowing together.

'Nice to meet you.' Max gestured a handshake, holding his hand out towards Dave. Gina had obviously mentioned Max, as it was clear Dave's drunken mind was reviewing her ex. I felt the urge to wrap my arms around Max, pull him to my side, but how obvious would that be? Awkwardly, Max pulled his hand away.

'So, how have you been?' Max turned back to Gina.

'Great ... yeah ... brilliant.' Gina smiled, but her lip quivered as her eyes began to water. Suddenly tears erupted as she fell into a burst of emotion.

Instinctively I went towards her. Sitting back down, I wrapped my arm around her tiny shoulders.

'Are you okay?' I asked softly.

'She's drunk, I'll call for a taxi,' Dave said, pressing numbers into his mobile.

'Look at you.' She met my eyes. Her nose had started to run and she rubbed it with her hand. The elegant, petite figure I'd first met was washed away in this wrecked state. 'You're so lovely.'

'So are you.'

'I'm not,' she cried dramatically. I glimpsed at Max, who was frowning at us both. 'This man loves you.' She pointed at Max, then dropped her hand to the floor. 'He really loves you.'

'Come on Gina. I think we should get you some fresh air.' Max stepped in.

'I tried to get him back, you know …' She peered at me, her eyes rolling slightly.

'I know.' I nodded, remembering how Max had told me they'd had one last date before we'd officially got together.

'No … you don't understand.'

'Gina, I think it's best you go outside.' Max knelt beside her. 'Come on, you need some air.'

She gazed at him, then gently stroked his face. My heart swelled, beating at a faster rate as my breath echoed in my ears. She turned back to face me, smiling. She then lifted her hand and stroked my cheek. I found myself suddenly feeling sorry for her. She would be so ashamed in the morning.

'I asked him to come back to me when Joe and I split up,' she announced.

'You did?' I glared at Max, who was shaking his head.

'I did.' She swallowed, and sitting up straight she circled my bump mid-air with her finger. 'But I didn't know you were pregnant.'

'Taxi will be here in five.' Dave stated, as if this conversation had nothing to do with him. I acknowledged him with a smile, whereas Max and Gina totally ignored him.

'He told me it was you he loved and that he would never leave you.' She started to cry again. Max shook his head, his face slightly ashen. Although she'd revealed this truth, I still felt sorry for her. I was a little annoyed that Max hadn't told me, but pleased, without wanting to gloat, about the outcome of the conversation.

'Do you want me to come outside with you?' I asked her, watching her head sway in her hands.

'But we did kiss,' she suddenly admitted.

'You did!?'

'Gina,' Max warned, I glared at him, my insides churning.

'It was a goodbye kiss,' Gina said. I nodded, my gut retching as if she'd punched me. 'Oh, God, I think I'm going to be sick …' She jumped from her seat and ran from the room, her hand covering her mouth, her heels tapping rapidly against the wooden floor of the hall. The downstairs toilet door opened and slammed shut.

I stood up to face Max, who shook his head in what seemed like bewilderment. 'I'll go and help her,' I offered.

'I'll go.' Dave lifted himself from his seat, his tall lanky body carrying him slowly forward, swaying as he grabbed the door on his way out.

'I hope she's okay,' I said, remembering many a time I'd been in that situation. Maybe not making such an announcement, but I'm sure I could think of numerous occasions where I'd totally embarrassed myself.

'About what she said—'

'You should have told me.' I abruptly stopped Max.

'I know, I'm sorry, but she made it sound more than it was.'

'But you kissed her.'

'It was nothing … I promise.'

'I wish you'd told me.' What else could I say? They'd kissed, but he'd told her he wanted me. That he loved me.

'I wanted to, but I didn't see the point in bringing something up that could cause an argument, when it meant nothing.'

'I appreciate what you said to her,' I mumbled.

Each week that had passed seemed to dig a bigger gap between us. As we looked at each other, the barrier was obvious. I was scared to move forward, to hold out my arms and pull him close to me.

'I meant it, Kat.' He shuffled his feet slightly, as he peered up sheepishly to meet my eye. 'But I'm not sure where we are at the moment.' Heat was rising through my body; tears pricked as I fought them back.

Don't do this here? Not now. Not in front of everyone.

Suddenly, as if reading my thoughts, he leaned forward and kissed my forehead, pulling me close to him, so that my face rested against his chest. I could smell his aftershave, and the alcohol on his breath.

'Let's get back to this party.' He ended the conversation that would need to be finished later.

We left the room, as Gina, pale and deathly-looking, stumbled towards us. Her mascara had smudged under her teary eyes. Her perfected black curls had lost their vitality, and a few dirty strands stuck to her cheeks. She leaned towards me, hugging me close, her vile breath assailing me, as again I thought I might throw up myself. 'I'm sorry,' she murmured.

Dave forcefully grabbed her arm. 'Come on, the taxi's here,' he snapped rudely at her. I assumed his curtness was because the sofa antics didn't look as if they were going to reach the bedroom.

As she left, my heart went out to her. I really wouldn't want to be her when she awoke in the morning. Max took my hand and led me through to the kitchen. I followed, a tingle of warmth and pride running through me. I knew that it could so easily have been Gina showing a united front with Max.

But it wasn't her, it was me.

His words, though, were troubling me, '... *but I'm not sure where we are at the moment.*' Did that mean he wanted to leave? I hadn't thought it was that serious. In fact, I'd wondered if Max had even noticed our distance.

But I couldn't lose him. I was already on the verge of the salon being ripped from my hands.

So, I would have to do whatever it took to make this relationship work.

5

'Let's go out for tea tonight.' Suzy was jovial, but my heart wasn't in it.

'Suz, I really can't–'

'Yes, I know, that's the problem. I need to get you out.'

'Get out? I was at Clare's party only a few nights ago.'

'No, that's not going out and enjoying yourself. That's pressure, that's not relaxing with a friend.'

'Max will be home later.'

'What time?'

'Ten-ish.' I contemplated lying, telling her teatime, but he never arrived home that early if he was travelling back from London.

'So, we'll go out for tea.'

'I'm happy to stay in and have my bath–'

'I can't believe I'm competing with a bathtub.'

'It's not you–'

'I'm not taking no for an answer.' She paused, while I thought rapidly how I could get out of this. 'You'll be home by seven or eight.'

'Alright, then,' I tried to hold the sigh in, but failed.

'It will do you good.'

'If you say so.'

We decided on a venue before saying our goodbyes. I appreciated Suzy wanted to take me out, ensuring I wasn't wallowing away on my own, but the last few months had been so hard. Every day was an effort; trudging through each second was really taking its toll on me.

Since Melanie had announced her not-so-wonderful news, I'd struggled to find suitable staff. The college would send me unreliable candidates who were either hungover or had never performed a treatment since leaving college. The first two weeks had been horrendous: Mandy and Melanie had literally wiped out my diary.

Sophie still denied all knowledge, but they'd told nearly all the customers who'd walked through my door their plans, so their regulars were bound to follow suit. They'd built a relationship with them, especially Melanie: she'd formed some strong connections over the last few years. I'd encouraged her to do this. It was what we were about.

Admittedly, I hadn't expected it to backfire.

It had also become apparent they'd gone through my database and systematically acquired every customer's contact details. They probably had an identical file of customers on their computer. It was Marianne who had convinced me that this had happened: she'd received a promotional leaflet the week they'd opened their new salon. If they hadn't deleted Marianne from their list, then they couldn't have deleted anyone.

I'd been secretly pleased they'd messed up a little, to be honest. Telling Marianne this was good in a way, as we could keep an eye on their promotional literature: offers, discounts and new treatments. I'd know what they were doing without having to ask customers, or drive past at night trying to scan their windows for evidence.

Yes, I may have dressed all in black a few evenings – hoodie included – pen and paper in hand as I'd copied down their offers, scanned their premises with my face squashed against their window. You see, they even promoted at night, with their flashy lights, big welcoming signs. I'd contemplated leaving my shutters up, but my lights weren't as contemporary and sleek – we were cosy and traditional. I'd always liked that about my salon; I'd convinced myself this since I'd studied the bank balance wondering if I could invest in some blue and white external uplighters that would brighten the skies, our logo shadowed in the air like Batman's. But even when I'd considered the cheaper lights, it wasn't the cost of the lights that scuppered the idea, but the labour involved in making them work.

When Marianne had handed me the first promotional leaflet she'd received, a silver and pink feather had fallen from the dusty pink envelope, and I nearly tore it up in a rage.

They'd used the feather motif. How dare they?

We placed feathers in our vouchers, and they'd stolen our personal touch, our identity, and cloned it. Could they not think of their own ideas? Clearly not. Maybe the business wouldn't last. If they couldn't develop their own trademark, stamp their own distinctive feature on their business, what chance did they stand?

I'd tried to convince myself, but I knew it didn't matter. She could have hearts, balloons, flying bloody elephants on her leaflets: the damage was done. She'd already worked her way through the core, drilling into the foundations and overturning what I'd worked so hard to achieve.

The business that had taken me years to build could be theirs instantly.

We had half the customer base we used to have, but still an extra pair of hands was needed. I was trying to think ahead; the babies were coming, and I was hanging on by a thread. I didn't want to give up. I wanted to show them they couldn't beat me. I wouldn't go down; not without a fight anyway. The problem was, that fighting spirit had declined rapidly. I was so exhausted, so tired, I just wanted to sleep.

In the first week, I realised I had to take some action, as another customer had said she'd received a phone call from Mandy, inviting her to try one of their treatments for free. I couldn't compete with free treatments. However, we upped our promotions to our loyal customers, enabling them to buy one treatment and get another free. Within a week, they'd matched my promotion but undercut all my prices. I knew I'd have had more of a chance if I hadn't let Melanie run the salon for months on end.

But hindsight is a wonderful thing.

Most of the customers I used to treat had been passed over to Melanie and Mandy, so they wanted to stay with them, knowing I'd be off soon having babies. Even though I knew this, I tried so hard to get our customers back; I made a point of ringing every single one of them, I didn't ask Sophie to do it, I wanted them to see I was still here. My personal service was still available. I offered them loyalty cards, discounts, free products ... anything I could think of that would entice them. I even attempted a few networking events, but people were more interested in my bump and what had happened with Melanie than they were in helping me save my business. Some booked appointments, but many cancelled. Everyone was so busy. People are busy.

We'd even had a bit of revamp, changing the room around a little. I bought some new red and black towels that were a bit different from the pink we'd had for years, new candles, a new chandelier and a vibrant black and red luxurious rug with matching cushions, in hope the expenditure would show our customers we were here to stay.

I even enrolled Sophie on a permanent make-up course. It seemed more viable for *her* to complete the training. We'd have done it together, but one of us needed to stay in the salon, try and keep the customers who had stayed with us.

I was willing to tackle Mandy and Melanie head-on. I'd also made an agreement with a woman I'd met through networking, a nurse who'd moved into the Botox arena. Mrs D being my first port of call, I'd hoped I hadn't sounded as if I was begging when I'd casually phoned her to explain our new service.

'I'm already using Mandy's therapist,' she'd told me.

'But you do realise they should be a qualified nurse?'

'She is. It's Mandy's sister. She *is* a nurse, but since the salon opened she's qualified so she can perform Botox.'

The conversation had ended quickly, as I fought the urge to throw the phone across the room. I'd wondered if her sister was a partner in the business, as well as Melanie. But then, she couldn't be as Melanie had said she owned half the business. I assumed Mandy had offered Melanie such a large stake because she needed her. Mandy – or her father – was the one with the money, but Melanie was the one with the large, loyal customer base: the bloody base she wouldn't have had if I'd not given her the opportunity.

Mrs D had been right: many customers had made elaborated excuses, while others had not bothered to turn up. Sophie was still adamant that Mandy and Melanie never discussed their new plans in front of her, but if that was the case, how the hell did all my customers know about their new venture? Every single customer knew what was happening; they were poaching my customers before they'd even left. Mandy, not Melanie, had apparently been promoting her new salon while working for me.

This was supposed to be our busiest time of the year. It was December in a few days; our diary should be chock-a-block. But instead it appeared bleak. I'd felt the urge to scribble made-up names into the gaps, in hope it would make me feel better. I used all my energy to promote the salon, but it seemed whatever I did, Mandy and Melanie were already doing it, or they'd undermine my efforts by offering a better package. Not only was my strength dwindling fast, but so were my resources. My bank balance was expending more than it was expanding. I couldn't go on spending to promote the salon if we weren't reaping the rewards.

I'd tortured myself over and over about my failure to see the signs. None of my customers had admitted to me what was going on while Mandy had worked for me, but I remembered how a few of my loyal customers had warned me indirectly: 'I don't gel with her.' 'Bit too loud.' 'Bit obnoxious.' And I remembered how one of them had told me, 'I'm not too keen, there's something about her, I think you need to be careful.' At the time, I'd thought she was paranoid; maybe she didn't really like anyone. I didn't believe her. But then, I wouldn't have: Mandy was putting on a huge act for me. I know I was looking out for my babies, ensuring my health was as good as it could be, but I couldn't have been so blind. Surely.

Mandy had been so polite, so friendly and warm-hearted, to me anyway. No wonder she'd been so eager to please, willing to help at the drop of a hat. All along she'd planned to sabotage my business; take away all that I'd slogged my guts out for. It had taken me years to build a reputation, to have loyal customers, and I wasn't anywhere near my goal. I hadn't fulfilled my dreams in the world of beauty; I was just beginning. Melanie knew this too, yet still she'd come along and whipped the carpet from underneath me.

The babies had been a huge hurdle, but one I was willing to work with. I would put my expansion plans on hold for a few years; my own building blocks, goals and desires would take second place while I concentrated on my little ones. But I'd thought I was in a stable enough place to do this; I'd thought I could keep afloat a business that I knew inside out. I was fine with this. But now, I could see the blocks I'd built smashing down around me.

Every morning, my first thoughts were of Mandy and Melanie. I tried so hard to push them to the back of my mind. I wanted them to rot away in my memory, so that I could forget they existed. It was harder in the first few weeks as every customer wanted to know how the drama had unfolded. I tried my best not to slate them, but it was hard when some of the customers were really angry, especially with Melanie. 'All you've done for that girl and she does this now. It's absolutely disgusting,' one customer had said. I took hope in their support that we could turn this around, that I could survive, but every hour of every day the battle was becoming harder.

So, as I waited for the next interviewee to arrive I knew I'd hire her because I had little choice. I needed someone to help out. Although we weren't getting any new clients, I needed to service the regular, loyal people who had supported me. Whether I liked her or not had little relevance, because there wasn't much choice out there.

The door chimed as a young girl entered, I concealed the fears that hit me. Her short, dyed black hair covered one eye, her dramatic make-up would have been great for theatrics, a silver wolf aggressively pounced from her black T-shirt, while her short denim skirt drew attention to her holey tights. The whiteness of her skin shone through as her spindly legs seemed fragile in her Doc Martens.

'Laura?' I hoped she would say, 'No'.

'Yeah, sorry I'm late.' She had a slight drawl, as if she'd just woken up.

'Let's take a seat and have a chat.' I didn't tell her it was fine she was late, because it wasn't. However, as she sat on her hands, her hair still covering one eye, her holey tights winking at me, I'd decided these things could become my new pet hates, rather than lateness.

'I've done loads of treatments. All my friends love that I do this. I should charge them but I don't,' she told me before I had the chance to ask her a question.

For the next twenty minutes Laura seemed to talk at me. Every question I asked got an answer that seemed to go on for ever, about things that weren't relevant. I had to keep stopping her, especially as she kept giving me renditions of what her friends did. I'd already found out one of her friends had a baby.

'She was only fifteen,' she'd told me, shaking her head dramatically, dark wisps of hair moving across eyes, showing her smudged eye-liner. 'I don't want to be a young mam. I plan on having kids when I'm about twenty-one, cos I don't want to be an old mam either.' Yes, those were her words.

She either thought I was a larger lady or I looked very young for my age. I really wanted to believe the latter, but I doubted that was the case, especially with the supermarket bags that had been created under my eyes after the endless sleepless nights that seemed to haunt me. So, I went with the fact that she wasn't the brightest, and actually felt a little sorry for her after she'd obliviously insulted me.

'And what are the hours again, and what will I be paid?' She was blatant, but it held an innocence that was quite endearing. She nodded when I reiterated what she'd been told by the college.

'As I said to the college, I need someone quite urgently. So, if you're happy to start, how does tomorrow suit you?'

'Oh ... yeah, great.' She seemed a little shocked, but smiled.

'I wondered, if you don't mind, because our customers would love to see your pretty face, if you could maybe wear a hairband ... or a clip ...'

'Oh yeah, of course.' She pushed the fringe away from her face, 'Should I wear my uniform too?'

'Please, that would be great.' I smiled warmly. What else could she possibly plan on wearing?

As we said our goodbyes, she seemed pleased to be starting with us. Although her image could be construed as scary, she was actually very sweet. I liked her.

But then, I'd liked Melanie. In fact, I'd loved Melanie.

Sophie was pleased we'd finally hired someone. 'Even if they only last a few days it takes the pressure off a little,' she'd said.

Sophie had been great. But we both knew that if we were to survive we needed another qualified and experienced therapist. Someone who could not only perform treatments but help us promote the salon. Laura knew the position was temporary, until I could find someone who could help me save the business; although I'd been trying for two months now and I felt as if I was running out of time.

Marianne was one of my last customers of the day. She'd become a regular in the salon. I'd never thought I'd say it, but I enjoyed her company. However, I could easily have cancelled her today, I felt so drained. I'd not slept well the night before, which wasn't unusual. I'd tossed and turned, pulling at the quilt, puffing up the pillows, sleeping on one pillow, then two, then back to one; plus I went to the loo at least six times. I was fidgeting more than the babies. Even though it was their most active time, I think I kept them awake. Luckily Max was away working. Otherwise he'd probably have slept in the spare bed. The way things were going I think he'd prefer to be in there anyway.

We'd still not discussed his cutting remark at Clare and Henry's party. He'd left earlier on the Sunday than he normally would. His excuse was: 'I've got to sort things out for Monday.' He would normally work from home if this was the case, but even my suggestion of eating out, was responded to with a flippant remark: 'Maybe you should be promoting your business instead of spending money.' He'd apologised before he left. 'I'm really stressed with work at the moment,' he'd told me. 'I know you've done your best …' I'd not answered, as I'd swallowed the lump that blocked my throat.

As I waited for Marianne, I quickly demolished a bag of crisps and a can of Diet Coke. I could hear Max's words: 'And you wonder why you've put more weight on than most women!'

My response was generally that I was carrying two babies who needed more grub. He'd shake his head at me. Often I wondered if I disgusted him. Suzy's words chimed with Max's: 'A banana or an apple would be much better for the babies.' I pushed their voices from my mind as I ate my way through the zesty, chilli-flavoured crisps.

I hadn't actually had any cravings; I'd been enjoying all my food until Melanie had left me stranded. Before this I'd been taking pleasure in being pregnant and the fact that it took away the guilt about eating too much. I'd relished the need to put weight on. It would be the only time in my life I could stuff my face and not have that irritating voice at the back of my mind. You know the one: 1 crisp = 5,000 calories; 1 bar of chocolate = no food for a week.

'How are you, pet?' Marianne distracted my thoughts, as I licked my fingers to remove the chilli dust.

'Good.' I lied. But Marianne knew me, and I appreciated the comforting hug, as she wrapped her arms around my sizeable figure.

'They're very busy around the corner.' She shook her head as we both cast our eyes over my empty salon: not another body to be seen. I'd sent Sophie home early as it seemed pointless her tidying any more shelves. It was hard, as we needed the extra help to cover when we had our mini-overloads; then at times like this I wondered what I was fighting for. 'Honestly, it's unbelievable,' she said, hugging me. 'Just remember, the Lord is watching.'

I showed Marianne over to the nail station, where she made herself comfortable. We talked colours, her usual pale-pink matt varnish being changed for a slightly darker shade; this would be as adventurous as Marianne would get.

'I've been meaning to talk to you.' She was shaking slightly as I worked gently on her cuticles.

'Is everything—'

'I've met someone.' She spoke quickly, and bit her lip as our eyes met for a second, before I peered back down at her hands.

'Oh!' I managed.

'I wanted both you girls to know because I respect your thoughts and he in no way replaces your dad.'

'Does Libby know?'

'I was going to tell her tonight, but I wanted to tell you first.'

'Oh … well, I'm fine with it.' I shrugged, not meeting her eye as I gently filed away. 'Let's face it, you had a tough time with Dad.' I felt I was betraying him as soon as the words were out.

'I'm not forgetting your dad. It's about me finding someone who can keep me company. Derek is so attentive. It's nice to be around someone who cares about me.'

'Where did you meet him?' Maybe general chit-chat would show her that this was okay. This was allowed. I had to accept the fact she would want to move on.

'At the church.' I could feel her eyes burning into my head as I focused on beautifying her nails. 'We've been friends for years, but it's only recently with your father passing that we decided to take our friendship further.'

Was she talking about sex? Oh God, I didn't need to know. But, I couldn't help but wonder if she was lying; had they really waited? Oooohhh … I couldn't go there!

'I'm pleased for you.'

'Are you, Kat?' She begged for my approval, me once again being the authoritative figure. 'It would mean the world to me if you meant it.'

'I do. You deserve to be happy.' I smiled, meeting her gaze, hoping the part of me that *did* mean it reached her, and the other, childish part stayed deeply hidden. I felt sad that Dad missed out on the lovely life he could have had with Marianne.

'I'd love you to meet him.'

'That would be lovely.' Wouldn't it?

'Great. Why don't you come over on Sunday? I'll do us all lunch. Bring Max too. I think he and Derek will get along.'

'Great.' How on earth could I say, 'No thanks, I can't think of anything worse?' Lunch, in my dad's house, with her new boyfriend: wasn't that disrespectful? She was doing it again: playing happy families. The familiar feeling of Marianne taking Mum's place rose within me, but I pushed it away firmly, feeling ashamed of myself.

Marianne had become a friend rather than the mother figure she'd always wanted to be. Our relationship had moved forward immensely since I'd let go of resentful feelings. Maybe Dad would be pleased for her, pleased that she'd moved on and found someone else. If I focused on that angle, maybe I could get through lunch.

Hopefully Max could join us. It had been a while since he'd visited Marianne's. He was always working; his projects were starting to seep into our weekends. The thought made me feel slightly guilty that I was a little upset with how distracted he was lately. He enjoyed Marianne's company, had encouraged me to invite her for dinner once Dad had passed away. But when the contracts had started becoming bigger and more consuming he'd closed himself off. To be honest, he'd not really seen Clare much either, which she constantly nagged me about. But I'd tried my best to make the visits on my own, not wanting to stress Max out, more than he already was.

For some reason, I felt slightly relieved that even our outside worlds were being affected, because it must mean it wasn't me he was unsettled with, it was obviously his work. He wasn't making excuses, he was focusing on his business. Which, let's be honest, I really needed him to do, especially the way mine was heading.

As I chatted with Marianne, a weight seemed to float off my shoulders.

When I got in from seeing Suzy, I'd cook him a nice meal ready for him coming home. I usually stuck in a ready-meal but maybe I'd make a lasagne from scratch. Unfortunately, though, my cookery skills hadn't progressed much. So, although I'd love to whip up some fine cuisine, it would probably end up in the bin.

If I didn't eat much with Suzy, maybe Max and I could eat together. I could arrange a romantic, candle-lit dinner. I hated eating so late, though: it didn't help with the indigestion.

However, I really wanted to make this work.

Hopefully, he did too.

6

The restaurant was packed. It's a bit hard trying to push your way through a crowd with a huge, distended bump attached to your front. Luckily, most people were nice; they'd move out of your way apologetically, as if they'd trodden on your toe. Most were probably petrified I'd go into labour.

'Just here, ladies.' The young Italian waiter directed us to our table. He whipped out his pad and pen, poised at the ready. 'Can I get you ladies some drinks?' I wondered if the Italian accent was fake, or exaggerated for effect.

'Glass of water, please,' Suzy ordered, as she picked up a menu.

'Same, please,' I heard myself saying, although I really wanted a full-fat Coke. But I wasn't in the mood for Suzy's lecture about calories, how caffeine can cause disabilities or any other information overload that took the enjoyment out of food and drink.

'So, how are you and Max?'

'The same, really … I'm going to cook a meal tonight for when he gets in.'

'He has to make an effort too.'

'I know, but he's so busy.'

'But so are you, when you should be resting.'

'It's just hard, Suz …' I scanned the restaurant. There were several tables set out for what seemed a special occasion. Attached to them were, silver, blue and white helium balloons, tied together with flamboyant silver ribbon. 'We'll be fine. We'll have to be when these babies arrive.'

'I know he's busy, but he needs to be there for you.' Suzy raised her eyebrows.

'I'm probably to blame as much as him.' I shrugged my shoulders. I wanted to tell her that he was there for me. But he hadn't really given me a reason to fight his corner when it came to this argument. But I'd probably not helped things: my mind was also elsewhere. Trying to save the salon had practically taken over my life.

I browsed through the menu, as the crowd of around twenty people that had congregated at the door started to cheer. Suzy and I turned to observe the jovial group as they swooped, whistled and clapped at the two young women who entered through the main entrance.

It was her long lean legs that I noticed first, the slit from her tight-fitting red dress teasing onlookers with a glimpse of her tanned thighs. Her head was held high, her shoulders were back, practically forcing her bulging cleavage from its very low neckline.

Mandy kissed those who had come to greet her, laughing loudly, behaving like a celebrity. Melanie was a few steps behind her, not so brash, taking off her black woollen coat to reveal a plain black A-line dress.

'Are you ready to order?' The waiter placed the glasses of water on the table.

'What's going on there?' Suzy asked him, pointing in the direction of the rowdy group as I turned away from them. The beating of my heart grew faster and I could feel my legs shaking uncontrollably.

'Celebration … new business or something. They've done amazing, they only opened a few months ago.' His Italian smoothness didn't soften the words.

'I can't stay here.' I pushed back the chair.

'You're leaving?' He frowned.

'I'm sorry.' I shook my head, pulling on my coat, desperate to get some air.

'I'm sorry,' Suzy said to the waiter, who was obviously totally bewildered. He didn't speak but I could feel his eyes upon us as we walked away from the table.

I edged around the group, hoping not to be seen, but the hand that clutched my arm felt like a vice. 'Kat …'

I turned to face Melanie, who was not letting go. The sparkle she'd always held was missing, as she desperately searched my eyes. Her own glint had disappeared.

'You look great,' she said, finally removing her fingers.

'Kat?' Mandy was behind her. 'Oh, wow, haven't you grown?' I stared at them both in disbelief as a silence fell between us. Mandy reached her arm towards me, placing it on my shoulder. 'Kat, seriously … no hard feelings.'

I couldn't speak. The words stuck as I gritted my teeth. Shaking my head, I walked away towards the door. 'Come on, Kat, if you'd not left us to it—'

Suzy words rang out behind me. 'Do you know what you've done to her?'

'Oh, seriously ….' Mandy laughed. 'I saw an opportunity.'

'How do you sleep at night?' Suzy's voice was raised. A hush settled across the crowd they were with.

'Fantastically, thank you.'

'You would be nothing without Kat.' Suzy was glaring intensely at Mandy.

'Do you see all these people?' Mandy raised her hand, signifying the crowd who were with her. 'They're all here for me.'

'Did you hear that, Mel?' Suzy turned towards Melanie, who bit her lip. 'They're here for her … not you.'

'She knows what I mean,' Mandy growled.

'I know what you mean …' Suzy stared at her, disgust apparent.

'You don't know me.' Mandy stepped forward aggressively, her body twice the size of Suzy's, her breasts seeming to sit beneath Suzy's chin.

'I know you're a fake.' Suzy stepped back from Mandy, turning to Melanie. 'Kat never made everything about her. She always made sure you were okay.'

Melanie caught my eye, but I turned away. 'Come on, Suzy,' I urged, uncomfortable with the huge scene that had been created.

People who had previously been enjoying a meal were turning to stare at the commotion.

Suzy shook her head at them both as she turned to walk towards me. Muttering stirred through their crowd, and Mandy's stare could have turned Suzy to stone. Melanie's tearful eyes burned through me, as we walked out of the restaurant.

'I'm glad you're on my side,' I joked, as we exited into the cool evening air. As we walked back to our cars, I was so pleased to have Suzy with me. Our friendship was locked together by shared experiences. Her protection reminded me of our schooldays, when she would stand up to anyone who tried to question me about Mum.

I kept seeing Melanie's tortured face in my mind, but the anger and bitterness that kept tearing at me, the hurt that they had caused, were far too raw and painful for me to easily forgive.

I'd thought Melanie would be relishing her new-found opportunity, but even before she'd seen me she'd looked forlorn as she walked behind Mandy. Her head was down, her usual bright appearance had gone. She seemed lost. Her downcast figure was hidden in Mandy's shadow, whereas Mandy's presence had been formidable when she'd entered, exuding her powerful charisma.

I couldn't feel sorry for Melanie, though. She'd made her choice. She'd chosen to go with a woman who appeared soft, bubbly and enticing from the outside, but inside she was rock. Her hardness allowed her to breeze through life, trampling on those who stepped in her way.

Before we left each other, I kissed Suzy on the cheek, hugging her close as I thanked her for being an amazing friend. Driving home, earlier than I'd anticipated, was great because it meant I might get my bath before I started on the lasagne, which I could now share with Max.

As I guided the car back along the narrow roads, I couldn't erase Melanie's face from my mind. I couldn't help hoping that she was okay. But I pushed that thought away: she'd hurt me too much to have my pity.

7

Back at home, I felt exhausted. Every bone that usually ached throbbed angrily. Pain penetrated through all the familiar areas but my lower back was the worst. My bump was heavy and uncomfortable; I could hear its cry for help. My routine bath helped to ease the pain, as did the paracetamol. It was the only thing I was allowed to take, but even then, the midwife had said, 'Only when you really need it.' Tonight, it was definitely needed.

I knew it wasn't only the babies that were playing havoc with my muscles. Since Melanie and Mandy had set up their own salon my shoulders seemed to have gathered a mass of rocks and knots underneath them.

If Melanie had been with me, I'd have asked her to treat me to one of our therapies for pregnant ladies. I didn't want to ask Sophie because I was still trying to put on my brave face at work. She'd been an amazing support, but I could tell she was still nervous in some areas. So I had to be the strong one. I'd surmised she didn't expect anything less of me: I was the boss, if I'd crashed in front of her, I'm sure she'd have crashed with me.

I suppose with all this going on, I wondered if it was me who'd pushed Max away. The distance that been created: had it mainly been my fault? We needed to talk about things properly. We seemed to avoid the conversation, either diverting onto another subject or ignoring the wedge that had been driven between us.

At that thought, I pulled the groceries from the carrier bag. I'd called at the shops on my way home, picking up all the ingredients for the lasagne. Yes, I did have to search the internet on my phone for the recipe, but still, I was making the effort.

I followed the recipe faithfully: I thought it best not to add my own bits. I often wanted to be like the professionals who seemed to throw any old thing in, but they knew what they were doing. I on the other hand simply wanted to impress Max.

I was secretly pleased with my bubbling mixture of mince, onions, mushrooms, chopped tomatoes and other herb bits, and after wiping the tomato juice from the kitchen sides, cupboards and floor, I thought it best to leave it to settle, while I dived (or climbed gently) into my regular hot bath.

I was becoming a little bit too large for the bath. I'd put on a good two stone (at least) but it wasn't my size stopping me: it was the ability to get out. I had this fear I'd be stuck for a week before Max returned home. Oh well, if it happened tonight at least he'd be at hand to rescue me … although the romantic night would be out the window and he'd probably be slightly turned off.

You see, this was the other thing about our relationship: I'd always imagined settling down with someone who knew my body, intimately. However, Max had only known my old body for six months before this new one had formed.

A belly button that stuck outwards – apparently, it's quite common, but it was so noticeable, and reminded me of a wart. My breasts had practically doubled in size – most men would have found this a bonus, but Max had not mentioned the balloons that rested floppily on my chest. Lawrence had mentioned over dinner one night that, 'a pregnant woman is so sexy,' and winked jokily at me. Max had retorted, 'You haven't seen her naked.' A deathly silence had followed, until he laughed and said, 'I'm joking.' I laughed along, but admittedly it stung.

As I lay in the bath caressing the large, mountainous island of my stomach, my belly button being the palm tree (my way of making myself feel better), I wondered if I could turn this around. Over the past few weeks, I'd watched Max's behaviour carefully, analysing his every move: how he would kiss me on the forehead instead of the lips, how his hugs seemed to lack feeling: a pat on the back would have felt more attentive.

But was it my fault? My mind was elsewhere at the moment: on my efforts to save the salon.

What if I'd pushed Max away?

I changed into the comfy bottoms that had become my daily attire since I'd reached twenty-five weeks. Scraping my hair back from my dry, tired face, before leaving the bedroom I glanced in the mirror, the image stopping me sharply in my stride.

What was I doing? I was trying to make an effort. Although the thought made me want to crawl under the sheets and not venture back out, I pulled my maternity jeans from the wardrobe. I'd not had much chance to wear them: if I wasn't dressed in black for work, it was jogging bottoms for home.

I know jeans aren't exactly the most romantic of clothing, but I wanted to be casual rather than glamorous. I'd lived in them when we'd met. He used to rub his hand across my arse and tell me how gorgeous it was. It was sizable then, so now … well, let's just say tight-fitting maternity jeans do wonders!

I found a white maternity vest top after delving deeper into my wardrobe. Another item I'd bought at the beginning of my pregnancy and never worn. But it flawlessly covered the bra that pushed my breasts together. I causally released my hair and pulled the straighteners through the dry ends, noting that I really needed to get some oils on the frizzy mop. After finally making it look half decent, I sat down at the dressing table and pulled out my old make-up bag. The one with the special goodies, not the regular one that I flicked through blindly every day. The one that would brighten my skin, enhance my eyes and transform me into a picture of health.

Before leaving the room, I pulled on a small pink cardigan, which wasn't maternity but maybe added some cuteness to my style, but then I took it off: it was obviously too small, the sides not stretching around my huge breasts. I pulled on a large grey cardigan, which I loved, but the outfit became too casual. I decided that, although it was the middle of winter, the heating was blaring, my internal thermometer was doing its job, so I'd go for the fresh summer look.

Back in the kitchen, I was aware that I was feeling excited about Max's arrival, although for some reason a little nervous. Every day recently felt like a test for us, forcing us to strengthen our relationship; but the effort had seemed colossal. Although I didn't think a push-up bra, jeans and a lasagne would fix us, it could be a start.

I read each section of the recipe again. Simply pour in mince, place on lasagne sheets (fresh sheets from the supermarket freezer section, rather than the box version, as advised by Suzy) then add béchamel sauce, repeat this three times. I wanted to make sure I got it right. Mmm ... perhaps only two layers were needed, I wondered, as the sauce ran sloppily down the side of the dish. As I grated cheese onto the top layer, before wiping away the excess with a cloth, thoughts of cooking baby meals swarmed into my mind.

Oh God, I needed lessons ... I didn't know where to start.

After placing the lasagne into the oven, I poured boiling water onto the powdered Horlicks which had become my favourite night-time drink. Too many lectures from Suzy had forced me to seek an alternative to tea. She wasn't overly impressed with my hot chocolate choice: 'Hot chocolate contains about 140 calories and 3 grams of fat. Yes, Kat, it is healthier than a bar of chocolate but seriously, can't you stick to something healthy? Like herbal teas or boiled water.' So, I'd reduced my tea intake. I'd totally gone off coffee; I couldn't bear the smell, let alone the taste. 'Our mums drank alcohol with us,' I'd argued, but she'd soon put me right about the research: stillbirths, low weight gain and all these other pertinent facts. I listened, and in some cases I took notice. I wondered what all other clueless women did who didn't have a friend who was a health freak like Suzy.

The shrill from the phone startled me, as I hurriedly placed two teaspoons of sugar into the malted drink. No, Suzy didn't know about the sugar!

'Can you believe it?' Libby's abrupt but quiet voice addressed me. I knew what she was talking about, but she seemed more annoyed than I'd thought she would be. I'd expected her to be laid back about the whole thing. 'Good on her,' is what I'd presumed she'd say. But she seemed genuinely put out. I could hear myself calming her, telling her maybe it wasn't a bad thing. I wondered when our roles had changed.

'I think she was seeing him beforehand,' she said.

'I don't think so, Lib.' The thought *had* crossed my mind but I decided it was best not to rile Libby any more.

'It all seems to be falling perfectly into place, doesn't it?' she whispered.

'I think he's just been there as a friend.'

'Did she tell you he lost his wife a few years back?'

'Well then, it's great they've got each other, isn't it?'

'If you say so.'

'Have you met him?'

'No, she wants us to do this family lunch thing, bloody farce.'

'It'll give us a chance to weigh him up. Ask a few questions and suss him out.'

'Mmm ... I'll be weighing him up alright.' Libby's agitation was completely out of character. I wondered if there was something underlying. Was she worried she'd be pushed out?

'Anyway, how's uni?' I purposely changed the subject.

'Great, I love it.' She lightened immediately. I was pleased she still had the ability to change focus quickly. I also hoped Marianne hadn't been listening outside Libby's door. 'Anyway, I'm going to go, I'm popping out with Calvin.'

'As in Calvin who puked all over my room?' I shouldn't have been so curt, but I wanted to know more about her involvement with Calvin. I wasn't sure he could be trusted.

'Honestly, he feels terrible about that and so do I.'

'Lib, I hope you're concentrating on your course—'

'Oh don't start lecturing me,' she snapped.

'I'm not—'

'I know you don't like Calvin, but really he's been such a good friend to me.'

'Is there something going on between you two? I thought he was gay.'

'He *is* gay, but that doesn't mean we can't be friends.'

'I know. I didn't mean it like that. I wondered if there was more to your relationship.'

'No, don't be stupid. Jesus, he'd shit himself if I came on to him. Anyway, I'm going, Marianne is calling me.' I doubted if that was true: there were no muffled noises in the background.

I needed to give her a break. Maybe Calvin's sickness incident had been a one-off; maybe he'd had a bad turn because he'd not been used to the rubbish they were putting in their bodies. Libby seemed to have placed him on a pedestal but I couldn't see why. I didn't really know him, though. She seemed to be getting her life back on track and that's all that mattered. Maybe it was losing Dad, being chucked out of my home or living with Marianne, or a combination of all three that made her need a saviour. If Calvin was that saviour, then so be it. It wasn't up to me to choose her friends.

This is what it would be like with my own children. I wondered, if we had girls would they be closer to Max than to me: Daddy's girls? Something I'd wanted to be in the latter years of my own dad's life. If we had boys would I scrutinise every girl who walked through the door? Would I judge her before she'd even spoken? Visions of my imaginary son bringing home Laura flashed through my mind; scary eyeliner and dirty hair. Yes, I probably *would* judge her.

I often wondered how Max would be as a father. I hoped he'd be like the dad I remembered from all those years ago. I often fantasised about taking our children to Lampford Park. I imagined us chasing each other through the labyrinth, having a traditional picnic with cucumber sandwiches like the ones Mum made, the warmth of the summer sun beating down on our fresh faces, all of us laughing as we blissfully revelled in each other's company.

The table was set to restaurant standard: chic glass mats, a tall, thin red candle elegantly placed in the centre, which I'd light when I could hear Max pulling up, and a wine glass that would allow him to finish the red wine I'd needlessly poured into the mince. (Another hint from Suzy, although she told me she only used it when making spaghetti bolognese, I thought it would add a bit of flavour.)

I sat on the sofa, waiting for Max, allowing the cushions to embrace me. I picked up a pregnancy magazine. I'd not read any in the beginning of the pregnancy, but now I couldn't put them down. Learning about our babies was fascinating. As I ran my eye over an article about toddler tantrums – although I knew I had a long way to go before then – the ringing of my mobile made me jump.

'Hi, Clare.'
'Hello, Kathryn, how are you?'
'I'm fine.'
'I've bought some more gorgeous things today—'
'More things …'
'I know, but I can't help it. Anyway, I wondered if you and Maxwell would like to come for dinner on Thursday evening. We haven't seen him for a while.'
'He's not home yet. Can I check when he comes in?'
'Of course … he's working so hard lately.'
'I know …' The beep indicating a text distracted me.

She continued to tell me about more baby paraphernalia she'd seen and suggested we should go out shopping together. As she mumbled into my ear, I lifted the phone back to see who the text was from. It was Max. He was probably just texting to say he was only an hour away. Not that he'd done that in a while, but maybe he was going to make an effort, too. Perhaps we *were* in tune with each other.

I listened as Clare waffled, willing her to hang up, and when she finally did, I checked his message.

'Just setting off now, will be early hours when I get home x'
'What!' I realised I'd spoken aloud. I found myself scrolling for his number, clicking the button that would connect us. But he didn't answer.

I stared at my phone, rubbing my fingers across the touch screen. Biting my lip, I tried him again, but I was greeted with his recorded, professional tones.

How had he sent me a text, and now not be near his phone?

Suddenly my phone lit up, his face peering at me. 'Hello,' I quickly answered.

'Hi, everything okay?' he asked loudly, pitching his voice above the car engine.

'Yeah, I just wondered how come you're only setting off now … it's eight-thirty.'

'It's been a manic day. I'd stay if I didn't need to be in Leeds in the morning.'

'Oh … well, drive carefully.' I didn't know what else to say. How could I tell him I'd prepared a meal for him … a romantic evening? How guilty would that make him feel?

'Will do.'

'Oh, before I forget, your mum asked if we could go for dinner on Thursday night.'

'Thursday.' He seemed distracted, as he clicked his tongue, the noise irritating. 'Yeah, should be alright. I'll move things around if not. I'll be in Leeds anyway.'

'Great.' I tried to smile, wondering: if he'd known what I'd had planned this evening, would he have cancelled his meetings? 'There's a lasagne in the oven, if you're hungry when you get in.'

'I'll grab something on the way home.'

'Okay.' I tried to tell myself that of course that was easier for him. Who'd want to come in and eat at 2 a.m.? Unless it was a drunken night out; then there was nothing better.

'You get some rest.'

'Max …'

'Yeah?'

'I love you …'

'You too …'

We hung up after saying the words that hadn't been spoken for weeks.

8

The next morning the rain hit the salon windows as if we were situated in the middle of a waterfall. The letter was sitting on the reception desk, daring me to open it, its edges wet where it had been manhandled by the dishevelled postman. 'IMPORTANT' was stamped across the top of the envelope. My name, salon name and address were typed in bold capital letters, shouting its urgency.

Two months ago, I'd have flown into a panic that an invoice was overdue, but now, bills were of no interest to me. I placed the letter to the side of the desk. It could be a supplier, the electricity bill or council tax. I didn't care.

I hadn't been paying myself a salary. I'd used that money to promote the salon and train Sophie in areas that could enhance the business. I'd planned to do some training myself by now, but I was worried about leaving the salon. It was bad enough having a few hours out, let alone being away for days. I still felt stupid for giving Melanie and Mandy too much control. It probably would have happened anyway, but I knew I'd have had more of a fighting chance if I'd not practically handed my business to them on a plate.

Another problem I was faced with, which I'd somewhat tried to ignore, believing it wouldn't be a problem because I would stamp all over Lush Lucia, was the rigid salon contract that was hanging over my head.

I'd initially signed a year's contract. My landlord was lovely. He'd given me a great deal. He'd said I reminded him of his daughter, who at the time was travelling the world. I'd never actually had the privilege of travelling abroad since Mum died.

We'd had few holidays before that but even trips to the beach had ceased when she was no longer with us. So how I reminded him of his daughter was beyond me. After the first year was up, I'd agreed to sign a five-year contract. I did it for my benefit more than his. He was obviously thrilled, but I wanted the security to run the business without anyone coming and taking it away from me. The flat was included in the contract, so I'd made the whole place my home, my safe abode. Now I had just over three years left. I really hadn't imagined I'd be in this position.

So, I was trying to think from all angles. Having a business with no clients wasn't much good. Because of this, I'd substituted my salary for marketing, it meant there were plenty of funds at the moment, but my takings had dropped. Although I didn't have Melanie and Mandy's salaries to worry about, still the deficit was significant. So, although there was money to pay these bills, I'd been forgetting them lately. I'd always had one night a week when I worked on my accounts, but now I couldn't remember the last time I'd looked at my receipts and invoices or updated my spreadsheets.

Max had asked if I'd spoken to Jack Haslow. Apparently, Jack had chased Henry wondering why I'd not called him back after Clare and Henry's party. Henry had then made it quite clear to Max that Jack really needed to speak to me. I knew should call him, but I was worried about the news he'd give me. I was convinced he'd have someone who wanted to buy my business, which financially would be great news: it would give me a break and time to get to know my babies. However, I didn't want to let go of my business.

I didn't know anything else ...

Maybe this was why Max was irritable at the moment. Was he frustrated with me for trying to save the salon? He'd not said. But he'd not told me to fight for it either.

I'd ventured to the loo at about 4 a.m. and he was snoring quietly next to me. I'd laid on my side to watch him, my hands wrapped around my bump. His breaths had gently wafted across my skin. I studied him while he was sleeping. His strong features seemed tense even in sleep.

I'd cleared the table before coming to bed, not wanting him to feel guilty when he realised he'd unwittingly stood me up. I'd waited for the lasagne to cook. Fighting away the deflation, as the smell of the baking meat and cheese suddenly turned my stomach. I'd blamed the food, but I'd known it was the disappointment that swayed through my body.

Max was obviously distracted at the moment. We were heading towards a new chapter that we'd not planned for. And we couldn't have predicted what would happen to my business. Although his work seemed to be doing well, and he was winning more contracts than he could deal with, maybe he was worried about the finances. He was constantly watching my spending. I'd found this hard to deal with as I'd always been so independent. I'd accepted, though, that this was a partnership. He was working hard for us, so I did my best not to overspend. My biggest budget used to be on my clothes, but now I'd buy for the babies: I was trying to stock up on nappies, creams and other baby stuff. I'd add to our collection whenever I was at the supermarket, and yes, the bathroom resembled the supermarket's baby aisle, but I wanted to be prepared. 'What? For a year!' Max had exclaimed.

He was quite happy that Clare was buying most of the outfits, if I found anything I loved, he'd ask: 'Do we really need that?'

In searching for a pram, he'd asked me keep the cost low: 'We don't need any of that fancy celebrity stuff.' I'd tried to convince him that because we needed a twin pushchair we'd have to pay a lot more. He started searching for a better deal. I'd given up the fight for the Bugaboo Donkey Twin Pram and Pushchair, '… but it comes with a free car seat, we'd be saving money,' I'd tried and failed.

'We need two car seats. I'm not paying over a grand for a bloody pushchair.'

I could have argued. But I understood. I was maybe being a little excessive. And, he was right, it was his money. He'd worked hard for it. But I needed my own financial independence. I couldn't ask him for handouts, or be given weekly budget limits. I'd never lived that way.

That was the main reason I'd not contacted Jack Haslow. If I let go of this business, what would I do with my future? Yes, I'd have a lump sum to play with, but that would soon dwindle. There were alternative options, such as becoming a mobile therapist, but still the promotional aspects would take up as much time as the treatments. Plus I'd have two babies to take care of. So, while I still had the salon, I still had some of my freedom; I still felt as self-sufficient, as I'd always been.

These thoughts occupied me as I stared at the corner of the salon where the Christmas tree would usually be up by now. Melanie and Mandy had a huge tree in their bay window. I'd not been able to resist driving past on the way to work. Their salon wasn't directly on my route, but sometimes I couldn't help but divert. It was torture every time, but it was as if my car had its own mind. It was worse when I'd see my old customers venturing into their place. I was dying to stop my car and ask: What did I do wrong? What can I do to bring you back? But they'd think I was neurotic. At least this way without accosting anyone I could be neurotic alone.

Melanie always put our tree up before the first of December. I wondered if she'd decorated their elaborate tree, and enjoyed it in the way she used to. It looked three times bigger than any tree I'd placed in my salon. She would normally have had the decorations up by now, with the jovial Christmas tunes blaring in the background. I wondered if she'd happily sung away, filled their new business with the joy she'd spread in mine. I hadn't had the inclination or the energy to even buy a tree, let alone put one up, and Sophie hadn't mentioned it either.

I suddenly realised I missed Melanie. I'd been so angry with her, so hurt, not allowing myself to think about our friendship, believing it had all been fake. But as I thought about how Melanie would be in her element, spraying each window pane with a sprinkle of fake snow, bordering the bay windows with fairy lights and building a village of cotton wool, with Santa's sleigh and presents galore, I fought back the tears.

I'd found Christmas gruelling ever since Mum passed away, but I had tried to become more accommodating to the season's festivities over the last few years. Melanie had helped in bringing her excitement into the place.

It was Marianne who'd made the effort when we were younger but she and Dad didn't have much money, so I knew it was hard. She did her best, although I didn't appreciate it at the time. But even as I'd grown into an adult I still found Christmas intense. It was as if it made me think about how life could have been; or should have been. Families everywhere were forced together by the yuletide season; it felt false but at the same time I was envious. Customers would tell us all about their huge family dinners, the extensive list of presents they had bought for loved ones and the cheerful celebrations that would last for weeks.

As 'bah, humbug' as it may sound, I wanted every Christmas to pass quickly. This year would be the first without Dad. Although this filled me with great sadness, I knew it wouldn't be much different as he'd usually be in a drunken, comatose state anyway. I wondered if things would change now that I had my own little ones on the way. Would I get excited about filling the house with decorations, wrapping presents until the early hours or standing in queues awaiting the release of a new toy? I could think of nothing worse, but I was sure the emotional exhilaration would hit me at some stage. Even Max had commented it was great the babies were due after Christmas.

'We'll have all that expense to come,' I'd laughed.

'They're costing a fortune before they've even arrived,' he mumbled. I pretended I'd not heard him. It would only lead to another fight.

Laura was running late again. I was waiting for her excuse. I wondered if the day could get any worse. It could: three clients cancelled because of the weather. I didn't believe them. They were all Melanie's regular customers, so I knew exactly where they were going. You'd think I would be used to the cancellations by now. When the phone rang I never wanted to answer it; it pained me every time we lost a customer.

Sophie placed a hot lemon and water in front of me. We'd sort-of had the coffee conversation, as it had become slightly embarrassing that she made me coffee every morning. Although I was truly grateful, I'd told her one morning as I heard the kettle boiling that I'd prefer a lemon and water; coffee knocked me sick recently. I didn't see the point of telling her I hadn't drunk it for months.

'So, do you think Laura will turn up?' She gestured towards the door, wrapping her hands around her own cup, her cardigan protecting her from the cold air that had seeped into our usually cosy salon.

'I hope so.' I'd barely finished my sentence when the door flew open and banged against the sofa, swinging back against Laura's face.

'Fucking hell,' she practically screamed, as she rammed the door back. It swung towards her again. Sophie jumped in, stopping the swing of the door before the whole thing came off its hinges. I cringed as a customer walked in behind her.

'Like I haven't already had the morning from hell, then your door tries to attack me. What a fucking morning. Can I put the kettle on before I get started?'

My jaw must have hit the floor, because I literally felt it drop. My eyes must have been on stalks as I glared at her as if she'd just landed, as her dishevelled figure strutted past me into the kitchen. This sociable girl, who I'd interviewed, who I'd liked, had developed into the Devil.

'Mrs Garney.' I greeted the customer who'd followed Laura in, hoping I could take control of the situation. Mrs Garney, probably my oldest client, looked as if she'd swallowed a wasp. I felt her disapproval, as I removed her coat and ushered her quickly into a treatment room before we heard any more foul language. Mrs Garney loved her facials, her monthly treat since Arnold had passed away. A lovely woman who seemed so grateful for everything in her life, she would often talk about her deeply missed Arnold. I hoped that Max and I survived these early years so we could build that unconditional love for one another. I assumed she was in her eighties, but she never told me and it would be impolite to ask.

Once she was settled I excused myself for a moment, asking her to relax.

'Laura, can I have a little word?' I found her and Sophie in the kitchen, Laura obviously giving an exaggerated account of her morning events. Sophie got the hint and left.

'I'm so sorry I'm late. My mother hadn't dried my clothes, the bus was late and—'

'That's fine; these things happen.' It wasn't fine, but I thought it best to leave that part. 'But I wanted to talk to you about your language. Now, don't get me wrong, I can have a good swear.' I tried to laugh, not wanting to lecture her too much but needing her to understand her behaviour was unacceptable. 'But we don't do it in front of the customers.'

'Customers?' She poured the hot water into her cup, the tea bag floating to the top. 'I didn't see anyone.'

'Mrs Garney was behind you.'

'Who, that old woman?' Laura screwed up her face. 'Really?'

'Really.' I was soft but firm. 'So, can you please be careful.'

'Yeah, sure, sorry.' She backed down, relief sweeping over me that she wasn't going to storm out of the door. Although, with that type of entrance maybe we could cope without her.

The rest of the day passed us by without a hitch. Laura's vibrant personality filled the salon. Although it did feel at times too much, she'd added a spark to the place that we'd lost. But I think it was definitely official: my judgement of character was not my best talent.

As I worked alongside the girls, listening to the customers gossiping – Melanie being brought up frequently, as she always was – I felt lost. I felt as if I didn't belong. That feeling crept over me most days. I swallowed back the lump that kept forcing its way up, not wanting to cry in front of the customers. I wouldn't allow anyone to see my weakness. Many would sympathise and understand but even so the news would travel. Melanie and Mandy would find out I'd crashed. I didn't want them to know I was panicking, that many a sleepless night I wondered if my business would survive. That I was constantly beating myself up about how the hell Melanie could have done this to me. So, I fought back the tears, laughed in the right places and communicated with all my customers in a professional manner; in the way I always had.

By the end of the day we'd had a few more cancellations for the following day. I was trying to stay positive and focus on the customers we had: the loyal customers who had stayed with me. But maybe they would only stay with me if I was their therapist, which would be pretty hard to do when I would be giving birth to two babies in less than seven weeks.

***

As I drove home through the darkness, the early dark nights making it feel later than it was, I tried to push back the tears of frustration.

I felt worthless.

I knew I would be going back to an empty house as Max had informed me earlier he would be working late again.

'The Leeds office have fucked a load of jobs up.' He'd been a little upset, to say the least, so I'd thought it best not to tell him about the lasagne. I was actually pleased he'd rung in good time before I'd squeezed into my maternity jeans again.

I needed to take my mind off things, so a night of watching *One Born Every Minute* helped in easing my over-analysed thoughts. I really had tried to understand the importance of the breathing techniques. I couldn't believe how much I enjoyed watching women give birth. It was a strange feeling, as if I was indulging in some kind of intense training, which was needed because I had no clue what I was doing. It was a sad episode, though, that had me crying. This poor baby was born with its bowel on the outside of its body. All was calm as they whipped the little wrinkled chap away, explaining that it's more common than we think; they could operate and all would be fine. It seemed so simple; but still it terrified me.

How common was this?

I'd never heard of such a thing, and I'd had years of women talking about births and the trials and tribulations of pregnancy. I started to investigate the internet, but then started to drive myself insane; clicking from site to site to site to site, and more sites, discovering more and more defects.

'Our babies will be fine,' I said it aloud, as if this was more definite confirmation.

I'd decided it was best to turn my education tools off as my frantic thoughts were turning into hysterical apprehension.

After making myself a Horlicks, I'd spoken briefly to Suzy. I was hoping she would take my mind off babies. She did slightly, as she didn't relay any statistics to me about babies born with disabilities.

She did, however, beg that I would still go to yoga in the morning. 'You can't give up now, you need it more than ever.'

Yoga? I can hear you asking. Me and yoga? I know, but, it had been Suzy's idea: 'Pregnancy yoga will help your mind and body prepare for labour,' she'd said when trying to persuade me.

'Nothing will help me prepare.'

'It helps to relieve tension around the cervix and birth canal by opening up the pelvis. I'll come with you and be your supportive partner.'

'Oh, for God's sake, please stop!' I'd wanted to say, but instead I found myself succumbing with a simple, 'Okay, I'll go.' And at the same time, wondering how Suzy and I were friends.

To be honest, I'd agreed because it meant I could definitely see Suzy once a week. But a morning's performance of stretching my lady-bits felt too much to bear this week. I couldn't think of anything worse than pretending to be a spiritual being who was in tune with her uterus.

'But maybe this is the reason I'm losing the salon,' I'd told her.

'What? A morning's yoga session that isn't even an hour long? Don't be silly.'

She was right but still I felt as if I was inviting misfortune because I was being selfish by taking this timeout to myself: Well, let's face it, it wasn't really me-time, it was so that I could spend time with Suzy. My quality me-time wasn't about bending my arse over for all to see.

Suzy was on an extreme fitness mission, more so than her usual three-to-five hours' daily workout (and that was between clients). She and Lawrence were debating which marathon they could compete in. They'd decided they not only wanted to do the London Marathon, but they were thinking of heading to Rome next March to compete and make a holiday out of it.

'Make a holiday out of it?' I'd tried not to insult them but seriously it made absolutely no sense to me. If she'd spoken to me in Spanish I'd have probably understood her more.

It was at this point, I'd realised that Suzy and I had an 'opposites attract' friendship.

Max had decided not to do any events next year. I'd told him he should; life couldn't stop because we had babies. But he'd insisted. He said it would be bad enough with one baby, but two? That would be unfair. Secretly I was delighted. I wasn't sure I was going to cope with Max, let alone without him.

My thoughts edged towards the loving and more supportive things Max had said, when he'd finally got over the fact there were two fuzzy shapes on the scan monitor. After our first scan, he would talk to my bump, okay, flab: I knew I was just bloated – I had enjoyed the white bread, pizzas and any other carbs that made me look six months pregnant when I was only four. For the first few weeks Max would tell stories about his day, and sing daft songs that would have me doubled over with laughter. He would kiss my ballooned, stretched skin tenderly, his hands caressing gently around the babies. He was affectionate in a way I'd never really imagined possible. But by the time we'd experienced our second scan, which was only four weeks later, I'd realised his first rush of affection had abated. I put it down to his workload. I didn't want to create a fuss: he didn't need me nagging at home while he 'worked his bollocks off.'

Later, Max finally appeared and climbed in beside me. I checked my clock. It read 12.03 a.m. I'd turned the light off an hour ago, but the elbows or heels that were digging in my ribs were causing me some discomfort. He kissed his own fingers, then pressed them onto my cheek as if transferring the kiss, as he crawled under the covers, explaining how tired he was. I nodded, exhausted myself.

I remembered how he used to warm my side of the bed for me when I'd been the one out late. This was before we moved into together, if he'd waited at my flat for me or I'd gone to his house. Our midnight lovemaking had been the thrilling, exciting highlights in our relationship, full of sensational lust and energy.

As he quickly fell into a deep sleep, I listened to the rhythm of his gentle snores that had taken him into a different land: a world of fantasy, nightmares and delusions. I wondered where he was; what was he dreaming about?

Brushing my hand over the cheek were he'd casually placed a kiss with his hand, I bit my lip as I pushed away the thought that he was slipping away from me. Internally wrestling with the fear that I actually wasn't sure how to make the next move. I knew that I needed to do something bigger, more extravagant than cooking homemade lasagne.

It will be fine, I told myself, I'll think of something. We will be fine.

I leaned over to kiss his back, to feel his softness, touch his skin …

Then the smell hit me – perfume!

Melanie's perfume.

9

'I've read somewhere that if you're around someone who wears really strong perfume it can transfer onto your clothes and even into your hair,' Suzy informed me on the way to yoga: the yoga I'd told her there was no way I could face today. But she'd turned up at the house, practically dragging me out by my hair. That's a little exaggerated, but my head throbbed so much she might as well have.

'You need to stop reading,' I said flatly.

'It's true!' she exclaimed. I loved her for wanting to make me feel better, but it wasn't happening.

I'd tossed and turned most of the night. I'd debated whether to wake Max up … but I couldn't.

I'd cried. I'd stomped around the bathroom in anger. Then I'd collapsed with weakness and cried some more. I'd had the urge to pack his suitcase, but then remembered it was his house.

I could pack *my* suitcase, but where would I go?

Back to the flat? There was no furniture.

Marianne's? What if her new man was there?

Clare's? She'd side with Max out of loyalty.

I wished Mum was here.

I'd tortured myself until my last glance at the clock at 4.36 a.m. when my brain must have decided it'd had enough: it was time to sleep. My plan to confront him in the morning failed, as when I awoke at 8.07 a.m. Max had already left.

Trying to figure out how on earth I'd slept through the 7 a.m. alarm, I realised I'd forgotten to put it on. (I'd done that twice in the last month: I'd heard my customers talking of baby brain, but I thought it came afterwards.) He must have left before 7 a.m. or he would have woken me. It wasn't unusual for him to set off so early. He liked to miss the traffic: it would generally take an hour and a half even without the added problem of rush hour.

I did think about calling him, but I wanted to see his face. Look into his eyes: which are said to be the windows of the soul.

And I needed him to see mine.

Suzy got the full brunt of my emotions, as I'd told her it all made sense, his lack of interest in Melanie setting up with Mandy: he was behind them.

Why hadn't he left me, though? Was he staying because of the babies?

Suzy was adamant that Max was not seeing Melanie; or anyone, for that matter. 'Lawrence would know and he'd have told me.'

'But there is no other explanation.' I shook my head.

'Right … look here,' she ordered as we pulled into the car park of the community centre where the yoga was held. Parking quickly in a tight space, which if possible would have made me pull my stomach in, the car engine still running, she tugged her phone from her bag. She then clicked a few buttons on her screen. 'Can … perfume … transfer … onto … body … from … someone … else's … clothes,' she sang as she typed the words into the phone.

'What are you doing?'

'I've definitely read it somewhere, so it will be on the internet if it's true.' She scanned her phone, tapping against the screen as she made a clicking sound with her mouth. 'Here we are.' She turned her phone to me so I could see the screen. Lists of articles about fragrances appeared. She quickly read some evidence out to me: a discussion forum complained about women who wear too much perfume and how it's frustrating when the smell is transferred onto their clothes and hair. Some workplaces actually have a fragrance-free policy because a condition known as Multiple Chemical Sensitivities (MCS) can cause some people serious illnesses if they're exposed to fragrances.

'I've never read anything like it,' I said in disbelief.

'I have a client who must bath in the stuff before her session—'

'What, before you train her?' I shook my head, wondering why someone would bother showering before a workout.

'Yeah,' Suzy nodded, 'I swear she still smells the same after I've made her sweat buckets and I can smell it for hours after.'

'You're just trying to make me feel better.'

'I'm not, I swear.' She clicked off her phone before turning off the engine. 'Have you smelt it on him before?'

'No.' I bit my lip, not adding but when had we last been that close in bed?

'So, if he was having an affair with Melanie, don't you think you'd have smelt it by now?'

'S'pose.' I was still unconvinced.

'You need to talk to him about it.'

I didn't admit my turbulent thoughts had said the same thing all night. Actually, talk hadn't been an option: shouting and screaming was probably the more viable of outcomes. But now … would it be silly of me to hold onto the internet evidence?

I really wanted to find out that Max had been working with a woman who didn't understand the limits of fragrance use, but he'd not mentioned anyone new. Maybe he'd had a meeting with someone … but what, until ten o'clock at night?

It sounds laughable, but in his line of work, it could be true.

He could have met a client after work … I wouldn't know: he didn't really tell me what he was doing or with whom. But that wasn't unusual either. When we'd first met, he'd tell me about the big contracts, but he had other smaller contracts that he never talked about. I'd always asked if he'd had a good day, and he would reply with a fair, moderate or good answer. He would sometimes tell me about little incidents that happened, but if I was asked to reel off a list of his clients, I wouldn't know where to start.

My worse fear before falling pregnant, was actually falling pregnant, but I was here now. I'd learned to grow with my babies;

with slight apprehension, but I was working through it. In fact, in all honesty, over the last two months saving the salon had been more at the forefront of my mind than the babies. Although I'd become a sponge when it came to learning about them, taking in all that I could about being a parent, my focus had been on my work. The babies were there with me constantly, so it wasn't as if I could forget about them. But the salon had been a good distraction in easing the anxiety.

As we walked into the community centre, with other women who waddled instead of walked, I realised how relaxed I'd actually become about them arriving. But I also knew it was because I had Max. I wasn't doing it alone.

I hoped this was still the case.

My eyes were sore, my body ached severely as we entered the yoga classroom, but the distraction would do me good. Back in the salon, I'd only wallow and let the nausea overwhelm me. Suzy was right: I needed to do this. I needed to do anything apart from sit in the salon and dwell.

'So, how's it going at the salon?' Suzy whispered, once the class had started. So much for a distraction …

'People are still cancelling daily.' Hoping my hushed tones reached her. I stretched one leg out in front of the other, my arms extended, my warrior pose looking more like a charades mime for a wobbly bridge than a refined, purposeful position.

'Really!' Suzy's voice echoed across the high-ceilinged hall.

Other pregnant and non-pregnant women (or supportive partners, being the correct term) peered at us. The yoga teacher raised her eyebrows in our direction, daring us to interrupt this tranquil time.

'They keep undercutting my prices, and offering new treatments that I can't afford to think about, let alone do.'

'Where the hell are they getting the money from?' Suzy stared straight ahead, speaking from the side of her mouth.

'Mandy's father.' The teacher glared over at us. I smiled as if listening intently to everything she was saying. 'I did a bit of research on him. He owns nursing homes and other investments … he's minted,' I said quietly between the teacher's glances.

'What're you going to do?'

'I don't know. I can't keep the business going while my customers are going to them.' We all followed the teacher to the wall, placing our hands against the cold brick, walking our feet outwards so our backs were straight and in line with our arms, pushing our heads forwards.

'Feel the stretch in your back, ladies.' The teacher spoke softly, as if she was walking on air, while I felt as if my bump would bounce on the floor.

'The best of it is, Mrs bloody Donnelly was right: not one of them has had the guts to tell me where they're going,' I said, as blood rushed to my head.

'Maybe the others had genuine reasons.' Suzy, always the optimist, stretched her lean, flawless figure up to the sky, away from the wall. I did the same, feeling as if I was eighty years old.

I knew Suzy didn't want to dwell on Mrs Donnelly. It was a part of her life she seemed to have stored away, a part that she didn't want to examine. I'd never asked her if she'd discussed it with Lawrence; I assumed she must have at some point. But we all had parts in our lives we wanted to store in a locked, bottom drawer.

'They were crap reasons, like other appointments, illnesses; one said her cat had died.'

'Aw, Kat, that could be true.'

'I don't think she owned a bloody cat.'

'Oh.'

I breathed deeply, as we walked away from the wall. Back in our positions I mirrored the teacher, arching my arm uncomfortably over my head for a side stretch.

'Release the blood flow, ladies.'

What? I don't think so! There was no blood flow being released: I felt as if I was squashing my lungs.

'I don't understand how the hell I got here, Suz. Not only losing my business but now this with Max …'

'Max is *not* cheating.' Her words vibrated across the quiet hall, above the peaceful waterfall music that was meant to be soothing but really just made me need the loo.

The teacher cleared her throat, making it very clear she disapproved of our behaviour.

'Thanks for that,' I muttered, as a few of the women squinted at me, sympathy or horror showing in their faces.

'Sorry. But I don't believe anything is going on,' Suzy murmured when the stiff-faced teacher had doubled over into an extended forward bend, which had me and several other women with huge bumps simply watching the process in a bemused manner.

Suzy followed her lead, her head resting against her knees, her arms swinging against the floor, her natural flexibility making it a pleasure for her. This position wasn't recommended for the pregnant ladies in the class; it was to help the 'supportive partners' stretch out their muscles. I liked that this was a position for supportive partners only, and never admitted, not even to Suzy, that I couldn't touch my toes before I was pregnant so there was no chance now.

'I don't know what to do, Suz,' I said quietly, as she stretched her body back up, her arms reaching upwards, her back arching gracefully. I wondered if she even felt any of her muscles stretching, she was so flexible.

'You need to talk to him.' She glared at me sternly, her eyebrows raised as she came back to an upright position. 'But, I think you're wrong. I'd know if he was cheating with Melanie.'

I was quiet as the teacher told us to sit down cross-legged to help stretch our pubic area; her words, not mine. Talking of stretching uteruses and cervixes felt so wrong with all these other people in the room. I also felt like an uncomfortable lump next to Suzy with her bendy suppleness: I resembled a sumo wrestler compared to her lithe body.

'You're pregnant, not fat; it's beautiful,' she'd once told me when I was complaining about the lard-arse I'd acquired.

'But it's meant to go on my front, not my arse,' I'd replied. 'I suppose you're going to tell me the purple marks surrounding my hips are picturesque story lines, like laughter lines.'

'Bio-Oil is fantastic for stretch marks,' she'd informed me. Guess she didn't think they *were* so beautiful then!

Suzy stretched her enviable body. Her stunning features, her flawless skin were made more beautiful because of her charming personality. I watched as she effortlessly pushed her body into positions it wasn't designed to reach, and I knew she would probably never smell perfume on her man – unless her theory was right, of course. She'd had a glow about her since meeting Lawrence. She radiated happiness, her eyes were alight, her aura full of energy. Lawrence would be a fool to let her go; *any* man who had her in his grasp would be stupid to let her go. I thought about Steve Donnelly: how could he compare Suzy to Mrs D, when really there was no comparison?

'Ladies, if we're going to attend next week, could we please leave the conversations outside? It's very distracting for the other pupils.' The teacher addressed us when the class was finished, her soft words direct, and very clear. Suzy and I apologised for our bad manners, making excuses that we had things to talk about. She told us, 'That being the case you should go and catch up over coffee rather than disrupting my session.'

'Sorry,' we both mumbled, like reprimanded children, embarrassed that she'd made a point of telling us off in front of the whole class. We left, debating whether we would actually go back.

'You're going through a stressful time,' Suzy said, shivering against the cold winds, as we walked to her car.

'I know.'

'Do you want Lawrence to have a word?'

'No … no …' I shook my head. Yes, I did, but what would that solve?

I wished someone could sort this out for me.

Make it go away.

If I'd not leaned into Max, I'd not have smelt the pungent scent that now had me in such turmoil. It could have been the nicest, freshest fragrance ever, but at this moment to me cow-dung would have been more appealing. And, for that reason, I had to deal with this. No-one else could sort this out but me and Max. 'We're s'posed to be going to his Mum's tonight … I'll ask him on the way there … or maybe after …' I was distracted as I spoke, unsure how I would start the conversation with Max.

'Lawrence is always saying that Max is so happy about the babies coming.'

'I wish he'd show me how happy he is.'

***

I arrived at the salon about an hour later. It was nice that the lights were on, that someone was already there. It was better than the bleakness I'd faced every morning. Sophie and Laura were sitting at the nail table, chatting.

There were no customers in. I peered at the diary, sure that there should have been at least two appointments booked in. Sophie came to the desk, her solemn expression speaking a thousand words.

'More cancellations?' I asked.

'Three more cancelled for this afternoon.'

'Jesus.' I breathed out loudly, rubbing my eyes, too tired to focus. 'What is going on?'

'Did you drive past their salon?' Sophie grimaced.

'No … why?' It was probably the only time I hadn't, but my focus was on Max, which hadn't been the case over the last few weeks.

'I think they must be having some kind of launch.'

'What do you mean?'

'They've got music blaring, balloons hanging outside and some kind of promotional girls handing out leaflets that offer free treatments all day today.' She handed me a glossy A5 leaflet, grey and pink feathers adorning the logo. My heart sank. Had Marianne not got one of these? She'd not mentioned it.

'How did you get this?'

'Courtesy of me,' Laura said smiling, obviously very pleased with herself.

'They don't know who Laura is, so she went and had a nosey.'

'Excellent.' I was impressed with their detective work, wanting to show my appreciation but wishing my gut would lift from its pit.

'I'm sorry, Kat, it doesn't matter what we do, they seem to be …' Sophie shrugged, not finishing the sentence that could have ended with: 'better.' Or 'wiping the floor with us.' Or 'winning.'

'Don't you be sorry.' I decided to ignore the fact that she couldn't, or didn't want to speak the words that would have me in tears. I flicked through the next few pages. It was starting to look more like a child's scribbling book than a professional diary.

It was decided there were only a few customers left to come in, so I sent Laura home. Sophie and I worked our way through the remaining clients, but queasiness shadowed me all day, more so than it usually did. I had no energy, no time or inclination to start again. Even though I was trying so hard to hold onto the place that was my haven … the place where Mum would have been so proud of me … the place that was my second home … I had to be realistic.

How long could I carry on like this, before it was too late? How long could I go on before the bank was chasing me?

I remembered the days when I started my business. Before I even opened the salon, I was out meeting people, networking, mixing in every corner possible. I had the flair, the excitement, pushing me forward. I met amazing people who helped me launch my business. It was hard work but it had been so much fun. I would attend breakfast meetings at 7 a.m. before the salon opened and I would ensure I made it to evening events when sometimes I didn't get home until the early hours of the morning.

I suppose most of the activity started to dwindle once Max came into my life. I didn't mind at the time. He was a nice distraction, a welcome interruption to my busy life. I was so focused on making a success of the business that sometimes I lost myself inside its world. Every time I gained a new customer a flutter of satisfaction and excitement would drive through me, urging me to try and find more. It was an adrenaline rush watching my business grow, customers loving the treatments and word-of-mouth being my best form of advertising. It was an amazing feeling that kept me high.

When Max entered my world I didn't lose the enthusiasm but I gained some of my personal life back. I enjoyed it; I relished having some fun time. Since falling pregnant I'd taken a further step back, away from the business.

Not purposely, but I'd been so tired. I'd also felt guilty that I'd actually considered not going ahead with the pregnancy. So, I tried to make up for this, I thought that by resting, and ensuring the babies were healthy while educating myself on their tiny developing bodies, and soaking up as much information as possible, it would help me become a better parent. It would somehow redeem my initial uncertainty about continuing with the pregnancy. However, there was so much information that I'd often confuse myself on what was right and wrong, or if there *was* a right or wrong way. 'Follow your own instincts ... do it your own way ...' I'd read in one baby book.

I would do it my own way ... if I knew what I was doing!

I'd had appointments with the midwife, and routine scans. I'd trusted Melanie if I'd taken the afternoon off, or when I attended my weekly yoga session; which she'd encouraged me to do. I'd had a few late mornings when I was trying to settle into Max's house, trying to put my stamp on my new home; even though that wasn't working. I was trying to adapt to that thing people talk about: 'work-life balance'.

So, with the babies being my focus, I'd let go of the reins a little ... something I said I'd never do. I took a back seat and let people help me.

I'd let Melanie have more control, more responsibility ... but isn't that what a good boss would do? Personal development, encouragement ... wouldn't that make them better employees?

Having to be in control had always been one of my downfalls. But look what happens when you let go, when you sit in the passenger seat for a while.

Here I was, left with a shell, a building.

As we worked our way through the few clients, my thoughts collided, battling endlessly. Could I move the business forward any more? Did I have the fight in me? Or more so, the resources? I'd tried to tackle them head-to-head ... but look what was happening. My bank balance was declining. And my sanity was in tatters.

A heavy weight was pushing on my heart. My salon had offered me a life that was different. A life that was special. A life Mum would have been proud of. And now it was being ripped from me. The thing I couldn't grasp, that choked me to the core, was that Mum's death had happened so suddenly that it seemed like one of the only instantaneous things that would ever happen in my life.

It felt as if the things that mattered, the things that were important to me, could be taken away so quickly, snatched from my life, as easily as blowing away a feather.

10

Clare greeted us both with open arms, a different woman from the one I'd been introduced to a year ago. Smells of a succulent fresh dinner drifted through her hospitable home, tempting us inside. 'Hospitable' was probably a word I wouldn't have used a year ago. Not that her home had ever been a cold, unwelcoming place; but the ambience hadn't been one I'd adored.

'Hello, Kathryn, how lovely to see you.' Henry kissed my cheek, his eyes on my bump. 'Oh, haven't you grown?'

'Dad!' Max jested.

'In a good way,' he laughed.

'That's no way to talk to a lady.' Clare smiled as Henry poured us all a drink, the three of them enjoying the sparkling vintage wine, while I enjoyed the supermarket's own-brand sparkling flavoured water. Henry did, though, use a wine glass for the sparkling juice.

'It must taste better in this,' he said as he handed me the long-stemmed crystal glass.

'Of course,' I smiled, appreciating his warmth.

We sat around the table, a large cream candle in the centre setting the evening mood. As the hours passed, I watched Max talk with his mother and father. I studied him as he hardly met my eye. He told them stories of his work, then asked both Henry and Clare about their lives, catching up on the weeks he'd not seen them; but as he did this he didn't seem to be involving me. Not in a spiteful way; I don't think he was deliberately ignoring me but he wasn't making any effort to include me either. I wondered if I was being oversensitive. Was I now trying to pick out bits about our relationship that weren't right? Justify that he must be cheating on me?

Our journey to Clare's house had been quiet. As we drove through the dark, winding roads, our conversation was limited, as if being in each other's company was an effort. I didn't broach the perfume subject, concerned it would escalate into a row. If he could justify his answer and he wasn't having an affair, then he'd be upset. If he admitted to cheating, then I obviously wouldn't be going to Clare's. Both conclusions made my insides churn.

Once we were in the car, I didn't want us falling out before we reached his mother's. I didn't have the energy to disguise a huge argument.

The candle flickered across the room, shadows forming elegantly, dancing smoothly against the soft light. The bi-fold doors closed out the cold night, but the perfect lawns were emphasised by small lights that surrounded the neatly trimmed garden. The decking displayed an in-built array of blue lights that shone up towards the sky, an ideal setting for a stage, though maybe slightly elaborate for a back garden. I thought about how our children would run freely on Clare's unspoiled, flawless lawn. Would she cope with it? She was so thrilled and excited about the babies, but when reality hit could she really handle sticky fingers touching her polished cupboards, or messy faces stamping their mark across her sparkly windows?

'So, Kathryn, how's things with the salon? Any better?' Henry asked me.

'Not really.' I shook my head.

'Clare says you've had quite a few cancellations.'

I nodded, not wanting to elaborate.

'It's not for me to interfere, but I've seen many businesses go under in my time. If you can do something about this now, I would do it.'

'What can I do?'

'If the bank is in profit and you don't owe anything, then you have no debt; it could be an idea to walk away now.'

'Really!' I put down my knife and fork, grateful that someone was giving me their honest opinion, because no-one actually had. Not even Max had discussed the next stage. 'Do you think so?'

'I'm trying to look at this from a business and health point of view. You don't want to be running that place, taking care of babies and getting yourself into debt. A vicious circle to get into. Once you're in it, it'll be harder to get out.'

'I have thought about it.'

'Have you?' Max frowned, seemingly bewildered.

'A personal question, but are you in profit?' Henry was frowning, intensely analysing my situation, which was more than Max had done.

'Yes, I'd be okay for about six months if I closed it now. I doubt it would be that easy, though, I still have three years left on my contract.' I felt as if I was talking about someone else. Giving up my business, just walking away. It didn't feel real.

'If I was you, Kathryn, I'd look into this further.' Henry sipped his red wine. 'Have you made that appointment with Jack Haslow yet?'

'No … he did approach me at your party, I've just not got around to seeing him.'

'I think you must. I think you could be interested in what he has to say.'

'But what about my contract?'

'Can you chat with your landlord and explain your situation?'

'Don't you think you're being pessimistic, Kat?' Max asked, staring at me.

'I'm not sure of anything anymore, Max.' The words struck across the room. A heavy silence fell upon us as if I'd announced a loved one had died. Max looked away from me as Henry reached over and took my hand, telling me it would be okay.

***

I drove back through the dark roads, cat's eyes my only visible lead, as our heated words were thrown at each other.

'I can't believe you've not come to me,' Max said sternly.

'When? You're never here.'

'My work is busy at the moment. Are you begrudging me that, when yours might stop?'

'Do you think I want mine to stop?'

'I'm not saying you do, but I still need to know what is going on. I'll be the one supporting you, remember.'

'Do you want *me*, Max?' I said, after a short silence.

'What?' He shook his head in bewilderment. 'Of course, I do.'

'You're not having an affair?'

'Oh my God, Kat you're—'

'I smelt perfume on you last night.' The words hung in the air, the silence filled the car. 'Is it Melanie?'

'Are you serious?'

'It was Melanie's perfume.' The tears burned as I tried to focus on the darkness ahead.

'Perfume?' he stuttered. 'I don't know what you're talking about.'

'Please tell me the truth Max,' I begged.

'Stop the car.'

'What?'

'Stop the car.'

'You're not getting out!' I panicked, as the dark, unlit road surrounded us.

'No. Just stop the car,' he said, more softly than he'd spoken to me in a while.

I found a place to pull in about half a mile along: an entrance to a field, which was situated off the narrow country road. The wheels squelched on top of the wet mud, which splattered against the paintwork.

I left the engine ticking over and dimmed the lights slightly. The glow, lightly projecting into the car, casting shadows on Max's face as he turned to look at me. He took hold of my hands. 'I'm not seeing Melanie.'

'But you've shown little interest in what's happened with the salon.'

His usual deep blue eyes looked black against the night. 'I have … I've tried to … but, Kat, you've always been so independent, I've never interfered in your business. I didn't want to tell you how to run it, or what to do next. That wouldn't be fair.'

'But you've never talked to me about it.'

'I'm sorry, I didn't think you wanted me to. I thought you were getting on with it. I thought you'd come to me if you wanted to talk. When you were talking to Dad tonight, I was a bit peed off you'd not come to me first.'

'I tried, in the beginning. I rang you, remember, but you were far too busy to talk to me.'

'You rang at a really awkward moment.'

'But you didn't want to talk to me about it when you came home.'

'You seemed so upset that night, running off from the table when Suzy and Lawrence were there. Even Lawrence put it down to your hormones.' I remembered hearing the end of that conversation, and having had the idea that Max was slating me. 'I just thought that night you needed to sleep on things; there was no point us analysing anything.'

'But I needed you to be there.'

'Then you should have come to me. I've always said there is no point us discussing any business matters when emotions are running high.' He *had* always said that, and he always followed his own advice: if he was stressed about a project, he'd step back from it until he was properly focused.

'But when my emotions calmed down, you still didn't talk to me about it.'

'Did I not agree that you don't pay yourself a salary, so you could promote the place?'

'Yes.'

'So, I've supported you, Kat, in the best way I know how. I thought you were dealing with things. I've been so busy at work, too. If you needed me you should have come to me.'

I hated the way he was so black and white about the whole situation. I'd wanted him to ask about me, or at least take an interest in what was happening in my life. But he was always so busy, though it seemed pointless to throw this accusation at him. Why? Because he could throw it back at me. I always asked if he'd had a good day. Without fail those words passed my lips every day. But did I ask about his clients? His work colleagues? The ins and outs of his meetings? Never.

'But where were you last night?' I thought about the perfume and how he'd not answered me.

'Working. I told you that.' He let go of my hands, running his own through his thick blond hair.

'Where?'

'In the office. We've got a huge shopping complex to finish. Someone had fucked up the plans, so I was trying to save it before we lost the bloody contract.'

'But who was with you?'

'Jesus, Kat, what is this?' He shook his head, frustrated. 'I've told you where I was.'

'I know, but who was there with you?' I still needed some kind of confirmation. A background picture of where he'd been. A woman who may have been overzealous with her sweet scent.

'John, Stu, Kevin and Yasmin.'

'Yasmin?' Ah, was this her?

'I'm not having an affair with Yasmin.'

'I'm not saying you are, but who is she?' I'd only heard of John and Stu. Had Max employed new staff? Wouldn't he have mentioned that before? I would have, if I'd employed someone new: he knew all about Laura.

'She started about a month ago. Stu employed her through our graduate scheme. She's training.' He sounded exasperated. Did she perhaps wear a lot of perfume? As if reading my thoughts, he said, 'I remember now, she sprayed perfume all over the office—'

'What?'

'Because we were working late, John went out and got us an Indian. Stu was farting so much afterwards, she couldn't face it and sprayed perfume all over. It smelt worse than the farts.'

'You are kidding?' Part of me wanted to laugh at his ridiculous excuse, while the other part of me wanted to kiss him, forget we'd even had this conversation.

'No, I'm not kidding,' he said indignantly, as if I'd insulted him. 'Shall I ring John now?' He pulled his phone from his pocket, pressing the button to bring up his contact list.

I put my hand on his, stopping him from getting anyone else involved.

'Actually, I'll ring Stu. You know what John's like: he'll wind you up.' I didn't know what John or Stu were really like. I'd met them once, the night of the dinner, the night I fell pregnant. John had seemed like a joker, but I'd put that down to the drink.

'No.' I kept my hand on the phone. 'Don't ring anyone,' I said quietly. Would they lie for him? Would I believe them? I didn't know what to think. 'So, you're trying to tell me the perfume must have been from her?'

'I'm assuming so, Kat, because I swear on our babies' lives, I'm not seeing Melanie, or Yasmin.' That was a strong promise to make.

I peered out into the darkness. The low beam of the car headlights dimly lit up the bushes, the different shades of greens and browns sharply segmented, glistening under the mist and drizzle.

Should I believe him? Had Suzy told Lawrence, who in turn had told Max about our conversation?

I didn't know what to believe.

'If I was seeing someone else – anyone – not even Melanie, don't you think I'd have stopped out last night?'

True.

'If I'd been with a woman, don't you think I'd have showered when I got in?'

True.

'Kat, you have to believe me, I'm not seeing anyone else.'

I suddenly had the overwhelming desire to believe him.

***

As we drove home, after he'd slowly kissed my lips, my face in his hands, running his fingers through my hair, giving me a feeling I hadn't had in a while, I knew I had to believe him, because I was scared of the alternative. This relationship was no longer only about the two of us. We would be part of a bigger family soon, so I had to believe him, because I couldn't do it on my own.

When we later climbed into bed, he wrapped his body around mine, my back against the wall of his chest as his hands caressed my bump. We stayed in this position until he fell asleep.

Could he sleep so soundly, so quickly, if he was cheating?

I'd slid from his grasp, not only because I needed the loo, again, but because I needed some air. With his body next to mine, I was so hot I thought I'd pass out, but I'd stayed as long as I could within his grasp, because it felt so nice to have him so close. To feel his love in a way I'd not experienced in such a long time.

When I climbed into bed again, listening to his deep breathing, my mind began to wander. What if he was seeing Melanie, but they had nowhere to go, so he had to come home? If he was seeing her, she couldn't take him back home to Bobby. That would be a little awkward. What if Melanie had left Bobby for Max? I'm sure Bobby would have told me if that was the case.

Oh my God. I was driving myself insane.

I pushed away the thoughts, closed my eyes and knew I had to hold onto the belief that he was telling the truth …

11

In between holding onto the belief that Max was telling the truth, Henry's advice had also been swimming through my mind all night. Unless a miracle happened, I wasn't sure what I could do to save the salon. I tried so hard to fight against Melanie and Mandy, but they kept knocking me back, so God Damn slickly and easily. No matter what I did they seemed to do it ten times stronger. They had the money and the investment that I didn't have.

In the beginning, when the excitement and exhilaration of opening my salon kept me awake at night, I'd never thought it wouldn't work. As the business grew, as customers were reeled in, not for one minute did it occur to me that this could happen.

I really needed to think about my next move quickly. I really needed to do something about it now before Henry was right, and I built up mammoth amounts of debt. It wouldn't be long before the debt letters were arriving because I couldn't pay, and not because I'd become purely unorganised. It happened all the time. Did I want to fall into that category?

But I didn't want to close the salon. Realistically though, this wasn't about me anymore. It was about the two little beings that were relying me. Although, I wanted to hang on for dear life, strap myself to the building with a huge chain and tell the world I would not be beaten, what good would that do anyone? What good would I be to my two babies, who'd need me more than the salon needed me?

But what if I couldn't sell it? Or what if the landlord wouldn't let me cease the contract? My head was pounding with all these mixed thoughts.

I'd expected Sophie to be in the salon when I got there. It was a little after 8.30 a.m., although we didn't open until 9 a.m., Sophie had got into the habit of coming earlier to help me get sorted, in the way Melanie always had.

The salon was cold, the freezing air chilling my body. Shivering and rubbing my hands together, I checked the timer on the heater. My first customer was booked in for a spray-tan; I couldn't expect her to strip off in this arctic temperature. The heating had flicked off for some reason, so I pressed the buttons which enabled it to come back on.

'God, it's cold.' I spoke to myself, my breath showing in clouds in the freezing air. Oh Jesus, it must be illegal to spray-tan someone in such low temperatures. She'd become an ice sculpture. So, I dragged the heater that was normally placed in the reception area into the room where the woman would be naked while I caked her with bronzing solution. My back pulled as I heaved the metal unit. I grunted as I used muscles that hadn't been used in a while.

'Kathryn, you shouldn't be doing that!' Clare startled me, as she entered with force, the door chime vibrating through the room. She rushed towards me, taking the heater from my hands and dragging it into the treatment room where I needed it.

'What are you doing here so early?' I asked, surprised to see her.

'I've been thinking all night about the discussion we had at dinner,' she said. I shook my head, unsure which part she was referring to. 'I've spoken with Henry and Maxwell about this briefly this morning. I've come up with a fantastic idea.'

'You have?'

'I could fulfil the rest of your contract with your landlord.'

'What?' I shook my head. 'I don't understand. You want to take over the business? But you know nothing about beauty therapy.'

'No, I don't.' She grinned, her eyes blazing with enthusiasm. 'But I was thinking along the lines of getting you out of your contract. I could turn it into a hair salon.'

'What?' Had she lost her mind? 'You haven't touched hair since Max was born.'

'I have slightly; I cut Henry's hair. But you're right. I could hire a few girls, though. I'll retrain, or something. The basics are simple; I just need a refresher.'

'A refresher? No disrespect, Clare, but it's been over thirty years.'

'I know, but this feels like … my calling, or something. It means I help you out, and I follow my dream. It feels like the right thing to do.'

The phone rang, interrupting our conversation. I told Clare to hang on a minute as I answered in my professional manner.

'Kat. It's Sophie.' Her voice was trembling and she sounded as if she'd been crying.

'Sophie, are you okay? What's happened?'

'I really didn't want to do this over the phone, but I knew you'd not want to see my face.' She went quiet and I couldn't answer her as my body slumped into the reception chair. 'I'm going to work for Melanie and Mandy.'

12

I picked up my mobile and searched for his name. The dialling tone was long and distant; instantly I knew he was abroad. The cheerful manner of my landlord as he answered the phone sent butterflies of anxiety fluttering in my stomach, as I asked him how I could get out of my contract.

'I'm really sorry, but there's nothing I can do.'

'Really?'

'I would love to help you, Kat, but I have commitments based on our contract.'

What commitments? Endless holidays? 'What if I could find someone to take over?'

'If you can find someone to transfer it to, then I'm happy with that.'

'What if she wanted to make it into a hair salon?' I hinted at Clare's ludicrous idea, but who was I to judge her?

'Same rules apply, as long as it goes back to its original state.'

'Thanks. I'll ask around and keep you updated.' I didn't want to commit yet.

'Okay, pet. I'm sorry this has happened. I'm a big believer in karma, though.' I felt as if he was reading my mind, until he said, 'But business is business.'

'Business is business, you're not bloody kidding.' The phone was dead as I spoke my thoughts into the vacant, cold space.

I dialled another number into my phone. I wasn't sure if it was panic that was driving me forward, or the fact that I was merely going along with decisions that were being made around me. I didn't feel as if I had time to think about the next step. All I could see was my overheads flashing warning signs at me. I knew that with the number of customers who had cancelled I couldn't withstand these losses.

Now Sophie leaving me in the lurch, apparently, they'd offered her a better salary and further training. *Further training?* I felt sick I'd spent money on training her to compete against them. Would I ever learn?

Apparently, Mandy had plans to expand across the country, she could see Sophie running one of her salons, one day. I couldn't compete with that. But then, that had never been my intention when I'd opened the snug, tranquil place. Mandy however, deviant in her ways, had obviously took a few tips from 'Daddy'.

I didn't want to compete with any big corporations, that wasn't what I was about. Hence, the reason I'd stayed away from the cities. I wondered if Melanie knew about the bigger picture. Had she been lured in by the potential of what they could be?

In my determination to fight them, I'd had a fleeting moment of wondering if someone could come in and run the salon for me; but again, there'd be more overheads, wages to pay, and for what? It would at best be a break-even situation; or I'd make a significant loss. If whoever I employed decided to do what Mandy and Melanie had done, I'd be in a worse situation than I was now.

It was as if everything was telling me to get out. Move on to the next chapter in my life.

But it felt so hard.

But all I knew was, I had to do the right thing for the babies. No matter how difficult it was.

***

'Haslow Accountancy, how can I help?'

'I need to make an appointment with Jack Haslow, please,' I told the girl, who sounded very young. She advised there had been a cancellation and he had an afternoon slot. I took it.

Would Jack think I had anything to hang on to?

God, Mum I wish you were here.

As I placed the phone back down, I put my head in my hands, then looked up at the heavens and begged her to help me.

There was so much to lose by not taking Clare's hand and letting her help me. I could try and pass the business on, but who would want it when a sleek proficient outfit had set up around the corner?

Someone may have come along, who wanted to set up a small shop, their own cosy abode, but I doubted that would happen. It could take months, even years to try and transfer the contract to someone else.

Clare's face had been alight, she'd come alive; she'd seen an opportunity and she was ready to run with it, wanting to fulfil her little girl's dream. It wasn't about the money, I knew that. I asked about her and Henry's retirement. She'd laughed at me, 'I'm only in my fifties, Kathryn, I'm not dead.' I hadn't dared to question her after that. Whether she was making the right choice or not seemed little to do with me. Henry was behind her. She said she'd spoken to Max; so was he behind her too?

Laura was supposed to be in by now. To be honest I knew she'd only spend time embellishing her own nails or working her way through the products to see if there were any freebies going. There were a few appointments, but for a Friday the number was embarrassingly low, so I did something I've never done before ... I cancelled them.

I had no time to waste. No time to think.

If I delayed, I would decide to keep the salon going, a few more weeks would pass us by ... but I knew I would end up in a dire state.

***

'You could sell the business as a going concern.' Jack Haslow advised me, after I'd explained what had happened with Melanie. Although, he seemed to know most of it, I filled in a few gaps. His accent was quite sexy. He was a handsome man, probably in his early forties. His dark hair, sprinkled with grey, gave him that charming, distinguished demeanour that appealed to many women. Photos of his children and his wife cluttered his desk and office. Family skiing, water-jetting and camping holidays boasted of his happy lifestyle. I wondered if Max would have pictures of me across his desk. I wondered how much I was actually mentioned in his work life.

I explained to Jack about Clare, and how she could be my lifeline. How she could get me out of this before it became more unbearable than it already was. He tapped his pen and seemed to consider me carefully, his eyes mesmerising, deep and full of meaning. 'I need to look at your figures over the last few months. Have you had chance to send them through?'

'No. I'm sorry my head has been all over the place.' I usually sent him my paperwork every month, but I'd not sent anything since Melanie had left. I was blaming my messy mind, but perhaps it was having the reality spelt out for me. I had an idea of how much I'd lost, but to have it written down, figures in bold print to spell out my failure … that was like willingly torturing myself.

Jack was staring at me, his pen tapping against his cheek, 'Kat, I'm your accountant, but we've had quite a trusting relationship, so please don't take umbrage at what I have to say …'

'I won't.' Hopefully!

'You've got to make sure you are taking care of yourself, these babies need you to be healthy,' He pointed his pen at my bump, 'But no offence … you look beat.'

'I know.' A dramatic sigh escaped me. I appreciated his honesty; well maybe not the word 'beat'. He could have said, 'Less than your usual glamorous self,' and boosted my deflated ego a little.

'I'd been so interested to talk to you earlier, because I had a client who wants to expand her own salon. However, she doesn't have any funds so she couldn't *buy* you out. She would have taken over the contract, though. But, I think Clare's offer might be the better option.'

'Why?' I didn't want to upset Clare, but was interested to know his opinion.

'I did *hint* to my client that there could be an opportunity near your area,' he held his hands up, 'Don't worry, client confidentiality. I didn't say it was in Great Ayton, I just told her it was over that way. And apparently, my client has friends who have a salon in Stokesley and apparently Lush Lucia have been trying to steal customers from all over.'

'What Mandy and Melanie have been going around the other salons looking for business?'

'Apparently.'

'That somehow doesn't surprise me,' I leaned back in the chair.

'Kat, I've seen many companies fail. If you don't have the resources to fight them, then you've got to do what is right for you.'

'I can't keep using money to promote the salon, especially when they keep under-cutting me.'

'… but when I say resources …' he paused, twiddled the pen between his fingers, '… we can look at the financial side, but you've got to think about yourself. You are the main resource for that business and the babies are due very soon …'

'I know … but what if I'm making a rash decision?' I spoke to him as if he were a counsellor.

'I'm sorry, Kat, but I can't tell you that,' he sighed, loudly, 'All I can do is look at your figures and then we can go from there.'

I breathed out deeply, taking in the reality that I was talking about wrapping my business in. 'Great,' I managed to say. Hoping it sounded sincere and not sarcastic.

'I'll put the figures together. Who's your solicitor?'

'I haven't used one since setting up the business, but the landlord has one that he'd like to use for signing over the contract.'

'Okay, great,' he nodded. I could see that his mind was ticking over as he thought of another suggestion. 'If you're unsure of Clare taking over, I can go back to my client, but I think Lush Lucia have given them a fright. But, we can always use a commercial estate agent. They'll put the feelers out to see if anyone is interested in buying.'

'Do you think anyone will be?'

'It could be just what someone is looking for.'

'I'd probably be shooting myself in the foot, though, wouldn't I?'

'It is an option if Clare decides it's not for her, or if you would prefer to sell outside of the family.'

'I'll have a chat with her, make sure this is what she wants. I don't want her making any quick decisions either, then being stuck with a hair salon that she doesn't want. I don't want it coming back on me.'

As I drove away from Jack Haslow I thought I'd feel some kind of relief, like a sense that I'd either closed a chapter in my life or settled an unnecessary worry. I thought maybe he would tell me not to be so silly: of course I didn't have to sell.

I'd left some paperwork at the salon and I'd planned on looking at my accounts over the coming days, which was inevitable now, I'd have to get them to Jack: the truth to be revealed.

But heading back to the salon stirred up an unpleasant mixture of emotions. I couldn't get Melanie from my mind, it wasn't Mandy who tortured my thoughts, it was the woman who'd supposedly been my friend. I could never have hurt her in the way she'd hurt me, but maybe in her world her behaviour was acceptable.

Jack had asked me if I'd stated in her contract that if she stopped working for me she couldn't work within a certain radius. But I hadn't even given her a contract. Foolish, I know. We'd signed something in the beginning, but it was as if we were playing at it; it was fun.

As I drove towards the place that had once been my home, I felt as if I was travelling to a place I didn't know. A place where I wasn't welcome. It no longer felt like my haven … and for that reason I knew it was time to walk away.

At the salon, I grabbed the file I needed, feeling a desperate need to be away from these four walls. I scanned the empty room, in hope that I may feel a connection, wipe away some of the fury that was eating away at me.

But there was nothing.

The door chimed its acknowledgement of someone entering. My breath caught in my throat. I dropped my keys as my heart quickened its pace.

I recognised the older lady instantly. She'd not changed.

Her elaborate sense of style showed in her high black boots and black leggings, her long turquoise coat covering her slim figure, the matching, fur-trimmed enhancing her sophistication.

A peculiar sensation quivered through my body as I glared at the woman who could have been mistaken for my own mother.

'June?'

'Hello, dear.'

13

After the shock of Mum's sister arriving like some kind of paranormal vision, we hugged and I caught my breath as the reality hit me.

She then followed me along the wet, miserable roads, to Middlesbrough where I found a pub on the outskirts. I'd tried to ring Libby to come and join us, but she'd not answered her phone. I'd chosen to go back towards town in case she called me back; it would be easier for her if we were closer to Marianne's house (or Dad's, I was still trying to get used to it not being his home anymore).

We could have been sitting in a country pub: ornate wooden beams were adorned with golden tinsel, and an open log fire burned furiously. A small Christmas tree had been placed in the corner of the room; silver tinsel hung randomly on individual branches and mismatched baubles were unevenly placed. I wondered if children had decorated it; either that, or someone had been begrudged having to do the job. Christmas music was playing quietly in the background.

June removed her hat, gently easing her fingers through her wisps of hair. It was moulded into a short, cropped style, although it was much thinner than it used to be. Actually, I was surprised how thin it seemed. It was lighter too, with wisps of ash-blonde. I'd always remembered her with bright, funky hair: not bright pink or neon colours, but distinctive reds that would make her stand out from the crowd. It was lighter than Mum's ever was; mousy-brown with the odd highlight was probably the best way to describe her's. But it would be wrong to tell you I remember this; it was the few photos I had that told me. June's eyes though, were the same emerald green as Mum's, with the same softness.

'I can't believe you're here.'

'I can't believe I've come,' she laughed as she sipped an orange juice.

I wondered if Mum was a drinker. I don't mean an alcoholic, but had she enjoyed a glass or two? It was hard to imagine that they had enjoyed an alcoholic drink leisurely, especially with Dad turning to alcohol once she was gone. I couldn't remember him drinking when Mum was here. I couldn't ever recall any of my parents being drunk before Mum died.

But I wondered as June sipped her alcohol-free drink, had Mum and Dad relaxed on an evening with their favourite beverage? It was these things I couldn't remember and now June was here, I could bombard her with the hundreds of questions I'd stored away over the years.

'So, where have you been?' This was my way of asking why she was here now, without the rudeness or ignorance those words would have conveyed.

'It's a long story.' She sipped again at her juice.

'I've got all night.' Max was working late again. 'On a Friday?' I'd quizzed him. He'd ranted about it not mattering what night of the week it was; he was trying to run a bloody business.

'It was hard when your mum passed away. I found it hard to stay around here.'

'Where did you go?'

'We moved to Devon. Ernest had been poorly, so we took our savings and moved away. It was for the best. As you'll know, your father could be difficult sometimes.' I didn't want her to see her harsh words against Dad had jarred me slightly, so I sipped my drink hoping to draw away the tension. 'But, I'm not here to bring up the past.'

'So why are you here?' The abrupt words sprang from my lips as if they were on springs. Hastily trying to amend my impoliteness I found myself spluttering, 'I don't mean that the way it sounded.'

'No, it's fine. Don't be silly.' She made a dismissive gesture with her hand, instantly reminding me of Mum. The same movement and expression. It was only a flash but it was there. 'I've recently been cleared of cancer.'

'Oh my God …' suddenly understanding the fineness of her hair.

'I'm fine now. It was breast cancer. I'm absolutely fine. All the treatments went well. It's been a few years of hospital trips and operations but I'm okay.' She spoke as if she was telling me she'd had a common cold; brushing off the severity of the condition. 'When I got the all-clear I decided to come back and see you girls. I realised I had another chance and I had to grab it with both hands. Things were not good back here when your mum died and I probably shouldn't have left you; but I couldn't stay here.'

'But why?'

'Oh, Kat, things were so complicated. Everyone was at each other's throats. It was a bad time.'

'I remember,' I said as she gently rubbed my arm. 'I just don't understand why you had to leave so suddenly.'

'Oh, many reasons.' She shook her head. 'I'm sorry to hear about your dad. I didn't even realise he'd passed away. It was Marianne who told me–'

'Marianne?'

'Yes, I had the old address so I went back there. She gave me the salon address.'

'Right.' I nodded.

'I've come to see you and Libby. I haven't come here to drag up the past.'

'I'm glad you're back.'

'I've thought about you girls every day and I knew I had to come back.'

'Is Uncle Ernest with you?' Even after all these years I sounded like a small child, but it felt disrespectful not to use his title of Uncle; though for some reason it felt strange to call her Aunty June.

'Unfortunately, he died six months ago.' Her voice was lowered, her pain obvious.

'Oh, June, I'm so sorry.'

'It's fine. It was a heart attack. A long time coming, I can tell you.' She joked, but the sadness reached her eyes.

I remembered them being so close. As she sat alone, without him by her side, I wondered how she'd coped since he'd gone.

'Is that another reason why you're here?'

'Kat, life is too short. When your mum died I thought my world would end. She wasn't only my sister, she was my best friend. We did everything together. We talked every day. It felt as if I'd lost a part of me when she died.'

'I know how that feels.'

'I don't want to intrude into your life, but after losing the most precious people in my life and surviving cancer—'

'You're not intruding.' A silence fell between us, the enormity of her arrival hanging in the air. 'Dad never got over Mum.' She didn't answer me, just nodded slowly, but I could see a glimpse of scepticism. 'Do you not think so?'

'Oh … probably.' Another silence fell, more uncomfortable than the last one. Suddenly she smiled and cheered up instantly. 'Anyway, tell me about what's going on with you. When are you due?'

I wanted to go back to discussions of Mum and Dad. I thought she'd understand how Dad had been feeling, and how he suffered, but her apparent lack of concern surprised me. 'In about six and a half weeks, unless they come early.'

'They?'

'I'm having twins.'

'Oh, how lovely!' She smiled warmly. 'I know sometimes twins are delivered by Caesarean, not like our day where you just got on with it. Many women didn't know they were having twins.'

'I've heard that before. I think it will be a normal delivery. I've had scans every four weeks to check everything is okay, but both babies are head down, so there seems no reason for a C-section.'

'Every four weeks?'

'It's routine with twins; non-identical twins anyway.'

'Do you know what you're having?' Her excitement filled the air.

'No.' I smiled, shaking my head. 'We wanted it to be a surprise.'

'Good, it's better that way.' We both sipped our drinks. 'Your mum had a Caesarean with you. She was devastated, she really wanted to live the experience. She could be quite earthy sometimes.' June smiled, obviously remembering Mum for who she really was.

Maybe me and Mum weren't so similar: I couldn't think of anything worse than 'experiencing it' I'd told my midwife to write in big capital letters across my file 'EPIDURAL OR GENERAL ANAESTHETIC!'

'Why did she need a Caesarean?' I loved that I was finding out these details. Questions that I probably wouldn't have thought to ask, but helped to build a picture of Mum.

'You didn't want to come out. In those days everything took so long. You were stuck for a while. They actually said it was lucky you survived.'

'Really?'

'Really. Please don't tell Libby this, but because of the trauma your mum went through with you, she didn't really want any more children.'

'So, Libby was an accident?'

'I don't like to use the term 'accident', but she wasn't exactly planned.'

I nodded, refraining from telling her Libby probably wouldn't care. But then, Libby's reactions of late had surprised me; so maybe she *would* care if she found out she hadn't actually been put on their calendar, just like my babies might feel unwanted for being 'unplanned.' The thought filled me with fear.

'You were both loved very much, though. Your mum doted on you girls. You were her world and she did all she could to protect you. I'm so glad I've come back. We've so much to catch up on. You must tell me all about your life; I can't believe you own a beauty salon. Your mum would be so proud; she and I went weekly to a beauty therapist.'

'I remember Mum always used to say, "Every woman should have a therapist."' We laughed as we finished the sentence together. I pictured how beautiful Mum was, I assumed June was doing the same, as her eyes glazed over slightly.

'She wanted to be a beauty therapist,' June said, telling me something else I hadn't known.

'Really?' I frowned. 'That's a bit different from a science teacher.'

'I know. When we were younger she was forever doing my nails, wanting to put face masks on. It was me who wanted to be the teacher.'

'Why didn't you?'

'I left school and was offered a job in an office, so thought that was my best option. Anyway, Lanie was the clever one.' As she referred to Mum by her family pet name, Mum became another person. A woman who'd had a life before me and Libby. 'Everyone loved her, you know.'

'Did they?'

'She would light up a room when she entered and she had such a loud, horrendous laugh.' June smiled and shook her head, staring at her drink.

'I remember her laugh, Libby inherited it.' It suddenly occurred to me I hadn't actually heard Libby laugh in a while.

'Yes, she did. I remember even from a young age Libby had the same loud deep laugh.' June smiled. 'How is Libby?'

'She's fine. She's living with Marianne. She's studying to be a teacher too.'

'Oh, that's brilliant.' Her eyes met mine, a sparkle of delight shining through. 'I just needed to know that you girls are okay.'

'Honestly, we're doing fine,' I lied. I was intrigued by some of the secrets she may be hiding, so didn't want her distracted, 'I'd really like to know more about Mum.'

'Like what?'

'I don't know. Everything.'

'God, I could tell you some stories.'

'I'd love to hear them.' I was practically begging her to give me more.

'Well, I tell you what, why don't I take you and Libby out for tea one night next week? You girls can ask me as many questions as you like.'

'We only have one night?' I jested, but on a serious note I wanted to know all that she knew about Mum. Silly things like what was her favourite colour, food, drink; what music she listened to; what motivated her; what were her passions; what were her hates. I wanted the whole picture. I yearned for the gaps to be filled.

We chatted a little while longer, but June kept diverting the conversation back to me. I told her about the babies, about Max and how quickly things had happened. I sadly told her about the salon and how Melanie had taken my trust and thrown it back in my face. My anger was apparent as I expressed how hurt I was, how I was thinking of passing the salon over to Clare and how I was feeling stranded at the moment. Her words, 'Everything happens for a reason,' were spoken as if that would make everything better.

I felt as if for most of my life, or at least since Mum died, I'd been a square peg trying to fit into a round hole. The only thing that made me feel 'normal', if there was such a thing, was my salon. Although, even inside those walls, where customers came and went, their lives intermingling, I still wore a mask to disguise any real feelings or emotions.

As I sat with June, for the first time in a long time I felt a barrier was being broken down. A feeling that I wasn't sure I'd even shared with Max. Invisible obstacles seemed to be stacking up; were we growing apart, travelling a different journey? I so wanted to bring him back to me, although he said he hadn't physically gone anywhere. He had so much work on, and he was adamant things would change when the babies arrived.

I didn't share these fears with June; I needed to know more about her, more about Mum before I let her in further.

As we left the pub, the freezing cold air was refreshing. June shivered and I let out a long breath, enjoying the crispness of the night air, letting it surround my limbs, my coat open to let the breeze envelop me.

'I'm so pleased to be here with you, Kat,' June said, as we hugged. I felt as if a part of me that had been missing was being slotted back into place. 'As I said, I've got the cottage for two weeks, but I'm happy to stay for longer.' June had hired a cottage as she didn't want to put on anyone. It was cheaper than staying in a hotel for two weeks, she'd told me.

'I'd like that.' I really would. Two weeks wouldn't be long enough to find out a lifetime of stories; I needed her to stay as long as she could. While she was here with me, it was as if Mum was too.

'I'd love to meet Max,' she said.

Her words hung frozen in the air, as suddenly my lungs seemed to lose their function and my head began to spin. Under the orange glow of the streetlight there was no mistaking Max's car.

Sitting cosily beside him, in the passenger seat, was Gina.

14

I couldn't believe it.
He was lying.
He'd been lying all along.
He was supposed to be working late … had all his late nights been a lie?

The perfume … he'd lied. It was hers.

I should have known: I could tell the way she'd looked at him at Clare's party. Had he had a glint too? Had I purposely ignored it? Had I not wanted to see what was in front of me? Had I not wanted to be alone so much, I'd turned a blind eye to Max's other life?

How could I possibly stay with a man who lied to me?

A man who wanted another woman.

I pulled clothes from drawers, swearing, shouting into the open air, screaming with despair, frenzied animal behaviour taking over my body.

'Bastard!' resonated from my lips over and over again. I felt as if I was suffocating, the feeling overpowered me as I struggled to breathe. Weakness overwhelmed me as I collapsed on the side of the bed, the tears blurring my vision, my nose streaming.

I screamed into my hands. Shaking with rage. Nauseated by anguish. Our babies jolted together by my distress as I plunged into despair then shot back to anger.

Fury forced me from the bed. This couldn't be happening.

Oh God, what would I do?

I grabbed at clothes, underwear, make-up, shoes, the suitcase an endless pit for the things I would need. The shrieks of pain escaped me as I fought to get as much as I could into the case.

Marianne and Libby were expecting me; I'd called them on my frantic drive home. I'd made a quick excuse to June, who must have thought me slightly unstable, as I'd told her I'd remembered my car parking was up – we hadn't paid for car parking. She didn't have time to stop me as I'd quickly made my exit, shouting to her that I'd ring her about tea with Libby.

The case shut, I pressed the edges together forcing the zip to fasten. Swearing loudly, wiping my nose with the back of my hand, I blinked away the tears so I could see.

I didn't hear his footsteps, I didn't feel his presence. I just felt his hand and his breath upon me. 'Kat, what the hell are you doing?'

'What the fuck does it look like I'm doing?' I choked on my own tears, as I forcefully pushed his hand away from me, and losing my balance I grabbed the bedside table. The lamp jolted, fell to the floor and smashed into tiny pieces.

'Kat, seriously, should I call the doctor?'

'I can't believe you would do this to me,' I sobbed through the words, as I struggled to form them.

'Do what? … Kat … listen to me, what the hell are you talking about?' I ignored his pleas, as I continued to shove things into the case. 'I'm getting someone out, you're losing it.' He was adamant as he pulled his mobile from his pocket. The angry, betrayed woman inside me flew towards him, knocking the phone from his hand, forcing myself to reach it before he did, feeling the stretch of my stomach.

'How many times a day do you call her? How long have you been laughing at me?' I sobbed as I pressed the button on his phone. The screen lit up. He didn't move.

'Call who?' He sat on the edge of the bed, watching me intently, obviously knowing I wouldn't find a thing. There were no calls or texts to or from Gina, Melanie, Yasmin or any other woman. Well, a few from Clare, but that didn't count.

Was I going mad?

'This doesn't mean a thing. You could have deleted them.' I threw the phone at him. 'I saw you with her.'

'With Gina?' He sighed heavily.

I didn't dare answer. Was this a joke? Was he admitting it to me?

'I was giving her a lift home.'

'Of course you were ... just like the perfume was from that woman in your office.'

'It's true, Kat.' He exhaled loudly, a dramatic sigh of frustration, running his hand through his hair. 'Her car broke down. Mum rang me to see if I could help her.'

'Your mum rang you?' I'd registered Clare's number on his phone, so maybe it did count. The rage that had bolted through me seemed to shrivel as I felt my cheeks burn.

'Yes. Her mum rang my mum ... you get the picture?'

'Why did you have to help?'

'Because that's what people do, Kat, they help each other.' He signed deeply again. 'She was on her own, it was dark. She'd just left work when she broke down. Her mum was worried, Gina had phoned for help but they were going to be a while, so Mum asked me to help her.'

'But why would she ring you if you were in Leeds, surely someone else could have got their faster?'

'I was on my way home when she rang, she didn't know where I was, or obviously she would have phoned someone else if I wasn't ... oh, for fuck's sake Kat, I don't know why, but Mum rang me.'

I didn't answer him; again his plausible excuse floored me. Surprised me. Relief seeped from every pore. Could it be true? It sounded as if it could be. It made sense.

'I can help you pack this now if you want to go, but seriously ...' He shook his head, his jaw tense as he glared directly at me.

I sat down on the bed next to him, calmer, my hysteria deflated as exhaustion drowned me. 'I feel as if we're falling apart, Max.' My words were barely a whisper. He glanced down at his hands and didn't answer. 'I feel as if you're not there for me.'

Suddenly he stood up from the bed, turning towards me, his face taut, anger flaring. 'I'm working my arse off here, late fucking nights, early fucking mornings, I don't stop to pee because I'm trying to get as much done before these babies come and all I get from you is that I'm not here for you. This is fucking ridiculous.' He walked from the bedroom, bouncing the door from its hinges as he tried to slam it behind him.

My heart plummeted, yearning for him. Shit ... what had I done?

How had that just happened? How had the tables turned? How was I now the one in the wrong? One minute I wanted to kill him, the next I was longing for him.

The sound of the front door closing vibrated through the rest of the house as he left. Then I heard his car racing down the gravelled drive, leaving me here alone.

Nausea engulfed me as I left the bedroom, I made my way unsteadily downstairs, not sure what my next step would be.

Would he come back? Could I rectify this mess?

I rang Marianne to say I wouldn't be coming over, and that everything was okay. I'd not told her anything when I'd called earlier, although she'd probed me, before realising my distressed state she asked me quite curtly, 'So, how was it?'

'How was what?' I'd been shaking, trying to focus as my mind raced, choking back the tears although Marianne's terse manner had confused me; not used to her clipped tones, it had taken something away from my own drama.

'How was it with June? Are you crying? Has she upset you?' Her voice had increased a decibel.

'No—'

'I knew I shouldn't have told her where the salon was?' Marianne's harshness surprised me. Marianne was the person who I would have normally ran to in times of distress, because of her calm approachable behaviour but she was acting as if she was possessed. 'What's happened? What did she say?'

'She didn't say anything ... it was fine,' I'd struggled to speak, 'But ... can I come and stay tonight?'

'Here?' Her anger deflated as she'd seemed bewildered.

'Yes, is that okay?'

'Of course it is, pet.' Her stress still clear, but the resentment gone. 'Is everything okay?'

'I'll tell you later.'

When I'd rang the second time, alone, wondering where on earth Max had gone, she told me as sweetly as she always did, 'We're here, pet.' No mention of June, which pleased me.

After speaking to Marianne, I thought about calling Clare and maybe checking if Max was telling the truth, but I knew it would make the situation worse; she'd tell him I'd called, and if he was telling the truth, where did that leave us? What if he was also telling the truth about the perfume? Which had played on my mind constantly.

What did we have, if we didn't have trust?

My insides ached as I sat on the sofa. The tears formed again. I had no energy left. Exhaustion enveloped my entire body. Even my mind wanted to stop for a while. I placed myself carefully onto the sofa, a cushion underneath my bump, my head resting gently on the arm.

Was Max telling the truth? Had he walked away because I'd hit a nerve? Or had it simply been out of frustration?

Was I losing my mind, as well as losing my business?

Was I about to lose Max too?

15

As I lay on the sofa, wondering if Max was coming back? Creating images in my mind as to where he could have gone? Who he could be with? I didn't know who to ring, because I wasn't sure I wanted the answer.

I wanted to believe him. I craved that he was telling the truth. I prayed that he'd left out of frustration … we could work through that. As for the alternative, I doubted that we could. As my thoughts collided, I was worried about our two babies entering this world into this mess.

We'd been given January 13th as the due date, it may change they'd told us, especially if you're having a C-section. It's very common with twins, another fact that I'd been informed of several times. At each scan we could see their little bodies moving closer to each other. The tiny movements from their limbs sent small waves of excitement but also fear through me, with an intermingled sense of relief that the babies were healthy.

When they'd given us the 13th, I'd automatically imagined the babies' birthdays being on a Friday and decided I'd have to think of ways to banish the superstition. It was the same with magpies. I'd had a spate of seeing one magpie on its own constantly for weeks. I told myself and anyone else who was interested that seeing one magpie wasn't unlucky, it was very lucky: it meant the magpie was having some well-deserved 'me-time'. I thought of it as the Mummy magpie who needed some rest. I could do this with Friday 13th; make it the day that people had a party. Make it the best day ever to be born on. It was more than likely, though, they wouldn't be born on this day; apparently only around 4% of babies are born on their due date; another fact Suzy had stored.

I wondered if I'd been born on my due date. I suppose I could ask June now, another random question that would make no difference to my life, a question that wouldn't even allow me to know Mum better, but would somehow help me feel closer to her.

Max hadn't been born on his; he was eight days late. 'He was a nightmare, he didn't sleep, he didn't feed properly ...' Clare had told me.

I wondered if our babies would be good. I had no idea what I was like as a baby. Dad had never said. To be honest, I'd never asked. It was never something I was interested in knowing. Since falling pregnant, I'd also wondered if Mum had wanted girls. Had she been disappointed that Libby or I weren't a boy? Again, June was here now; I'd better start my list of enquiries.

We didn't know if we were having boys, girls or both. It was a shock when we found out we'd be having twins. I actually thought Max might faint: the colour had drained from his face. As for me I'd nearly wet myself. We were having scans every four weeks, which was the normal procedure with fraternal twins. After every scan I felt that same degree of relief. It was thought that the babies were non-identical because they had separate placentas and their own separate membrane. Apparently, my pregnancy was referred to as dichorionic diamniotic (DCDA). My notes stated this frequently. All the medical talk had become a second language, although it still felt strange because I never thought I'd have to listen to it, let alone understand it.

Since I'd fallen pregnant our lives had seemed somewhat disjointed. We were supposed to be in it together, but if that was the case, why did I feel so alone?

For some of the scans I'd had to take Clare, Marianne or Suzy with me, as Max had to work away. I'd understood this, but sometimes he'd forget I was going for a scan. I'd show him a picture, or bring it into the conversation that everything had seemed fine this week. I was trying to keep him updated, without pressurising him.

I often wondered if the babies would look like Max with his thick blond waves, his tall, thick-set figure and his deep-blue eyes. Or would they look like me; dark brunette, and coffee-tinted eyes. 'I could melt into them,' Max used to say. 'Swirls of chocolate, drinking me in.' I would laugh.

He didn't say that any more. I couldn't remember the last time he told me I looked beautiful or nice. Half-decent would have felt like a compliment, had he given one. If anything was to be said about my looks, it would be about the amount of weight I was putting on.

When we first started dating, I tried so hard to look good for him. But we all do it. Those first few months are crucial. I'd tried so hard to impress him. Had I stopped trying? Not intentionally, but I probably had. But isn't that normal? To relax and enjoy each other for who we were. Max had a habit of mentioning my weight gain, which was perfectly normal obviously, maybe not the rate I was putting it on, but it was better going on than not. (That was my theory anyway). The thing was, he'd put a few pounds on, if not more, himself. Since he'd stop working out, his waist line had increased, but I'd not mentioned it, because it didn't bother me.

I didn't think I'd let myself go that much. I still took care of the basics; washed and styled my hair, painted on the foundation and dressed accordingly. Yes, I did dress in the most comfortable clothes I could find. Work: the maternity dress; big, baggy and flexible. Home: the joggers; snug, luxurious and relaxing. Was I really supposed to get dressed up for him when I was carrying around two-tons of arms, legs and limbs? And that's just me.

And let's face it, when I did attempt to make the effort, he didn't turn up.

Even before I was pregnant, I was never one of those women who would stay fully made-up until late in the night. Most of the time if Max was working in Leeds, I was in bed when he arrived home. And it would be sacrilege to leave my make-up on for bed, I'd broken a few beauty rules since falling pregnant, but I couldn't break the basic rule.

But as thoughts of my appearance swam through my mind, I knew it wasn't my weight gain or lack of blusher that had caused this rift, it was so much deeper than that. Something had gone amiss between us. Had we both been so focused on our own individual lives that the only thing connecting us was the babies?

I hoped not.

We'd had no chance to deal with life as a couple. Life as Max and Kat. Life just the two of us. Six months seems a reasonable time to get to know each other, and we had, but maybe it was only the fundamentals.

Before I found out I was pregnant we'd not argued much. We'd had inconsequential disagreements about whether salt and vinegar crisps were better than cheese and onion. Actually, we'd both agreed that ready salted won hands down. None of our disagreements had been life-changing, nothing that would determine whether we could be partners for life and definitely nothing that would affect our suitability to be parents.

After laying on the sofa for an hour, there was still no sign of Max, I tried to push away thoughts that he'd ran back to Gina, Melanie or another woman.

'It was true, he must be cheating,' I battled with myself. 'He just needs some space, he's really stressed.' These thoughts crashed into each other as I thought about us as a family.

Would we survive as a family? A strong unit. Max and I weren't doing that great at being partners at the moment, how the hell would we survive being a Mum and Dad?

'I'm going to be a mother. Me – a mummy!' I shivered with anxiety, anticipation or excitement, as I always did when this reality hit me. I was never sure which emotion it was. I was definitely eager to start this new life, but, I was petrified: driven by the fear that I would be a crap mother, plus the underlying notion that one day I would lose them. Apparently, I would love them in a way that no-one could adequately describe to me; the only description anybody could offer was that I would die for them. That scared me more than most people could imagine; to love someone so deeply you would risk your own life for them. And what happens if the object of this love is taken away?

Banished, like Mum. What happens after that?

Max and I were both stressed and irritable, but we had other factors going on. His work, I know I keep referring to it, but he was majorly busy, plus with my salon … everything hadn't really gone the way we'd planned.

We'd only recently decorated the nursery, or I should say we'd hired people to decorate the nursery for us; we'd not physically lifted a finger, we hadn't had the time. I'd thought Max would have wanted some input into the colour scheme, the fabrics, the furniture but he seemed to show little interest. I thought he would want to discuss names for hours, but we didn't talk about names much. He always seemed to be preoccupied, or everything I suggested he hated, but he didn't offer any alternatives.

Two hours later, when Max still hadn't returned home, I wondered if we could rebuild the relationship we'd only started a year ago.

I let my tears fall as my heart felt sore, my chest was burning with confusion. I was filled with fear that the babies would be born into the sort of dysfunctional family I'd so wanted to avoid.

16

I awoke to a softness caressing my arm, and the sound of somebody whispering my name. I opened my eyes to Max, who stood over me, holding one of our large mugs; the mugs I bought in hope of making his place feel like mine.

'Morning,' he said, putting the mug down on the coffee table in front of me.

'Morning.' I wiped the saliva which had dribbled down my chin. 'I must have fallen asleep.' I lifted myself up slightly, a little embarrassed that he'd seen me only as he should if we were an elderly couple: wrinkled and salivating. Attractive! I realise it doesn't *have* to be like that when we're elderly, but it's more likely to happen when we're in our eighties than our late twenties.

He sat down on the edge of the sofa next to me. I quickly checked my watch. It was 7.30 a.m. I must have slept all night on the sofa. I needed to be in the salon in an hour. Saturdays were not a good day to be slacking, although, did it really matter now?

'I'm sorry I walked out last night.' Max didn't look at me. He stared into his hands as if they had the answer to this mess.

'I'm sorry too.'

'Look, Kat. I want this to work. I understand we started this pretty quickly and we're still finding our feet with each other. I understand you're hormonal, but this is ridiculous.' Don't use my hormones as an excuse I wanted to tell him: my hormones didn't plant perfume on you or place Gina in your car – but thought better of it.

'You have to see it from my point of view ... loads of late nights, we hardly see each other, you're distant with me, the perfume and then I see you with Gina in your car.'

'I'm telling you, Kat, I'm not cheating. I don't have time to think about it, let alone do it.'

'But I feel that you could be with me because I'm pregnant and you don't have a choice.'

'I want to be with you. I'm so excited about our babies,' he said, turning to look at me. I peered down at my cup, the steam from the hot water still rising. 'I'm asking you to trust me, Kat. I can't ask much more than that, because I don't know how to change anything. I can't stop working late, as we have so much going on.'

'I do trust you.' I looked at him, his eyes meeting mine. But he seemed so far away. 'I feel as if we're not connecting.'

'We have to work together ...' He placed his cup down, turning to face me. The urgency was apparent as he touched my leg. 'I want to be with you, Kat.'

'I want to be with you too.'

'So, we both need to make the effort.'

'Yes,' I agreed, and as he leaned over and kissed my forehead, I whispered, 'I love you.'

'You too.' He kissed my nose before lifting himself from the sofa. He stretched his back and drew a deep breath. 'I've got to go into the office today.'

'On a Saturday?'

'I have no choice. Honestly, we're so busy.'

'Are you working tomorrow?' I stopped him before he left the room.

'I should really.' He ran his hand through his hair, a frown appeared as thoughts seem to race through his mind.

'Did I tell you that Marianne has invited us round for dinner to meet her new man?'

'No, but ...' he shook his head. 'I'm really struggling. If I don't get these contracts finished, if we miss any more deadlines, I could lose my own company. You've got to understand: if you lose yours and then I lose mine, where the hell would that leave us?'

'I know.' I sighed, rubbing my bump where our babies felt as if they were having a tiny fight.

As he left me alone the calmness that surrounded us was unlike the destruction of the night before. The seething anger that had exploded from my body had wiped me out. I'd slept deeply and I ached. My head, my bones, my bump: everything about me wanted to stop.

As I showered, I thought about how things had changed between me and Max: when we met I told him everything, even things he didn't need to know. I would chat about my day, the customers who'd made me laugh, those who'd had a drama or those who'd been a nightmare. He knew my world inside out and now here we were ... I'd forgotten to mention something as simple as having dinner at Marianne's.

I couldn't stay in the shower for long these days: it was far too much effort to stand, plus too much heat would have me practically collapsing. The bath was great for the warmth, because I could just let the water take my body, but I'd no time this morning for such luxury. I dressed in the black dress I'd become accustomed to, a maternity one that floated around my bump, making me look humongous, but there didn't seem to be anything that could make me look smaller. Tight-fitting made me look as if I had a beach ball shoved up my top, and too baggy made me look as if I'd put twice as much weight on than I actually had. Quickly putting on my make-up, a façade that would be presented to the world, I was the refined image of the perfectly happy pregnant lady.

Max was in his office, focusing on the screen as his hands quickly moved over the keyboard.

'I've been to see Jack Haslow at the accountants about selling the business.' He turned his chair to face me. 'So, you've spoken to Mum then?'

I nodded, focusing on his screen rather than meeting his eye.

'Have you spoken to your landlord?'

'Yes, but there's no way I can pull out of my contract. He's happy for your mum to take it over, but I'm unsure.'

'What do you mean?'

'I'm worried it might be a whim your mum is having.'

'She seemed adamant when I spoke to her. I think you should let *her* make that decision.'

'So, you'd be behind her doing this?'

'Come on, Kat, it's a project she can play with. It's like all those charity events and women's stuff she gets involved in. It's not as if they don't have the money.'

'You're all so laid-back about it.'

'I'm not exactly thinking of this as an amazing career for Mum, but it would be something for her to get her teeth into; as she said, fulfil her little girl's dream.'

'I'll have a word with her, make sure she knows what she's doing.'

'Does my mother ever not know what she's doing?' Max mocked confidently. 'Did Jack think it was a good idea?'

'He's going to put the figures together. If your mum doesn't want to go ahead, he'll help me find a commercial agent.'

'Great.' He turned his chair back to his desk.

'Also, I had a surprise visitor last night.' Having his attention for a few minutes made me crave more, but he still kept his back to me.

'Who?'

'June.' I was still finding it hard to refer to her as Aunty June.

'Who?' Although, I couldn't see his face, his tone had turned to confusion.

'My mum's sister. She just turned up. She's been fighting cancer and felt the need to come back into our lives.'

'That's great news!' He swivelled the chair back to face me. 'I mean that she's here ... but is the cancer ...' he stuttered slightly.

'Yes, she said she has the all-clear.'

'That's really great, I'm really pleased.'

'Yeah, it is.' I smiled, walking towards him, kissing him on the cheek, wanting him to grab me like he would have done when we first met, but his mind, I could see, was already focused on the screen before I'd left the room.

✳✳✳

The fifteen minutes that had been added to my journey time since moving in with Max felt like thirty this morning. The drive from Stokesley to Great Ayton was quite tedious. I often thought I should have left some of my belongings in the flat, so that when Max was away I could have stayed there. The wipers pushed the rain aside, the dark clouds threatened overhead as if they were aiming at me, shouting at me from the heavens. The wet roads glistened, the wheels slashed through the puddles, water splashing across the grass verge.

I wanted to turn the car back round. I wanted to call the boss that I didn't have and say I wouldn't be coming in today. I couldn't put on my polite, happy face: friendly Kat, the one who seemed to have it so together, when in reality she was completely losing it. I tried to stifle the unsettled feeling that was eating away at me; I wanted to believe Max, I so did, but what was stopping me?

I decided to call Suzy, as I drove through the deserted country roads.

'If he was seeing Gina, then this was his perfect opportunity to tell you …' she was such a good friend giving me the answer I wanted to hear.

'But he told me he was working late …'

'What time did you see him?'

'About nine-thirty, maybe ten, I don't know …' trying to think back to the exact time, realising I couldn't remember.

'So, he could easily have been driving home when Clare called him?'

'It's feasible, yes.'

'I think you're analysing this too much …' Suzy sighed, 'I really don't think he's cheating on you with Gina or anyone …' she paused. I found myself struggling to answer her. 'You've got so much going on at the moment, with the business, preparing for the babies, you're panicking …'

'Suppose, 'I said, exhaling loudly.

I agreed I would push these thoughts away from my tired head, although I knew I couldn't. I explained about June turning up. I needed to keep talking to her, distracting myself as I drove to the place I was beginning to loathe.

'She just turned up out of the blue?' Suzy asked surprised.

'It was quite bizarre, really,' I admitted.

'What was her explanation?'

'She said things weren't good and she'd had to get away. She's had cancer, it made her realise how much she's missed out on.'

'Oh dear, is she okay now?'

'As far as I know.'

'It was strange how she just left though. Do you think she fell out with your dad?' Suzy asked, I could hear her munching on something. Probably a healthy bar of some sort, or a piece of fruit, knowing Suzy.

'Maybe. June had said something about him being difficult at times, and when I'd spoken to Marianne she was quite uptight—'

'Marianne was uptight?' Suzy was clearing surprised, as was I when I'd had the conversation with Marianne.

'Yeah, it was odd ... something has obviously happened.'

'I think June was probably upset that Marianne came on the scene so quickly. They probably had a big fall-out over it or something,' Suzy surmised as she chomped away. I nodded, although she couldn't see me. Suzy had lived through it with me, so she remembered how heartbroken I was when Marianne appeared suddenly in our lives. 'But she didn't say bye to you and Libby, did she?' Suzy questioned, as if the memories were tumbling back to her.

'Not that I remember, one minute she was there and then the next she wasn't. Dad told me she'd moved away, when I asked.'

'I remember ... oh I'm sure you'll get to the bottom of it. But it's good that's she back.'

'Yeah, it is,' I agreed.

'You'll have to tell me the whole conversation when we catch up.'

'I will.' There was a slight pause between us.

'So, has Clare mentioned any more about taking over the salon?' Suzy asked, as if understanding my reluctance to hang-up.

Clare's idea had troubled me and I'd shared my concerns with Suzy.

'No ... but what if she's lost her mind slightly?'

'Like, a mid-life crisis of some kind?' Suzy added.

'I thought only men had them.'

'They're very common in women too,' Suzy, with her amazing library of knowledge, informed me. 'Usually, it's about women trying to prove themselves in the workplace and finding themselves.'

'Do you think Clare needs to prove something?'

'Maybe she needs an adventure, fulfilling her dreams before she feels it's too late,' she offered.

'Max said it would be like a project for her.'

'There you go ... she's a classic case, Kat, spent all her life taking care of the two men in her life, she's not really had her own purpose as such, or her own goals.'

'So, do you think I should put a stop to it?' I asked. 'If it is a mid-life crisis she shouldn't really be making such hasty decisions.'

'Absolutely not. This will be great for her. Mid-life crisis or not, she knows what she's doing,' Suzy laughed. 'There is one thing we do know: Clare knows her own mind.'

'Yeah, s'pose,' I smiled. 'Anyway, how's things with you?' I was pulling into the village, and still wanted to keep talking until I had parked up. Until I could no longer drive, as driving allowed me to think too much: analyse every aspect of my life ... and this was proving to be distressing at the moment.

'Well ... you'll never guess what I'm going to do,' Suzy said.

'Surprise me.' I forced a laugh, sensing excitement in her voice. Wishing she could pass some my way, as I thought about driving past Lush Lucia, but couldn't face their sparkling contemporary presence today.

'The Ironman,' she announced. She *had* surprised me.

'What?'

'We're going to go to America.'

'Oh my God, I thought you were sticking to a marathon. What will you have to do?'

'A 2.4-mile swim, a 112-mile bike ride and a 26.6-mile run.' Suzy was practically screaming at me down the phone, as if she'd won the lottery.

'Seriously?' I was bewildered.

'I know, it's so exciting.'

'Really?' I laughed. I was so pleased she was so happy; even if the things she wanted to do filled me with total fear. 'So, how does that work, are you and Lawrence racing against each other or in pairs, like a partnership or something?'

'No, apparently we all set off at the same time, then the results are categorised into gender and age. Lawrence reckons he'll leave me standing, but I'll show him,' Suzy giggled. I could imagine them laughing together and suddenly I felt a weight of sadness surround me as I yearned for their chemistry. 'We're going to have a holiday for two weeks afterwards, travel to a few places around America.'

'That sounds great … well the holiday bit,' I laughed and she laughed with me. 'Has Lawrence told Max?'

'Not sure, why?'

'No reason …' I lied. I wondered how Max would take the news. He'd told me that he was desperate to get back into his fitness training. I'd tried to encourage him, but he blamed his work, and even the babies had been his excuse. Although, he never said, I wondered if he blamed me.

As Suzy told me about the amount of training she had to do, which sounded as if she may as well enter a torture chamber, I pulled up outside the salon, next to Clare's car.

Clare was sitting neatly in her sleek Mercedes, her fingers tapping away on her mobile phone. She noticed me, her white teeth gleaming from her radiant smile, I waved as I spoke into the air, my voice travelling over the hands-free kit, as I told Suzy I had to go, 'I've got company.'

'Keep me posted,' she said before hanging up.

I stepped into cold air, shivering as the low temperatures hit me, the bitterness catching my skin. I pressed the button that would allow the shutters to be lifted.

'I was passing through ...' Clare said, as she walked towards me. Her elegant polished figure, as always, strident and confident, '... and thought I would call in.'

'Where are you going at this time on a Saturday morning?'

'Shopping ...' she didn't say with who, I wondered if she was lying, as she said, 'So, have you had much time to think about things?'

Had she purposely come to see me? Couldn't she ring me?

'I've had a chat with Jack and he's putting the figures together,' I said, shivering against the coldness, urging the shutters to move faster.

'And, what about you?'

'What about me?' I was little confused.

'Forget the figures, how do you feel about it all?'

The noisy clang the shutters made when they reached the top, seemed to vibrate through the village. The loud echo pulsating through my head, as her question seemed to hang in the air.

'Mmm ...' I was stuttering. 'I suppose it seems like the best option ... if you're sure you want to do this,' I finally said, my heart fighting against my head, urging me say, 'No, stop this!' before it was too late.

'I *do* want to do this.' I could hear the excitement in her voice, as I turned the key in the salon door. I wanted to be pleased for her, but I remembered how thrilled I was when I took ownership of the place, and I found myself wanting to rewind, swallow the words back. 'It makes sense, though, doesn't it? All is not lost if I step in. It's not as if it's being completely taken out of your hands. Plus, I had a thought last night: perhaps when the babies are born you could use the upstairs for your beauty therapy.'

'Sounds good,' I said, because I suppose it did. It sounded perfect. But in reality, would I want to open in this tiny village – opposite Melanie? No, not really. Would I also want to be indebted to Clare? No, not really.

She followed me into salon, 'I'll put the kettle on,' she said, as if she already worked here: as if the place was already hers.

I dumped my bag on the floor, underneath the reception desk, and stared at the diary. There were enough customers to get me through the day, but I suddenly had the urge to cancel them all, like I had in my moment of urgency to see Jack Haslow. I couldn't do that though, I didn't want to burn my bridges: if I did decide to open upstairs, become a mobile therapist, or convince Max we could convert the garage, although the latter didn't really feel like an option, I needed to keep my existing customers sweet.

What else could I do with my life? I didn't know how to do anything else. I could retrain, delve into another field; but did I really want to? I couldn't think at the moment. But I knew the loyal customers I did have left would maybe use me later. I had to keep my options open.

As the names on the pages blurred, more tears obscuring my vision, I couldn't believe how things had changed in a matter of months … weeks even. My life had been gliding along in the right direction. How I'd loved entering my own little sanctuary … and now I hated walking over the threshold.

I didn't want to be here.

All I could see was the destruction Melanie and Mandy had caused; a steamroller flattening all that I had. Maybe I was being hasty, panicking; but my head was telling me to grab Clare's offer. Although, there was some kind of internal conflict between my heart and my head, an argument going on somewhere deep within:

'Get out.'
'No, stay and fight.'
'Fight for what?'
'You can't give up.'
'You have nothing left.'
'Don't be stupid, don't walk away from everything you've worked for.'

It was endless: the taunts, the pressure, the analysing over and over. But, I knew if I turned Clare down, I would regret it.

This was Clare's chance to prove whatever it was she needed to prove, whether to herself, to Henry or Max, maybe her friends, I didn't know. But she definitely wanted to do this. I shouldn't stand in her way.

As she handed me a cup of steaming tea, her smile beaming, her eyes sparkling with delight, I knew she would be undertaking a new quest, while I was closing the doors on my journey.

I just had to hope it was the right thing to do.

17

I hadn't visited Marianne at home in weeks. Her salon treatments had given us our catch-up time. Libby would call in at the salon, or I'd pick her up from uni and we'd go out for tea; but we hadn't done that for the last few weeks. I'd felt settled, though, that Libby was living with Marianne, although slightly concerned to find Calvin had joined them. This was revealed when I'd walked into the newly decorated living room to find them lounging across the sofa watching a film. Images of Dad flashed into my mind as beer cans were lined up across the table.

'Oh hello, Calvin, are you stopping for dinner?' I'd spoken quietly. Libby's eyes were rolling, only a touch but I could see she was trying hard to focus on me.

'He's living here now.' Libby seemed to slur her words.

What? Permanently? 'Oh ...' I wasn't sure what else to say. 'Did you get my message the other night?'

'Yeah,' Libby sighed loudly, turning back to the television. 'Something about someone is here to see us.'

I was annoyed she hadn't called me back, but didn't want to argue with her, especially in front of Calvin. 'Has Marianne not mentioned anything?'

'No.' She sighed again even more loudly.

'Right ... well, June is back.'

'Who?'

'Mum's sister.'

'Oh ... I thought she might have died too,' Libby said casually, as Calvin let out a laugh.

'She hasn't and she'd like to meet with you,' I said sternly, ashamed of her nonchalant behaviour. I could feel my shoulder rise, the tension seizing across my neck as I clenched my fists and gritted my teeth. 'So, we need to make a date with her.'

'Yeah, whenever.' Libby shrugged.

I left them to it, before I screamed at her. I thought things had changed, I thought *she'd* changed. I felt like throwing Calvin out, with his floppy dark hair, his long, lean body stretched across the sofa. He'd hardly lifted his head to acknowledge me, let alone speak.

Derek was awaiting my arrival in the kitchen, 'It's so lovely to meet you, pet.' He shook one of my hands with both of his. His closeness disturbed me. Creepy or friendly, I was yet to decide. 'I've heard so much about you.' He was well-spoken, but his accent was indistinctive, making it hard to tell if he was originally from the North East. As his hands slid from mine, he nodded at my bump. 'May I?' he asked.

I felt my head nod forward, giving him the permission that I didn't really feel. There may have been slight movement from the babies, but his strange hands upon my body, weren't touching them; they were touching me. It felt weird.

Suddenly, he started to pray loudly. 'God, please give these babies all that they need for a good life. Let their family protect them, help to lead the babies away from evil forces, grant them good angels—'

I stepped away from him. Marianne was smiling in the background, obviously proud of this self-assured man. A huge difference from the man Dad had been.

'I'm sorry, I didn't mean to …' Derek said.

'It's fine, it's me.' I smiled.

Marianne, obviously sensing my discomfort with the contact with Derek, changed the subject. 'So, is Max not with you?'

'I'm sorry. I should have rung you earlier. He's working.'

'He's working so hard lately.' Marianne smiled as she messed around with some dishes, preparing her unsavoury Sunday lunch.

'I didn't realise Calvin was living here now.' I tried, and failed, to sound unconcerned, as I changed the subject away from Max.

Not wanting to think about, let alone chat about what had happened over the last week.

'Oh, poor boy, he had nowhere to go. His father is not proud that he's, you know ….' She turned to look at me, the flames lightly heating the silver pan, her hand holding the spoon as she continued to stir whatever was boiling. Her eyes widened and she nodded at me as if she couldn't say the word because it was far too rude.

'Gay?' I guessed.

'Yes,' she said, turning back and switching off the heat, 'So I said he could live here for a while.'

'She takes far too much on if you ask me.' Derek added.

I didn't answer, wondering why Libby hadn't mentioned what was happening with Calvin. I suppose I'd showed little interest in him. She probably thought I'd have a go at her and she was probably right: I didn't think she needed a distraction like Calvin.

'Dinner's ready.' Marianne practically sang, ignoring Derek's comment.

I sat down at the new table. A replacement for the table Libby and I had carved bits out of over the years. I tried not to feel a stab of resentment, told myself to stop being so stupid; but even the replacement of the table was as if she was trying to eradicate Dad from the house. I was being dramatic; it had been an old tatty thing that needed modernising. But there were other changes that I'd noticed, but I didn't want to pass comment. Perhaps Marianne needed a new focus, a fresher outlook, something to brighten her day. Or was she trying to wipe out any memories of Dad from the house? His house, might I add. (Well not, officially; it was the council's; but still it had been his home.)

At the same time, I knew I was being unfair. Had Derek not been sat there, these thoughts wouldn't have entered my head.

The lounge had looked lovely with its cream woollen carpet, huge red flowers adorning the wallpaper. Wine-red velvet curtains replaced the purple fabric that she'd used previously as drapes, while red and burgundy cushions were used to dress the black leather sofa; which Libby and Calvin had spoiled.

I had no idea where the money had come from but I certainly had no intention of asking. Derek, maybe? To be fair, Marianne had probably saved a fortune without Dad's drinking. I wondered if she had decorated the upstairs. Probably not, as the hallway still had its old rickety staircase with missing spindles, exposing the tattiness of the house. Had she missed the hallway out, though, and gone straight to the bedroom to create a cosy nest for her and Derek? Seriously, I couldn't go there! I diverted my thoughts back to the performance that was being played out in front of me, trying to crush any thoughts of Derek and Marianne in the bedroom.

Derek and Marianne were laughing at each other's jokes, Libby and Calvin were clearly stoned. I remembered the last time we'd sat around this table. I suddenly wished Dad was with us; it shouldn't be Derek sitting in his seat … but then Mum should have been serving the dinner. I pushed these thoughts away too; wanting to focus on something that didn't make me want to cry.

Marianne placed our meals in front of us and I was surprised that her cooking skills had improved. Still not a patch on Clare's, however; but her meat was tender, the gravy hid the sliminess of the roast potatoes and the vegetables were crisp and fresh. It looked edible, even if I didn't want to eat a thing.

Marianne sat next to Derek and they held hands. They closed their eyes and loudly spoke to God as they recited the Lord's Prayer. How different Marianne had become; she'd always kept her whispered devotions quiet when Dad was here, never forcing her love for the Almighty upon us. Libby and Calvin caught each other's eye as they suddenly laughed crudely, the food they'd just put in their mouths, sprayed repulsively across the table. Marianne and Derek ignored them as they proudly said grace.

I wanted to leave.

We worked our way through the meal, Libby and Calvin not speaking a word as they devoured the food, both of them still high on the junk they'd taken that morning. Derek made noises that showed he appreciated his food, complimenting Marianne on her efforts. I, on the other hand, sat quietly, putting small amounts into my mouth, forcing the food down. Think of the babies, I told myself. No matter how ill it made me feel, I would force-feed myself and keep them nourished.

'So, do we have any names for the babies?' Derek asked me.

'Maude and Mildred,' Libby laughed, Calvin joined her. Giggling like school children.

I blanked her. 'We're still deciding.' I smiled politely at him.

'Do you know the sex?' Derek asked. I sensed Libby and Calvin glance at each other, again, unable to contain their laughter as Libby sprayed the table with her wine and saliva. 'You two really are a jolly pair. How much have you had to drink?'

'No Derek, we don't know the sex,' I told him, steering his attention away from my ignorant sister as my anger at their rudeness began to burn, while biting back the urge to tell him it was more than drink they were taking.

'That's good, dear.' He swallowed his food, then placing his fork into his other hand, he touched my arm with his free hand. Although it was a warm gesture, I felt uncomfortable at his touch. 'In my day, there was no way of knowing the sex beforehand. My wife—'

'You're married?'

'My wife died years ago.' Shit. I should have remembered that. 'Beautiful woman she was, so caring and loving. She bore three wonderful children. She had a stroke … awfully sad.'

'God, Marianne, all these wives! You have something to live up to.'

'Libby!' I scolded.

'What? I'm just saying,' she answered rudely, with her mouth full. Marianne gave a little unnerving laugh and I felt sorry for her.

'You're definitely exceeding expectations at the moment.' Derek winked at her, and as she turned from the table to collect more dishes he gently patted her on the backside. She jumped playfully.

I *really* wanted to leave.

As dinner finished, Derek thanked Marianne and then thanked the ceiling.

'We're going to finish our film,' Libby told us, already out of her chair. Calvin was behind her.

'I need you to think about when you can do tea with June.' I stopped her in her tracks.

'Who?' she asked me again. Was she really that far gone?

'Your mum's sister.' Marianne interrupted uncharacteristically harsh.

'Is she back?'

'I've just told you in there that she is!' I tried to keep myself calm.

'Yeah, whatever, let me know when you sort it,' she said as wandered out of the kitchen. I shook my head at her inability to function like an adult. I was so disappointed to see her this way. I hoped it was a one-off.

'How come you didn't mention to Libby that June was back?' I asked Marianne. I thought probing lightly may help to reveal all that had gone on between her and June.

'I forgot.' She didn't look at me.

I decided to change the subject as Marianne obviously wasn't comfortable talking about June, 'Are they always like that?' I asked, nodding towards the door where my inebriated sister had just disappeared.

'They've had a few too many this morning.' Marianne laughed, reverting to her usual self, as if our conversation about June hadn't happened. She gathered the dirty plates together. 'They're just kids.'

'No they're not, Marianne.' I couldn't allow their behaviour to go on, so I made no excuses for my firmness. 'Libby is a grown woman. At twenty-three I was supporting myself and her. I wasn't off my head and sponging off other people. She's supposed to be studying to become a bloody teacher. Jesus—'

'Don't use the Lord's name in vain, my dear, he has done no wrong here,' Derek said softly, but his frown told me he was serious.

'Sorry,' I muttered under my breath embarrassed that he'd told me off. 'I was going to say she needs to sort her head out or she'll never pass her exams.'

'I agree with Kathryn.' Derek smiled, placing his hand on top of mine, *again*. I pulled it away this time. What was his problem, with all this touchy feely stuff? He seemed unmoved by my gesture as his next words threw me. 'She should chuck them both out. I've told her, there is no need for their layabout behaviour.'

'I can't leave them on the streets,' Marianne whispered.

'I'd like Marianne to move in with me,' Derek suddenly announced. I tried not to show my surprise, but was rendered speechless, so I didn't do a very good job.

'But not yet.' Marianne sat opposite me, clearly in a panic that Derek had told me this news.

Isn't it a bit soon? I wanted to ask, but didn't. Was Libby right? Had Marianne been seeing him longer than she'd admitted?

'I'd have her move in tomorrow, but she won't leave those kids.'

'Derek, please,' she begged him. He nodded, but his taut face showed his unhappiness at her reluctance to leave Libby.

'I think Derek is right,' I heard myself saying. 'You should move in together.'

'Really?' Marianne's eyes lit up. I was sad that she'd felt she couldn't tell me her true thoughts. 'Anyway …' she waved her hand away in mid-air, as if brushing away an annoying insect. 'Derek's house is only small, it's not big enough for us all, so it's something we can talk about when Libby has finished her course.'

'You can't wait around for Libby,' I said.

'I won't see her on the streets.'

'You could both help her find her own place,' Derek suggested.

'She can't afford it,' Marianne said, shaking her head.

'Maybe we could lend her some more.'

'Lend her some more? What do you mean?' I asked, the *'we'* worrying me slightly.

'I just want Marianne to be happy …' Derek said.

'I am happy here …'

'But she needs to move on with her life,' Derek said, looking at me.

'How much has she borrowed already?' I directed the question at both of them.

'She needed to pay the fees for her course. I agreed I would pay them for her and when she starts teaching she can pay me back.'

'She won't be teaching at this rate,' I sighed heavily. 'What if she can't pay you back?'

'She will. I have faith in her.'

'Libby could move in with me.' I suddenly announced, as if my brain wasn't connected to my mouth. I thought about how I'd told Libby to leave the last time, and there was no way Max would have drugs in the house. But if she already owed Marianne (and Derek) money, I couldn't let her lend any more, as I couldn't see how Libby could begin to pay it back.

Marianne obviously wanted to move on with her life, and why shouldn't she? She'd practically lived her life for us, the least I could do was help out with my unruly sister.

'You're about to start your own family, so let's look at some other options first,' Marianne suggested.

'I think it's a great idea …' Derek said jovially.

'It's too much for you Kat,' Marianne said, shaking her head.

'It won't be forever.' I hoped.

Marianne bit her lip. 'What would Max say?'

'He'll be fine,' I smiled, having absolutely no idea how Max would react.

'Well, let's have a think about it.'

I smiled at them both, my stomach churned nervously. If Max wasn't already on the edge he probably would be now.

18

I spoke with June on my way home, ensuring she was okay. I'd wanted to ask her to Marianne's for lunch, but it felt inappropriate. Marianne's apparent hostility towards June was slightly unsettling. We arranged for June to come to the salon in the morning, and I'd treat her to a manicure. Although it was the last place I wanted to be, I wanted to know so much more about Mum. I'd thought about inviting her to stay with me and Max, but it didn't feel right. The way things were with Max at the moment, I didn't want her stuck in the middle. But then, I'd just offered for my sister to come and live with us, indefinitely …

How the hell I would broach that subject with Max was beyond me. Maybe I'd leave it for a while.

When I arrived home Max wasn't there. He'd left me a note in the kitchen: a problem had cropped up at work and he needed to speak to one of his consultants. It was poles apart from the little love notes he used to leave on my pillow.

My eyes stinging as the tears pricked, I read his familiar untidy handwriting, that didn't say when he'd be back. I was totally aware of the one kiss under the 'M' instead of the usual three, as I put the scruffy note in the bin. The one kiss stood out to me more than the words he'd written, but I told myself it didn't mean anything. He'll have been rushing.

It was a Sunday night, though, could he possibly be working this late at the weekend?

He'd worked late last night, up in his office. The door closed. He said he was really busy, he really needed to concentrate. I'd tried to offer a film, a night cosily on the couch, but he'd said there was no way. I'd phoned Suzy and relayed the previous night's events to her.

She believed Max. So, did that mean I had to? I wanted to. I *really* did.

But I just wished he'd let me in.

As the taps poured copious amounts of water into the bath, I stared at myself in the mirror. A young woman stared back at me, her dark locks tied untidily on her head. There was darkness under her eyes, her skin was pasty and dry. Her face was full and round, a second chin starting to appear under the line of the first.

I didn't recognise myself.

As I climbed into the bath, I wondered if I would have such luxuries when the babies came along. Deciding I probably wouldn't, I consciously appreciated the warmth, the delicate smoothness of the bubbles surrounding the three of us, and the peaceful ambience that filled the room.

My body still ached to relax after I'd managed to pull myself out of the bath. I stretched out on the bed and tried to watch programmes that offered escapism; but my mind couldn't connect with any of them. I tried to sit between the pillows on the bed, my bump resting on one of the cushions. I wondered if the babies would fight like this when they came out. Probably, but at least they would have more space to do it in.

I couldn't relax. Not only was I experiencing a heel, foot or elbow in my ribcage; my mind was a flowing album of terrifying images: me homeless, Libby homeless, Max taking custody of the babies because I had nowhere to live, no work, no-one wanting me because I'd failed at my own business.

I was driving myself insane.

I kept playing with the idea that I could work my way through keeping the business, but it had plummeted. It would definitely get even worse when I wasn't there to control things. Not that I could control anything at the moment. I couldn't leave Laura alone to deal with the customers.

Mobile therapists were in demand, I told myself. I had enough customers to keep me busy, so I could venture down that route. That would work better around me and the babies, I tried to convince myself. If Max's work calmed down, I could work in the evenings. Marianne and Clare had offered to help with childcare, but if Clare went along with this new project she wouldn't have time to babysit; while Marianne seemed wrapped up in her world, with Derek. But I couldn't focus on the obstacles though, I'd work something out.

Driving myself stupid with thoughts of me living on the streets and venturing into the world of prostitution (although I'd have to pay the clients at the moment) I decided to busy myself with the chores that I hated: sorting out clothes, cleaning away pots, relocating items from one side of the house to the other, even though they didn't need to be moved.

It was Suzy who interrupted me, her tongue sticking out playfully as her picture flashed at me from my mobile. I really needed to update to a more recent photo.

'Hiya.' I sat down breathlessly, my legs apart so that I could feel comfortable. I was glad that no-one could see my inelegant position.

'Hey you, how's things?'

'Well, I met Derek today. Marianne's new man.'

'How was he?'

'He was alright, but after Dad I assume it can only get better.' I forced a laugh, feeling slightly guilty that I was belittling Dad, again.

'If she's happy, then that's what matters.'

'Yeah, you're right.' Marianne did deserve to be happy after the crap she'd endured in her lifetime.

'But what about you and Max?'

'We're okay ...' I exhaled loudly.

'You sure?'

'I went on my own today because he had work to do. When I got back he wasn't here, just a bloody flimsy note saying he's popped out to see someone about work.'

'Look, I've been thinking. Is he still working at the Leeds office?'

'Yes ... why?' I asked, sure I could hear her mind ticking like an unearthed bomb.

'I have a plan.'

'Oh ...' a nervous flutter rippled through my stomach.

'You've tried cooking him dinner at home, but obviously with his work he may not always make it ...'

'Yeah,' I said, remembering the lasagne, most of it had ended up in the bin.

'Why don't you take the dinner to him?'

'What?'

'Why don't you go to his work and surprise him with a dinner? Show him you want this to work.'

'What! Are you mad?'

'It will put a bit of romance back into your relationship and it'll show you're willing to make the effort.'

'But what if he's not there? What if I upset him for interrupting his work? What if–'

'What if, what if, what if ... you can sit there and do nothing, or you can think of ways to try to save your relationship.'

'But what if he doesn't want me, Suz?'

'He does want *you*.'

'But the perfume ... Gina ...'

'If he's telling the truth, which I've told you, I think he is, as Lawrence would know if something was going—'

'How do you know that Lawrence would tell you?'

'Lawrence is crap at lying ... I've already asked him about Max, and he is adamant there is nothing going on. So the only question is, what are you prepared to do to make this work?'

I drew a deep breath, 'Whatever it takes.'

19

'Have you heard back from Jack Haslow, yet?' Clare was waiting outside the salon.

'No,' I said, unlocking the door to what had become something of a hindrance. I was secretly pleased she was with me. Her company was welcomed: taking away that initial pang that whipped through me every time I walked through the door.

'Why don't you chase him today?'

'Clare, he won't have had chance to look at the figures yet. I only dropped them there on Saturday.'

'I'm sure he'll have had a look through by now.'

'The office was closed when I dropped them off.'

'It's not what you know, it's who … I've told you this before.' Clare gleamed. I frowned at her a little confused. What was she talking about?

'I may have made a little phone call to Jack over the weekend.'

'Right.' Unbelievable!

'He said he would work on them yesterday.'

'On a Sunday?' Remembering Max had not arrived back home until late.

'He's a good friend. He knows I'll pay him back; free haircuts for him and Joyce.' She laughed, as she referred to Jack's wife.

'Look Clare, I know it's not for me to pry, but you have spoken properly to Henry about this?'

'Oh, come on Kathryn; like I *need* to speak to Henry *properly*.'

'You mean you haven't!?'

'Of course, I have.' She sat on our cosy sofa, leaning back, her arm stretched across the back of the cushions, crossing her legs as if the place was already hers. 'He's just happy if I am.'

'So he's supporting you, even though you've never worked in the hairdressing industry?'

'He thinks it's a great idea ... so does Max.' Max and I'd had a fleeting conversation about it, but I hadn't seen him jumping up and down in excitement.

'But what if you lose money?'

'We won't, it'll be fine.'

Her confidence was disconcerting. She had no idea how to run a business. I was worried she had some kind of fluffy image in her head. I was apprehensive about the whole thing. Perhaps that was because I didn't want to let go.

'I just don't want to be blamed if anything goes wrong.' Making more excuses, although this was true, I was stalling.

'Blamed?' She sat up straight to face me, concern etched across her face.

'It's my business that's failing and you're helping me out.'

'Kathryn, I see this as fate. This is meant to be. I've been thinking so much about my future. I could have thirty, forty or even more years left. I want to do something that's for me. Admittedly, I wouldn't have considered it had this option not come along; but it feels perfect.'

'Do you think you should have a word with a professional first?' I wasn't trying to discourage her but I was concerned she hadn't thought it through. Troubled slightly that it was a whim that sounded like a perfect dream. But in reality, it could be a complete headache.

'Jack has given some advice. Plus, Henry is sorting out some meetings with some people.' She waved her hand dismissively. 'He's devised a business plan. Trust me, Kathryn, it will work. I have so much faith.'

'Well, let's see what Jack comes back with. I'll call you later.'

But, I already knew what I had to do.

'Great.' Clare got up from the sofa, her face bright, as she clapped her hands. Hugging me close.

June entered, within seconds of Clare leaving. Closing the door on the gusty winds, she took my breath away once again, as she reminded me so much of Mum.

'Oh, that weather is appalling,' she said, taking off her fur-trimmed hat, running her fingers through her fine hair.

'I know.'

'You look tired,' June said, as I showed her to the nail table.

'I am tired.' I found myself laughing slightly, swallowing the need to burst into tears. 'This pregnancy malarkey is tiring work.' I tried to joke, distract myself from the conversation I'd had with Clare.

'I can imagine.' She smiled back, but I noticed a sadness in her eyes as she sat opposite me. We discussed the colours she would usually use. Her bright reds and vibrant pinks were miles away from the colours Marianne would have chosen.

'Did Mum like bright colours?' I lightened a little as I broached the subject I loved talking about: Mum, that is, not the colour of nail polish.

'Not really, she was a bit more reserved than me,' June said, as she watched me work on her cuticles. 'I was the loud one.'

'Bit like Libby then.'

'Yes, Libby was a confident child.'

'I remember.' I smiled. 'She hasn't changed much.'

'It would be nice to see her.'

'I know. She's mad busy, I hardly ever see her now. I'll talk to her tonight. Maybe tomorrow?' I didn't want to commit. I didn't want June seeing Libby in the state she was in yesterday.

'Sounds great.'

'So, tell me some more about Mum.' A little flutter of excitement ran through my body. 'Something random … like … what was her favourite food?'

'Cheese.' June laughed. 'She loved cheese. If she could have lived off cheese and toast she would have. Next question …'

Suddenly Laura entered, shivering, exclaiming loudly about how cold she was. I'd asked her to join me in the salon, to help me clean and give the place a boost. I could easily have dealt with all the appointments and the cleaning on my own, but I didn't want to. Loneliness seemed to be always around me at the moment, so it would be good to have someone with me, to stop me dwelling on my worries.

'God, I'm so tired,' Laura declared inappropriately, she had no idea that June was a family member, not that it mattered. Laura still hadn't seemed to pick up the customer etiquette rules. She slumped down in the chair, her elbows resting on the other nail table. 'I had a bit of a late one.'

'Oh dear,' I cringed.

'I've met this new guy,' she sniggered. 'My mother hates him.'

'So, that's why you like him?' June probed.

'Probably. He plays in a band, so I was watching him last night. He had all these girls around him. I was like, hands off, he's mine.'

'What type of band is he in?' June asked politely.

'Heavy rock stuff.' Laura beamed, 'He's really good. But I was so pissed – oh, sorry – drunk, I think I might still be.'

'Why don't you put the kettle on, make us a drink.' I realised I was so eager to hear about Mum, I hadn't offered June any kind of beverage. 'Get yourself a coffee. Might sober you up,' I said to her. June raised her eyebrows at me, and I shook my head as Laura made her way out of the room.

'Who'd like what?' she shouted from the kitchen, instead of coming out to ask us. June said she'd have a cup of tea. I shouted back, giving up on the need to be polite. In the midst of the kettle boiling, Laura came back out to tell us another 'hilarious' incident that had happened.

I never got to speak to June about Mum. Laura was as loud as ever. She had no intention of working. I could have told her to clean, tidy or do numerous tasks, but it seemed pointless. We just listened to her waffling on about her life.

Once June had left, I was no further forward in completing my image of Mum. So, I decided even if Libby wasn't available tomorrow evening, I'd still see June.

In between treatments, Jack Haslow rang me. I wondered if Clare had chased him, because I'd made every excuse not to call him. 'Your figures have dropped considerably.' *Tell me something I don't know*, I'd thought, as his depressing words formed the reality I knew I had to face. 'Once the babies are born, Kat, can you seriously say you'll be able to deliver the best service to your customers?' he added, 'Customers that only want to see you ...' when I hadn't answered.

'No ... I can't.'

'The figures will only get worse ...'

So, it was in black and white; my balance sheet showed that I had no other option but to accept Clare's offer.

I tried to push my thoughts away as I listened to Laura's scandalous tales. Surprisingly pleased that she'd become a welcomed distraction; if my thoughts didn't divert back to Clare, then I kept wondering how Max would react when I turned up at his work this evening, with a romantic meal for two.

When I was finally alone, Laura's raucous laughter no longer my excuse to put this off, I stared at the phone. It felt like an eternity before I finally picked it up and dialled Clare's number.

I shared Jack's thoughts with her, telling her my business was on a downward slide.

I verbally accepted her offer. I made it final.

20

The plan to deliver Max his dinner was made easier because, once again, he'd phoned to say he was working late. The last thing I felt like doing was delivering a romantic meal, especially after my conversation with Clare. She'd been delighted. For herself, of course. I'd tried to share her enthusiasm, but could have thrown-up while talking to her.

I fought the urge to run my routine bath, cuddle on the sofa and dwell in my own self-pity. But I'd just lost my business, I couldn't lose Max too.

My stomach felt like a washing machine on a fast spin. Not because two little bodies were fighting for room, but because anxiety was gripping every part of me. All this turmoil was working its way through my brain like woodworm.

'What the hell am I doing, Suzy?' I rang her before I left the driveway. 'This is ludicrous, I should just talk to him.'

'You could do, but this is a huge gesture. This is your way of saying you want this to work.'

I was unconvinced, as I sat in my car staring at his house. *His house*. Would it ever feel like *my* home?

'It'll be fine, Kat.'

'What if it's not? What if I upset him?' My head was telling me to run back in, instead of going through with this scheme that he'd probably hate. It seemed ridiculous, or I felt ridiculous, whichever, it wasn't a good place to be.

'You won't upset him,' Suzy said, 'Do you want me to come with you?'

'No …' Yes. 'I'm okay … I think.' I swallowed.

'Kat, things haven't been right for months now.'

'I know.' My thoughts wandered back to the last time Max and I had laughed, chatted about things in general, spent time together, watched a film, gone out for a meal or simply gone for a walk. All the things we loved doing when we met.

'You can fix it,' she acknowledged, encouraging me.

'Do you really think so?'

'Yes I think so. Kat, you can resolve this with him later, if that's what you want. You can drive yourself mad worrying about him seeing someone else. I'm not forcing you to go ahead with the plan, but you haven't got anything to lose by showing him how much you care.'

I breathed out slowly, trying to release the sickening tension that was eating away at me. I stared back at the house that I was finding hard to make my home. I could pretend nothing was happening. Eliminate our problems from my mind, wait until the babies were born. Carry on as if nothing was wrong. It wasn't as if I didn't have enough on my plate already.

But we needed to sort things out. It was Max who'd said we had to make an effort. This was one big move, the first move, but I had to make it. I had to make things right. Nerves rumbled through me. I felt as if I was going on a first date.

'I'm going. I'll call you later,' I said, as if I was making a huge announcement.

'Good girl, that's what I like to hear …'

'Thanks Suz.'

'You're welcome … now go.'

We hung up as I set off down the gravelled drive. I peered out of the window as the heavens opened, the downpour would make it slightly more difficult to concentrate. I hoped Max would appreciate my efforts.

I wondered constantly if we'd been forced together rather than our relationship growing naturally. Were the babies the only reason we were together? I hoped not. That hope was the thing I was holding onto as I drove down the A19 towards his office in Leeds.

Losing Myself

I loved Max. I had to do this. I told myself over and over to keep going, as the rain beat against the windscreen, the wipers fighting to clear it, I forced myself onward, repeating, 'Keep going. Don't turn around.'

Suzy and I had discussed the best plan. It was decided rather than me packing up a picnic basket of food, I would call at one of the Indian takeaways. I'd printed off a list of those near his office. Luckily there was parking near the one that I'd circled. The fifteen-minute wait felt like an hour. I felt as if I could be sick. I was shaking from either the cold, or nerves, probably both. As I waited for the food, I considered going home.

Finally, Max's favourite dish was wrapped ready to serve him: a lamb tikka green masala. I tried to imagine his face, as I placed it down next to the candles I'd brought with me.

As I got back into the car, I realised I should have gone with the basket idea; the Indian food was releasing some strong fumes. I wasn't sure how Max would feel about the smell, especially when it worked its way across his office.

I found his office as quickly as I'd found the takeaway. 'Well done, Kathryn,' I said to myself, proud I'd not taken one wrong turn. The huge building stood in front of me, a mass of offices. I'd never been here before and I felt as if I was trespassing. The building contained a wide range of companies, but I knew Max's office was situated on the third floor. The car park was quite full, but people were starting to leave. Groups of people came out chatting, but then quickly ran to their cars, I assumed anxious to be out of the horrid weather. I found Max's car parked near the entrance, a reserved space just for him. I managed to find a space nearby.

The car park was lit up by the lamp posts that were strategically placed in the middle to shed the most light, which was useful as darkness had fallen.

'I daren't go in,' I said to myself. I wished I'd taken Suzy up on her offer of coming with me. It would have been unfair, though, her sitting in the car alone while we enjoyed a romantic meal.

'Let's go.' I took a deep breath and picked up the food. I was shaking slightly, the paper bag wobbling gently in my grasp. If my heart was to beat any faster, I'd die.

As I opened the car door to get out, Max came out of the building. Quietly shutting the door, I watched as he walked towards his car, something stopped me from shouting him. His head was bent against the rain. He was on his phone, his briefcase in the other hand as he tried to press the button to unlock the car. Succeeding, he slid into the driver's seat.

My heart was racing, as his lights were switched on and he pulled out of the space. Switching my lights to a higher beam, I followed him out of the car park. It all seemed to happen so quickly.

He'd said he was working late. He must be going to see a client. If he was, I should stop following him. I should turn around. But I couldn't. My body suddenly felt numb. My mouth dry. The shaking had stopped, but apprehension was filling me. I turned down the heaters, finding the rising temperature unbearable. It took only seconds for the front window to steam up, so I turned them back on, pressing down the side window an inch, hoping the cold air would allow some freshness into my lungs.

Max drove swiftly. It took all my concentration to keep up with him. Cars passed by, people in their own worlds, their own bubbles of life. I wondered how many people were facing life-changing decisions. As I chased him through the streets, following his path onto the A19, I wondered about all these other people I passed. People, perhaps, who had been told they had a life-threatening disease, people who had recently lost a loved one, people who were suffering immense financial pressure, people who were trying to solve issues of daily life. These imaginings sent waves of guilt through me.

What was I doing? Where was I expecting him to go?

The perfume … Gina … flashed through my mind. What if he was meeting another woman, but she was a client? What if I'd got the whole thing wrong? I'd need to play this so carefully, as it could easily blow up in my face.

We raced down the A19 at 90mph, Max a little ahead of me, battling the rain that wasn't letting up. I hoped I didn't get pulled by the police: not only would I lose Max, I could end up with a hefty fine which I could do without. As we headed north, the lamp posts that were protected by the central barrier, lit up the lanes as if helping us along our journey. The Indian food, had toppled to the side, luckily not out of the bag, but it was giving off an unpleasant smell, which wasn't helping my nausea.

Maybe he was coming home. Maybe he'd had the same thought; he wanted to surprise me. He was making an effort too. But my hopes were shattered when he took the turn-off to Northallerton.

'Maybe not, then,' I said aloud, as I clicked my indicator to follow him. I was keeping a safe distance so he couldn't possibly know it was me. I had images of him stopping his car to confront me, my cover blown.

The cat's eyes now led the way along the narrow, winding roads, passing little rows of timeworn cottages. Tall trees randomly planted at the edge of large fields leaned menacingly. Pylons reared above us as if watching our every move. The utter silence increased the intensity.

A sign on an enormous rock at the side of the road stated we had entered Northallerton. I tried to remember who lived here. He'd never mentioned anyone from this way, not even through work. It could be a new client, or it could be a decoy; he knew I was onto him.

A car emerged from a housing estate blocking my view, and as Max indicated left at a roundabout the car followed him. Another car pulled in front of me before I had the chance to follow Max's left turn. I heard myself swearing. I watched him approach a smaller roundabout, taking a right. I was then directly behind him as the other cars had taken a different road. Probably just leaving work, popping to the shops or picking up kids; not involved in a secret mission, like me …

As I followed, Max pulled up in front of a row of terraced houses. Cottage-style homes with black panelled doors, bay windows and stained brickwork. There was ivy climbing up many of the old bricks. The hedges and walls defined the boundaries between each home.

I continued on, passing his car, hopefully unnoticed by him.

A roundabout was ahead of me, where I turned around quickly. My heart was pounding. My driving had suddenly become erratic as I completely cut up another car, the horn resonated into the skies. I shouted, 'Sorry,' but obviously they couldn't hear me.

The madness was all around me, the heat of the moment forcing me forward. I was desperate to know where he was going. I probably wouldn't recognise who he was visiting, but I couldn't stop now.

Driving back down the road towards Max's car, the windscreen wipers still struggling against the rain. I could see him walking briskly along the path towards one of the houses. I thought about pulling into the side, but it was as if my car had a mind of its own. I drove slowly, a risk that I hadn't meant to take but I had no choice as he was too close now for me to stop, reverse or try to disguise myself in some way.

The door to the house opened as I passed his car. I turned my head to see the person he'd driven so speedily to visit.

Winded by the sight, my gasp filled the air as my stomach tightened.

Gina greeted Max with open arms, as he wrapped his arms around her waist and kissed her tenderly on the lips.

21

Abandoning all attempts at being discreet, I slammed on the brakes, the tyres screeching piercingly. Max spun around, while Gina stared at the car, looking bewildered.

'Kat?' I couldn't hear him, but his lips mimed my name. He walked towards me, the usual healthy glow had drained from his face. A curtain twitched behind one of the neighbours windows. Gina stood at the door, her arms folded tight around her chest, looking wounded, as if she was the victim in all this.

I had the truth; it was here, fresh for me to see.

He came to the passenger side, clearly confused. Fear apparent in his eyes. But before he reached me I placed my foot on the accelerator and with wheels spinning, the rubber bouncing against the tarmac, I drove away.

The rain bounced from the window as my wipers did their best to cope. It took me forever to find my way back to the A19; between the blurriness of tears, the heavy rain and my crap sense of direction I had no chance of getting away quickly.

'He's seeing Gina,' I screamed into the mouthpiece of my hands-free set.

'What?'

'He wasn't giving her a lift the other night it was her perfume it's been her all along,' I rambled as a sob escaped. I wiped my nose and eyes with my sleeve.

'Kat, calm down. What the hell are you talking about?' Suzy was obviously worried that I'd lost it.

'Max is seeing Gina.'

'I don't understand.'

'I've just seen them together.'

'What? Where?'

'I followed him. He went to her house,' I managed, through a blocked nose and tears that were spilling non-stop. She was silent. 'Did you know?' Her silence worried me.

'Oh my God, what a bastard! Of course I didn't know.' I heard her asking Lawrence in the background, 'Did you know?' He mumbled something, but I couldn't quite hear him. 'That Max was seeing Gina?' Suzy asked him. I heard Lawrence much more clearly as he said, 'Don't be so ridiculous.'

'I'll meet you at yours,' she said to me. Lawrence was trying to talk in the background, but she ignored him. 'We'll get you some stuff and you can stay with us.'

'Thank you.' I choked on my words. I didn't want to be a nuisance. I knew I could go to Marianne's, or even stay with June, but Suzy's felt the better option for tonight.

The drive back felt like it had taken for ever. I stared listlessly ahead, my brain automatically taking me along the dim roads. I let the darkness absorb my pain. Silently, tears rolled down my cheeks, falling from my chin onto my hands. The expression *a broken heart* wasn't even close: I felt as if shards of glass were piercing around my body, the pain unbearable.

I pulled into the driveway. Suzy's car was already there. And so was Max's. I'd not seen him pass me. But then considering the million streets it had taken me to find my way out of Northallerton, I'd probably given him a good head start. Suzy stepped from her car before I had the chance to turn the engine off. As I got out of my car she wrapped her arms tightly around me, but I felt as if someone had taken all my strength as I struggled to lift my arms and hug her back.

'Are you sure about this?' she asked.

'They kissed …' I managed.

'Kat, I'm so sorry.' Suzy hugged me again.

We walked towards the house. Presuming Max would be packing my case for me, because, surely, he wasn't going to bother making further excuses, I opened the front door. Suzy was close behind me as we entered the place that I'd never found comfortable calling my home.

I'd known what was going on so much earlier. I'd ignored the signs. I'd made excuses for his distance. I'd wanted to believe the perfume and the Gina stories ... I loved him.

But I'd known. Deep inside; the hidden places where we don't like to admit realities to ourselves.

'Kat, please you have to listen to me.' Max was waiting in the hallway. His face was ashen, his eyes full of sorrow. I walked past him, holding the banister to help me climb the stairs. If possible, I'd have run up each step ... run away from him.

In the bedroom, I pulled my suitcase from underneath the bed. I grabbed my clothes, pulling out things from the wardrobe and drawers. I didn't feel as hysterical, as I packed for the second time in a week. I felt deflated. I wanted to take as much as I could so I didn't have to come back.

He grabbed my arm, 'Please listen to me.'

'There's nothing to listen to, Max.' I forced the words from my aching throat.

'There is nothing going on. Gina has come into money and she's building a house, she wanted my advice. I didn't tell you because I know how much you hate my relationship with her.'

'So, did she need the kiss of life when you got there?' A small laugh escaped.

'What?'

'I saw you Max ...' I said, he glared at me confused. 'I saw you kiss her ...'

His body seem to collapse onto the side of the bed, as he rested his head in his hands, 'I'm so sorry.'

I ignored him, as I continued to load things into the case, through the anguish I was trying to make sure I had everything I needed.

'I didn't mean for it to happen.' He was shaking as the words penetrated across the room. 'After Mum's party we met up, she was upset because of Dave, one thing led to another ...'

'That's it ... that's your explanation.'

'I don't know what else to say ... I'm sorry.'

The case now contained plenty of clothes to last me a few days. I picked up my blue bag that I would need in case I went into labour; which at this rate it could happen anytime.

'Oh God, Kat, I'm sorry. Please don't leave.'

I zipped up the suitcase and lifted it, its heaviness pulling on my back. Max tried to take it from me, whether to stop me or help me, I didn't know, both were unwanted. I pulled away from him, feeling a sharp pain shoot down my front. I breathed deeply, letting the agony pass, as he rushed to my side.

'Are you okay?' He asked fearfully.

I wanted to laugh; his question didn't deserve an answer.

I pulled the suitcase down each step, dragging it with all the energy I had left, adrenaline forcing me to move and not breakdown. Suzy took it from me, lifting it as if it was a feather.

'I can't believe you Max,' she said between gritted teeth, as she shook her head. She carried the case out of the front door.

'Kat, please stay, we can sort this out ...' Max gently touched my arm, but I shoved him away. I couldn't speak to him. There were no words to express how much he'd hurt me. He was another person who'd left me when I needed them more than ever.

As I closed the door behind me, I thought about Mum.

If I could cope with such a loss at twelve years old, I was more than capable of doing it now.

22

Sitting in the waiting room, I couldn't tell from those around me who was coming for a first-time scan, a twenty-week scan or a monthly check-up like me. None of them looked as tired as I felt. Most appeared to be a picture of health.

Max had tried to ring countless times throughout the night, but I'd put the phone on silent and ignored the happy face that kept flashing at me. I realised that I hadn't seen him smile like that in a while. There was no laughter between us, no fun or excitement.

Suzy had really wanted to come with me but she had appointments, and I didn't want to mess up her day. Marianne had offered too when I'd rung to see if she had room for me. I could have stayed with Suzy longer. She'd insisted, but I really didn't want to get in the way of her and Lawrence. I knew I'd have to find somewhere to live in a matter of weeks, ideally before the babies were born.

My name was called. As I walked towards the door I felt a presence behind me. Assuming it was a nurse, I turned, enabling them to pass, but I came face-to-face with a weary-looking Max.

'What the hell are you doing here?' I snapped through clenched teeth. My voice was so quiet I could barely hear it myself, but I was aware the waiting room had turned into an audience. He told me he'd needed to come, and we walked into the darkened room as if there was nothing wrong.

The same procedure was followed, except this time I wanted to tell the sonographer that Max wasn't welcome in the room. I didn't speak as the gel was wiped across my bump, and the machine showed up our babies; who were both fit and well.

'They're both head down, so it looks like a normal delivery. This is what you wanted, yes?' She nodded at me, as she referred to my notes.

I nodded back. I wanted to tell her that it would definitely be the better option now that I was doing it alone. It would be bad enough with all the other symptoms: swollen, leaky breasts, the baby blues and sleepless nights; without the added pressure of major abdominal surgery. I needed to be able to lift the babies. Be capable of moving around without the worry of pulling a muscle, or getting a stitch that could cause more complications.

Now, don't get me wrong: if pain was the only deciding factor, a C-section would have won hands down.

What mattered now, was I needed the flexibility. More so than ever.

God, it scared me. I wanted to listen to Max. But I couldn't. I couldn't betray myself. I was better than this. But I wanted to make it all go away. I wished I'd not followed him.

Before we left, the sonographer made us another appointment. I'd be just over thirty-eight weeks by the time we came back. It had been lovely to see the babies. Tenderness filled me every time I knew they were okay. 'They are fighting for space,' she'd laughed, 'but they're doing marvellous.' She believed they'd be around 4 lbs. each. One was slightly bigger than the other but there wasn't much in it.

The warm feeling of tenderness disappeared as soon as we stepped from the room. I walked away as if I was on my own, not allowing Max into my space. He'd spoken a few times in the room but I'd ignored him.

'Kat, we have to talk.' He was walking beside me, obviously trying not to let onlookers see that things were not good.

'I have nothing to say to you.' I had lots I wanted to say, but I was so angry with him. So frustrated.

'I need to explain what happened.' We were outside in the fresh, cold air, the chill sending shivers down my spine as I fastened my coat around my bump, keeping us all cosy and warm. 'I was scared …'

I carried on walking (okay, waddling) faster than I usually would. I could feel the pulling on my bump and between my legs, as my back begged me to slow down. But I couldn't. I needed to be away from him. If I'd been able to run, I would have.

'I couldn't turn to you ... you were trying to make sure everything was set for the babies, and then everything happened with your business ... I'm so sorry ... I wish I could turn back time.'

'Tell me Max?' I stopped walking, turning to face him. 'How long has this been going on? You said it was after your Mum's party, but that's a lie isn't it?'

'That doesn't matter ...' he said, shaking his head.

'It does to me ...' He still didn't answer. 'All the late nights, it's all been a lie hasn't it?'

'None of that matters, what matters is sorting it now ... for the babies.'

I shook my head and walked away from him.

'We need to talk about the babies.' I ignored him. Finally reaching my car, with Max's repeated, 'Kat stop, please let's talk,' ringing in my ears, I clicked off the alarm, unlocked the door and climbed in. I slammed the door in his face, inches away from the stubble that he'd not bothered to get rid of this morning.

As I reversed out of the space, he stood watching me, shaking his head, sadness etched across his face. As I drove away from him, I glanced in the rear-view mirror. He was walking away. His shoulders were slightly hunched, his head down. I felt the tears sting, as one escaped.

I remembered how he'd sworn on our babies' lives that he wasn't seeing anyone. As that thought entered, I realised that hadn't been his words at all ... he'd sworn that he wasn't seeing Melanie or Yasmin. He'd not generalised. He'd been quite specific, cleverly fooling me. I was so bloody enraged with myself; how could I have been so stupid?

I really didn't want to go back to the salon. Laura was seeing to the few customers who were booked in. I just wanted to put a sign on the door that read; 'It's all over'.

Entering the village was always the point where my stomach felt as if it was a seabed of rocks. It was as if the babies knew we'd arrived as they bashed together, somersaulting their own distress.

Clare's car was waiting outside, the seabed rocked a little more, I couldn't deal with her now. I had no energy.

She was waiting on the customers' sofa, flicking through an old magazine; they hadn't been updated in months. One of Melanie's jobs, but she'd obviously been building her own collection.

'Oh, Kathryn. How are you, dear?' She immediately stood to greet me. I was surprised by her concern. Had Max told her? For some reason, I'd expected him to keep his sordid secret to himself. It would have to come out eventually but I hadn't expected it to be so soon.

'I'm fine.' I forced a smile, fully aware that Laura and her customer were watching me. They had obviously been in full conversation until I'd walked in.

'Can we chat?'

I nodded in response. After checking the diary and ensuring Laura was okay, I told Clare we'd go upstairs. I didn't need Laura or any customers knowing more of my business than they already did.

'That would be great, because that's what I want to talk to you about,' Clare said, confusing me. I unlocked the door to what I'd always classed as my secret hideaway when I'd lived in the flat. Why would she want to talk to me about the upstairs? She'd already mentioned that I could do beauty treatments up here; but was it so urgent, we had to discuss it now?

The door to the flat securely closed, Clare stunned me by giving me a hug. Although my bump got in our way, it was a sincere, hearty embrace.

'I don't know what to say, Kathryn.' Her voice started to shake, her eyes brimming with tears, which startled me even more.

'If this had been a year ago, you'd have been very pleased.' I tried to joke; jesting was my way of trying to protect myself, but today it was painful for me and I wished I'd not tried.

Clare smiled a little, then shaking her head, she quickly wiped away a stray tear. 'Oh, look at me. I'm sorry.' She took a tissue from her handbag, blowing her nose delicately. 'I've been thinking, and I've spoken to Henry about this; in fact, all we did last night was talk … Kathryn, Maxwell is devastated.'

'*He's* devastated?' The sarcasm pulsated from me, echoing into the empty room. I turned to look out of the sash windows, where I used to watch families enjoying each other's company as they fed bread to the ducks or savoured the deliciousness of their ice-creams. I often wondered if they were really as happy as they appeared to be. What was going on behind those smiles?

'I'm sorry. I haven't come here to talk to you about Maxwell. What he has done is completely unreasonable … I needed you to know that we're here for you.' I wondered what, and how much he'd told her as her manner, that was often a little forceful and abrupt, was soft. I assumed she was worried. Was I going to take her grandchildren away from her before she'd even had the chance to start a relationship with them? I wanted to tell her this wouldn't happen, but I couldn't even think about these issues, let alone discuss them.

'Thank you.' I whispered, swallowing the lump that had formed at the back of my throat; from the tears I'd shed, though, I was sure there couldn't be any more left.

'So, as I said, Henry and I were talking. I realise you'll need somewhere to live when the babies are born, and I wondered if you wanted to live back here?'

'In this flat?' Her offer threw me. I'd not thought so far ahead. I wanted to try and get through the day; I couldn't focus on where I would be living now or, when the babies were born.

'Yes, I thought it would be a great plan.'

'Mmm … thanks, but I need to look around for places, look at the pricing.'

'Oh, Kathryn, I don't expect you to pay. Babies are expensive. Obviously, Maxwell will have to contribute but I want to help. Henry and I want to help. It's going to be hard, but at least I'll be downstairs.'

'Right …' I stuttered, wanting to crash at the thought of not being with Max. Living alone with my babies. That wasn't how it was meant to be. 'So, you still want to go ahead with taking over the salon?'

'Absolutely.' Her brusque manner was back.

'I really appreciate the offer of the flat, but I'll have to think about it.' Talking about moving back into the flat seemed surreal. Talking about moving anywhere away from Max seemed very strange, like a dream – or a nightmare.

My phone rang. It was Libby. I switched her off. I couldn't deal with her at the moment.

'You take all the time you need.'

My phone interrupted us again. Libby screaming at me to talk to her. 'Sorry, I just take this.' I answered it, exasperated, 'Can I call you back?'

'I need you. I think Calvin is dead.'

23

She told me that he'd passed out after they'd taken some illegal substances, or in her words, 'I'm not sure what he's taken.' Of course she wasn't! Screaming with distress, she told me she couldn't feel his pulse. Gasping into the mouthpiece as she struggled to convey what had happened.

Instructing her to call an ambulance, I told her I was on my way. Clare was frowning; her eyes narrowed together, she was clearly perplexed by my one-way conversation with my senseless sister. She didn't know Libby well: I'd tried to keep our families' lives separate.

As I drove along the country roads away from the village, after telling Laura to cancel the *four* appointments we had in that afternoon, the conversation with Clare kept turning over in my mind. Whatever Max had told her, it had nothing to do with us getting back together, obviously. She'd never once mentioned about us working it out, fighting for our relationship, making it work for the babies.

I knew she'd had the conversation with Max, I knew she would have asked him to try and make our relationship work. Had he blamed me? Had he told her the truth? But what *was* the truth? Was it his love for Gina or his lack of love for me? Did he mention anything about our babies? See so many questions, but I was so angry with him, I couldn't ask.

This was such a mess, and now on top of all of it, I had to deal with Libby and her dramatics. I'd felt like hanging up on her, telling her to deal with it herself. Harsh, I know, but telling me she couldn't feel his pulse had riled me. She was probably so high herself she didn't even know where to look.

When I arrived at the house, there was an ambulance outside, the emergency lights flashing. I parked a distance away; not that I could get near the house with the number of people that had gathered in the street. Women with their arms folded, surmising what was going on inside. Kids on scooters and bikes, shouting rudely at each other. One child got slapped across the head by his mother, her foul language setting him a terrible example.

I pushed my apologetic way through the crowds. Politely they moved out of my way.

I noticed the front door was open as a reckless child scooted past me shouting, 'What's going on?' I shrugged, not wanting to get into conversation with some random child.

As I walked down the path towards the house that had once been my home, and would be again from tonight, I felt estranged from it. Amazing how many places I'd called home; and now there was nowhere I felt safe.

I entered into the grubby hallway, and had a fleeting thought that Marianne really should have decorated this part of the house, especially with it being on display to the whole street.

I could hear sobs above the subdued voices that were coming from the lounge. I knew it was Libby and instantly I felt the need to be with her.

Perhaps this was more serious than I'd thought. I expected Calvin to be sat up in a chair wrapped in a blanket, a lecture being given to them both from the paramedics.

My annoyance turned to fear, panic starting to sweep through me as I pushed open the lounge door. Libby sat in the corner of the room, her legs up to her chest, her arms squeezing her knees tight, rocking herself as her screams filled the room.

My heart pounded. Sickness engulfed me as I watched them cover Calvin's face with a sheet.

24

The next week passed by in what felt like slow motion. Every day was like wading through treacle, watching every minute until the next day arrived. Libby had shut herself off from the world, her bedroom her saviour. She didn't want to talk, she wouldn't eat and she wouldn't venture from her refuge unless she needed the bathroom.

I'd agreed to take Clare up on her offer of moving back into the flat, but told her we'd sort things out in the next few weeks. I wasn't comfortable living back in the house I'd grown up in, but it felt wrong to want to leave when Libby was so distressed.

I'd also spoken with Jack Haslow and my landlord's solicitor, advising them to make the transfer between me and Clare. 'Take this headache away from me,' I'd told Jack.

He asked repeatedly, 'Are you sure?'

'Never been more sure,' I lied. I wasn't sure of anything, my decisions, my life, my future. I just knew I wanted some head space and keeping hold of the salon wasn't giving me room to think.

Would that be a bad time to make this transfer? Would that be a bad time to make such a precious decision? I had no idea about that either; all I knew was I needed quiet. I needed space to think about the babies, and our next step.

I'd taken Clare up on her offer because it would mean the babies and I could live rent-free. As merciless as that might sound I needed to think about finances more carefully than I'd thought about them in years. I was in a worse position than when I'd decided to open the salon. Now, I had no idea where I would get an income from, plus I had two little people to think about. It had been decided that Libby was going to be moving in with me and she wasn't working. In fact, she'd not been to uni this week either. I guessed she would leave it until the New Year now.

I didn't want to pressurise her: I knew Calvin's loss had impacted on her greatly. I was hoping this sad situation would make her see sense about the dangerous stuff she was putting in her body. Although I hadn't held much respect for Calvin, his death was a shock that rippled through us like a mini-tornado. Such a short life, a sad existence torn away so quickly, so disastrously. It frightened me to think it could easily have been Libby.

His parents came to talk to Libby. They'd been so kind to her. I was surprised; I'd thought they might blame her. If it had been Libby who had tragically taken a dodgy drug – as it turned out to be - I'd not have been so welcoming of Calvin.

Marianne and I had left them in the lounge to talk. Libby had told me they were so grateful that she'd been such a close friend. They'd had a huge argument with Calvin before his death. They knew about the drugs and had a problem with his sexuality; or his father did. Hence the reason, as Marianne had said, he had no place to stay. His father had told Libby he'd hoped for more between them; he'd hoped she would have put him on the 'straight and narrow'.

Libby had sobbed to me, 'He would have been perfect for me if he'd loved women. His dad made it sound so simple, I wish it had been …' I'd cuddled her. Although I didn't agree with this statement, there was no point in having that argument.

Her sadness filled the house. It reminded me so much of Dad when we'd lost Mum; how the all-consuming misery dragged on my own spirit, sucking light and vitality from my soul. I was hoping she would be okay after the funeral, which Marianne had agreed to go to with her. I didn't think my emotions could take much more, as selfish as that may sound. Every day I was fighting for my own survival, my own world changing significantly around me. I didn't have the strength to carry her, as I'd always done before.

Living with Marianne seemed to help immensely. I didn't think I could cope on my own, now or when the babies arrived. Plus,

Marianne was my protection from Max. He'd turned up several times, begging to be seen. Marianne threatened to call the police if he kept pestering me, demanding answers, when I thought it should be *me* demanding from *him*.

I couldn't face him at the moment. My anger towards him was colossal. I could kill him. Not metaphorically; I mean literally, physically kill him. These thoughts would make me cry, because at the same time, I still loved him. I wanted to forgive, make it all better, tell him to forget it, let's move on with our lives … be a family for our babies.

But I couldn't do that.

I felt completely lost. I couldn't talk to Max and make him feel better and let him know it was okay, because it wasn't okay.

I wished adultery was illegal so they could lock him up. I'd shout to the judge in the courtroom to throw away the key. I couldn't sit with him and discuss custody, visiting rights, child maintenance or any other child-related matter that would allow him to feel better. I knew I couldn't stop him seeing his own children and I had no intention of doing so. But they weren't here yet, so I needed this time and space to sort myself out, to understand where I was going.

Clare rang me a few times, obviously wanting to know if I was okay, but also keeping me updated on solicitor movements. I'd basically told her I would sign whatever needed signing. I couldn't believe how quickly things were moving in that respect, how easy the transition was. But I was struggling to imagine myself back in the flat; probably another reason I'd been reluctant to move out of Marianne's. I also felt I was moving backwards, and I couldn't bear the thought of that. I'd have Mandy and Melanie around the corner waving their success at me. All I knew was, if I'd had another option that was as economically viable I'd have taken it.

I visited the salon every day to attend to the few appointments I had in. I told Laura that unfortunately there was no work, so every time I entered I was alone. The emptiness was eerie, the loneliness would hit me with a fierceness that was hard to cope with. Panic would claw at me, plunging me into a state of claustrophobia.

I needed to be away from the place. I was worried I'd feel the same sense of being smothered when I moved back to the flat. But, I couldn't live with Marianne for ever, I didn't want to impose or feel like a burden. I'd always been so independent, I was always the strong one once Mum had died and now here I was in need of support and feeling so weak. I felt as if I was drowning.

June had offered for me to live with her. She'd visited a few times but the hostility she received from Marianne was not only bad-mannered and embarrassingly rude, it was so unlike Marianne. Her usual pleasant and pleasing character was seething with resentment of some kind. I asked June to tell me the tale of her and Marianne, but she brushed me away and told me Marianne had always been that way and they'd never been friends.

June tried to accuse Marianne of taking Mum's place, but I stopped her. A year ago, sticking up for Marianne would have seemed like a betrayal of Mum. But she didn't deserve June's harshness; I'd discovered she was one of the nicest people. One of the kindest. The fact that we'd overlooked her compassion, when she'd given all she had, ate away at me. I wondered if one day I could ever make up for the hurt she must have felt.

When June had suggested moving in with her, I'd asked, 'In Devon?' and she'd nodded. It seemed an outlandish notion, but admittedly not one that I'd shunned straight away. I knew I wouldn't move away from Marianne, though, or Libby at the moment. Marianne was so happy to have us in her life, the happy family she deserved; so moving to Devon wasn't an option. Realistically, Max would have something to say about it, but I had no room for his opinions at the moment. But one of the other reasons it was impossible was that for the first time since Mum had passed away, I wanted to be looked after. And I knew I had more support here than I would have in Devon. There were two little babies who needed me more than anyone else ever had. But they were arriving when I was probably at my lowest and battling each day was an effort. I had to drag myself through the seconds, minutes and hours of every single day. It felt like torture.

During that week, Marianne and I put up the Christmas tree. 'We should have done this twelve days before Christmas,' she told me, 'but I'm sure ten days before will make little difference,' she laughed, seemingly thrilled at our bonding session.

We'd not seen much of Derek, and I wondered if Marianne had told him she needed to take care of me and Libby. 'I must look after my girls.' I could imagine her saying the words that in earlier years would have had me seething, but now were quite cathartic.

'Why don't you stay here until after Christmas?' she suggested as we strategically hung shimmering gold and red balls from the branches. 'You're more than welcome to stay until after the babies are born. You can stay for as long as you need.'

'What about you and Derek?'

'Oh, Derek, can wait. He's a kind man, he understands. We weren't planning our move straight away, anyway.'

'You're really happy, aren't you?'

'I don't want to disrespect your dad.' Her voice quivered a little as she quickly glanced at me, then turned to rearrange a bauble she'd placed on the tree. 'But I am happy, yes.'

'I have some presents that were meant for Max that you may as well give to Derek.' I flippantly made the remark to show it was okay to love another; she deserved to live her life now. 'I doubt he'll wear Issey Miyake or fit into size 11 trainers, but you never know.' I laughed, and she laughed with me.

'We have charity boxes at the church, if you want to donate some things.'

'That would be great. Although I'll have to go to the house without him being there.'

'Are you sure this is what you want, Kat? You know, to end it all with Max?'

'Not at all ... but I don't have a choice. It's him that's set up his life with someone else.'

'I can't believe it.' She shook her head.

'The babies and I obviously weren't enough.'

'It really would be best to talk to him.'

'I will, but I need to be a little calmer.'

She peered at me thoughtfully. Then she said, 'Well, you know I'm here, and I can soon disappear if you need the house to yourselves to talk.'

We decorated some more of the rather pathetic-looking tree. Although I felt downtrodden and defeated, I also felt tranquillity around me, Marianne being the reason. She made me feel secure and loved, offering me a shelter that I so needed at the moment.

That's why I asked her if she would mind if I stayed with her over Christmas. My voice was a whisper, fearful of being alone on Christmas Day. 'I really do need to move on, I know, but maybe I'll move into the flat between Christmas and New Year. I need to be settled before these babies arrive.'

'Kat, as I said, you can stay as long as you need.' Her softness surrounded me as I felt wrapped in her tenderness and warmth. The child within me enjoying the protection of her maternal nature. I smiled at her, wanting her to know how much I appreciated her without having to speak the words.

We turned back to the plastic pitiful tree that Marianne and I had dragged down from the loft; actually, it was Marianne more than me. I'd tried to use my feet to manoeuvre boxes and other Christmas paraphernalia as I couldn't bend. If I gracelessly tried to squat down, half the time I couldn't get back up. It had been disorderly, but we somehow managed to get the old tree and other pieces down the stairs. I'd have been quite happy not to put anything up, but Marianne was adamant we needed to bring some festivity into the home. Libby had stayed locked away, as we laughed at our shambolic effort. She didn't volunteer to join us.

As we continued to decorate the tree, forcing some festive spirit into ourselves and into the heart of the house, I ensured each bauble followed some kind of sequence. Controlling the beautification of the tree; the garlands, the wreaths, the hand-made embroidered cushions, ensuring each trimming was perfectly displayed, I fought back the tears.

Suddenly I realised that decorating the old, tattered Christmas tree was the only control I had in my life at the moment.

25

As I said, I assumed Libby would improve once Calvin's funeral was over. Even if it was only slightly. But she still locked herself away refusing to join us. She needed to be alone, she said, her firm words pushing us away.

When I dared to enter her room, she would usually be sleeping. Marianne had bought her a laptop, which she'd left at college. I'd offered to take her there to pick it up but she refused. It was worrying that she was having no communication with the outside world. No friends called. No-one seemed interested in her life. The depression Dad had suffered was at the forefront of my mind, especially when I would find her curled in a ball, no tears shed, just staring at the wall in front of her.

'Do you think we should get the doctor out?' I'd asked Marianne, she agreed, but when we suggested it to Libby she would bark at us like a vicious dog, claiming that there was nothing wrong, she just needed peace and we weren't helping. Marianne told me we should give it a few more days, hoping Christmas might pull Libby away from her pit, I assumed. If she was having the same kind of emotional turmoil Dad had suffered then I knew Christmas would simply come and go. Depression was clearly eating away at her but I felt helpless, as I always had around Dad.

I'd not seen much of Suzy but she rang me every day. She had tried to get as much information from Lawrence as possible, but apparently, he didn't know much. 'I've tried, Kat, I promise, Lawrence and I had a massive argument about it the other night.'

'Suzy, please don't you guys be falling out over this. It's not worth it. You've helped me out enough.'

'Maybe you should talk to Max,' she said hesitantly. This surprised me as she, at first, had been adamant that I should never see him again. In her anger, she'd even suggested I shouldn't allow him to see the babies.

I told her I'd talk to him when I was ready, but at the moment I needed him to leave me alone. She said she would communicate that back. I still wanted to scream at him, and release my anger, but I didn't see what good that would do. We needed to talk rationally, so when I felt as if I didn't want to attack him – if that feeling ever came – I'd talk, then. Beforehand was pointless.

There were only days left before I said goodbye to my ownership of the salon for good. Every day I dealt with the loyal customers that had stayed with me. This kept me busy, rather than wandering around the house that I never thought I'd live in again.

I was finishing my customer's nails when I heard the door chime someone's arrival, the privacy screen blocking the view, which made me anxious in case it was Max.

I hoped it wasn't Max.

I shouted politely for them to take a seat, something I'd never done before. I'd always made the effort to leave my chair, apologise to the customer I was serving and welcome the next with a big smile. I had little energy these days: just getting up would render me breathless. It was taking all my strength to chat cheerily to my customers. I'd told them my plans to close down the salon, not in the dispirited way I felt, but in a positive way: it was about my babies, it was time to move on.

All of them had told me that if I decided to come back, mobile or in another salon, they wanted to know. Most of them had said they would find somewhere else in the meantime, but it wouldn't be at Lush Lucia. It warmed me to have their support and I would keep their contact numbers for when I needed them. Becoming mobile would probably be the best option: no overheads, no employees. I could work my appointments around my life rather than the other way around. But that was something I would worry about once the babies were here. The profits for the salon didn't stand at much, but they would get us through in the beginning.

It was lucky I hadn't hastily renovated the flat as I'd initially planned. It had been decorated: fresh white walls which would be perfect when I moved back in. But luckily, I hadn't re-laid the floor or built the temporary wall which I'd planned to do before Mandy and Melanie had left, (all cleared by my landlord, of course). Most of my savings would have been lost in the restoration. Thinking back, I wondered why Max had kept holding me off from doing it, even before Mandy and Melanie had left, he'd been hesitant. One of his consultants had drawn up the plans for me, and I kept asking Max to chase him; I'd been stressing because I needed it sorting before the babies were born. His reluctance was explainable now.

My customer's nails were now beautifully varnished in a vibrant pink, a sparkling gem glittered from her thumb nails, an embellishment that she'd wanted for a weekend of parties she was attending. I remembered the days when I envied customers who were partying until all hours, drinking the night away; whereas now I couldn't think of anything worse. Don't get me wrong, I couldn't wait to guzzle a glass of wine (or bottle), but these days, going out meant achy feet, a bad head and tiredness; all of which I had at the moment anyway.

I guided my customer towards the reception desk, in order for her to pay. She told me I'd better keep hold of her number. I smiled, promising I would.

I pleasantly kept my professionalism, as I realised who was here to see me, not wanting to make a scene; my customers were aware of Melanie's deception but I didn't particularly want them to know about Max's.

I hoped I'd pulled it off, as Gina sat waiting.

26

'Can you please leave?' It wasn't meant to sound like a question, but I actually sounded as if I was grovelling. My customer had gone, and now my hands and legs were shaking. It took me all my strength to stand up and face Gina and not collapse on the chair behind me.

'Kat, you've left me no choice but to come and talk to you. Max has tried and—'

'I've nothing to say to you.' Proud, I was much firmer this time.

'I'm not leaving until you've spoken to me.' She stood up from the sofa, coming to face me across the reception desk. I was grateful the barrier was dividing us. The hatred I felt was boiling deep below the surface, the verbal missiles ready to be aimed straight at her, but at the same time I could have thrown up. 'So, we can stand here all night, but I'm not moving.'

'Don't you think you've done enough damage?' My heart was racing, my insides jumping hurdles, weakness pulling me down, but she seemed so calm, but fiery. Her eyes were burning.

'I'm sorry about what's happened between me and Max ...' I was silent, as she came further towards me, '... and I know you're hurting.'

'You have no idea how I feel.'

'Suzy's told me how hard it has been for you—'

'Suzy?' I was confused. 'You've spoken to Suzy?'

'Briefly.' Had she come here to tell me she was taking everyone away from me? I couldn't speak. Suzy hadn't mentioned anything. Why would she not tell me? 'I haven't come for an argument, Kat.'

'What did you expect? Did you expect that I'd put the kettle on?' My anger was rising quickly, fuelled further by her contact with Suzy.

'Look, I'm truly sorry about me and Max, really I am, but this needs sorting out.'

'I think you should leave.' I couldn't talk to her.

'We all need to work this out, for everyone's sake, especially the babies.'

'You think you can waltz in here and tell me I need to talk to you …' I shook my head.

She met my eye, a slight smirk edged across her glossed lips. 'If you don't talk to Max he said he'll have to take you to court.'

'Great. Tell him I'll see him there.' I totally didn't mean that, but how dare she threaten me. My firmness turned to fury. It had only been a week, couldn't she let me get used to the idea that they would be playing happy families with my babies, without throwing this at me.

'He obviously doesn't want to go down that route. He wants to try and sort this out amicably.' Her mouth was now a thin tight, line as her eyes widened slightly.

'So, he sends you to fight his battles?'

'He doesn't know I'm here.'

'Then I think it's best you leave.'

'I really want to help.'

'Gina, I'm not speaking to you about this. If he wants to take me to court—'

'He's happy to pay maintenance, or whatever else you need. The court doesn't need to come into it.'

'*You* mentioned court …'

'I know. I'm sorry, but it will have to be the final option if you won't resolve this with him.'

My shoulders straightened, shaking my head I turned to face her. 'I'm asking you, I think rather politely, to leave me alone.'

'This isn't doing anyone any good.'

'I'll ask you again, nicely, to please leave.' My teeth where clenched tight.

'You only have yourself to blame for this.'

'What?' I was confused, but cursing myself for not just asking her to leave, again. 'If you trick someone into having babies' then—'

'*Sorry? What the ...*' I glared at her in disbelief.

'It has been so miserable for him—'

'Gina, he wanted these babies ... trick him? ... I don't understand.'

'He's told me everything.'

'He's told you lies.' She didn't answer me. 'Please just go.' I struggled to catch my breath as I let myself collapse into the chair behind me.

'No, Kat, you have to understand you can't put a man in that position and expect that he'll stay with you while you—'

'You have no idea what you're talking about.'

'Now that he's developed that bond, he's excited and you're taking it away from him.' Her face was flushed as she stared at me. 'It's not fair what you're doing.'

'Please leave ...'

'Max is really upset about all this, the decent thing to do is to talk to him.'

I was quiet. I couldn't speak to her. I would, of course, speak to Max at some point. I wanted to ask him so many questions, but not like this. Gina demanding from me, was unfair. Couldn't she understand how much I was hurting?

My silence clearly making her realise I wasn't going to sit down and sort this with her. 'I can see I'm getting nowhere with you.' She stared at me a few seconds longer, before turning brusquely away.

'Gina ...' I felt the urge to suddenly stop her, part of me wanting to find out more, while the other part didn't want to know anything.

'Yes?' She turned to me looking hopeful, her hand resting on the door handle.

'How long have you two been seeing each other?' I was shaking, practically whispering as the words stuck in my throat, as I asked the question that I think Max had lied about. His claim that they had started seeing each other after Clare's party, had played on my mind.

'He came to me the night we all went out for a meal ...'

'When you were with Joe? The night you announced your engagement?'

The night I'd told him I was pregnant.

'Joe and I split up when me and Max ...' she glanced down.

I couldn't speak. It had all been a lie.

'He came to me when you guys had a fight ...' she continued, '... one thing led to another ...'

'But he begged that I keep the baby.' I was talking to myself rather than to her, trying to make sense of it all.

'He felt guilty, he said he couldn't leave you until the babies were here.'

'But we didn't have to keep ...' The words stung as I said them, knowing the right decision had been made, but still she needed to understand we'd had a choice.

'He couldn't live with himself if you'd had an abortion.' The word stuck me hard. Shame flowing through me that I'd actually considered that route. Since I'd seen several scans and felt endless movement it did feel strange that this path had been my less favoured.

'But Dave ...' I was confused, she had a boyfriend, Max and I had met him.

'After a few weeks, Max's guilt was getting too much, you'd moved in—'

'Which he'd insisted on.'

'Anyway, he said he was going to work things out with you, so I decided to find someone, anyone, to make him jealous. And it worked.'

I couldn't believe what I was hearing, she was talking to me as if I wasn't in the picture.

'Oh my God. Please just leave ...' I struggled to form the words, needing her away from me. She had a smugness about her, the innocent quality I'd found so endearing in the beginning had completely disappeared. An actress that could be on par with Mandy. I was pleased when she finally listened to me and left, but not before telling me I needed to talk to Max before things became much worse.

For who? I'd wanted to ask. *For them?* Because it couldn't possible get much worse for me.

I let the tears escape. Each drop splashed across the scribbled-out names in the diary. The wetness smudged the ink, making a black stain; similar to how my life had become; a fuzzy, blurred, smeared mess.

How could Max have done this to me? How could such a big decision have been made so whimsically? He'd told me he would be there, we were doing this together. Why would he be so forceful about us having the babies if he didn't want to be with me? It didn't make sense. All this time, I'd thought we were building a life together, and he was building it with someone else.

And now Suzy who was supposed to be protecting me, was joining forces with them.

I felt as if I couldn't physically hurt any more, I imagined the rawness of my insides as they cried for help. Cried to be released, let go of all the turmoil and pain.

Was there anyone I could trust? Was there anyone on my side?

I'd built an invisible cocoon around myself since Mum had no longer been there to help fight my battles, but I'd let Max inside it. And he'd ripped apart my trust.

The only thing I could do now was rebuild the cocoon that would protect me and my babies.

27

On my birthday which is the fifth of November, Max had bought me a box of chocolates. Nothing else but a box of Thornton's chocolates. Albeit, my favourite, and he'd made the effort to have them make up a box of the ones I liked best. But still, it was just chocolates.

Oh sorry, I did receive a card that was completely humorous; nothing about love, romance, being together or even actually knowing each other. I wasn't ungrateful; well, not to his face. He'd agreed that I could go on a spending spree after the babies were born, once Suzy had put me through a rigmarole of strenuous exercises. I remembered thinking, why not a spa day, a salon appointment, a treatment of some kind? Why hadn't he wanted to indulge me? It wasn't as if he didn't have the money. I put it down to his work. I actually told myself how lucky I was that he'd remembered my favourite chocolates.

He stood me up on my birthday, too. We were meant to be going to a restaurant. He was late home from work, some kind of crisis. I'd believed him. I'd made him feel better: I told him it was fine, we could do it another time, I was too tired anyway. Although I'd told him not to worry, I'd put the phone down and cried. I'd let the tears fall, blaming my hormones for my insecurity.

Had his excuse been true? Or the times he hadn't visited Marianne's with me because he was far too busy; had he been lying every single time? What about the number of Sunday lunches Clare had served, some of which I attended on my own because I felt guilty that we kept letting her down?

How stupid could I have been to think we could have worked it out? He'd had no intention of staying with me.

I watched the shadows on the ceiling and around my room, the same room I'd had as a teenager. The same room Calvin had stayed in for a short while. Had he joined up with Mum? Odd question, if you don't believe in the afterlife, God or any other form of being that's not human. But I could imagine her scolding him, though still taking him under her wing.

The room had been redecorated, although I'd say not to my taste but my original bedroom hadn't been to my taste either. The old green and brown vine that decorated the wallpaper had been replaced with a purple stripe. The plain cotton curtains matched the bedding. I wondered if she'd bought them as part of an offer: two for one; or buy bedding, get curtains free. There were no luxurious throws or cushions with intricate embroidery like there had been at Max's, or in my flat. In the bathroom, there were no his-and-her sinks, deep, sunken jacuzzi baths or vigorous power-showers. We had to schedule our preferred time for a bath. There was no proper shower, it was a do-it-yourself job; a plastic shower hose that was attached to the taps. But still I felt more at home here than I had at Max's.

That should tell me something.

Had I been holding onto something that wasn't really there? If that was the case, why did it hurt so much?

The knock on the door distracted me from my thoughts.

'Kat, it's me, can I come in?' Marianne's muffled tones echoed through the door. Although I wanted to say no, I told her it was fine. It was her home now, I no longer belonged here. I couldn't be that stroppy teenager who would have told her to leave me alone, although the lost little girl within me wanted to do just that.

'Are you okay?' Her head poked around the door. 'You've been up here a while.'

'I'm fine, honestly. It's been one of those days.'

'Is everything okay at the salon? It's only four 'o' clock?'

'There were no appointments so I didn't see the point in sitting there on my own.'

'No, of course not.' I could see she was wishing she'd not asked. 'Someone's here to see you.'

'Who?' Please tell me Max hadn't arrived again. Not after the drama with Gina yesterday. I couldn't face him, or more of his lies.

'Suzy.'

'Really.' I let out a sardonic laugh that sounded nothing like me.

'Are you two okay?'

'Yes, we're fine. Would you mind sending her up here?'

'No problem, pet.'

'Marianne.' I caught her before she left. 'I've not heard anything from Libby's room since I've been in here. Is she home?' Two hours had passed since I'd shut myself away.

'She went out after lunch.'

'Where?'

'She mentioned a friend. To be honest, I was so pleased to see her going out, I didn't really ask too much.'

'S'pose,' I agreed.

'I'll send Suzy up.' I thanked her before she left, as she closed the door on me. I felt I'd reverted back fifteen years. Suzy knocked seconds later but didn't wait for permission to enter. As she came into the room I remembered Gina's words. What could Suzy possibly say that would excuse this?

'This brings back memories,' Suzy said as she walked towards me, smiling.

'What do you want Suzy?' My abrupt manner stopped her in her tracks. I'd never before spoken to her with such aggression. She frowned, her innocent, sweet face showing her consternation as she bit her lip. Although, I felt slightly guilty, I couldn't take any more betrayal from those I loved.

'You won't return my calls and you didn't come to yoga this morning.'

'I'm fine. I need to be alone.'

'Kat, what have I done?' She sat down on the end of the bed, her stare intense.

'Who said you've done anything?' I glared coldly at her. It was as if this bedroom had also taken my personality back fifteen years: stroppy, inconsiderate teenager who was so wrapped up in her own world there was no room for others and their problems.

'It's obvious you think I've done something, because you're being a complete bitch.' Her words were thrown back at me like a brick. Not only had I reverted back to my thirteen-year-old self, it seemed Suzy had done the same.

'*I'm* being the bitch?' I laughed, scornfully. 'I think you need to look in the mirror.'

'What the hell are you talking about?'

'If I told you Gina came to see me yesterday …'

'And, what did she say?' Suzy seemed totally blasé about her and Gina's rendezvous. I'd say friendship, but that hurt more.

'She said quite a few things, actually, but the one that really sticks in my mind is her conversation with you.'

'Me?' Suzy put her hand to her chest.

'Yes, "Suzy's told me how hard it has been for you." Does it ring a bell?'

'Oh, Kat.' Her shoulders slumped, her pretty head shook as her sad eyes peered at me. 'Seriously, it was in passing.'

I didn't speak. Could she be telling me lies now? Was there a cosy little foursome going on while my life descended into a big black hole?

'Honestly, I saw them at the shops. She was being nice and asking me questions about me and Lawrence doing the Ironman thing, I stopped her in her tracks and basically told her I didn't agree with their relationship.'

'You did?' I said meekly.

'Did she make it out to be bigger than it was?' Suzy looked worried.

'She said something about briefly talking to you, but I put two and two together and came up with—'

'A hundred.'

'I'm sorry. She really threw my whole day.' I bit my lip, feeling completely foolish, forcing back the urge to burst into tears and sob into her shoulder.

'If that bitch made out that we're friends, I'll bloody—'

'She didn't,' I said weakly.

'Are you sure?'

'I'm really sure.' I managed a smile, shaking my head at my own irrationality.

'So, I have no reason to give her hell, then?'

'Not unless you're doing it for me.'

'I can do that.' Suzy smiled. I reached over to her and she took my hand in hers.

'I'm sorry.' I couldn't hold back the tears any longer. They rolled silently down my burning cheeks.

'Come here, you daft bugger.' She came towards me, knowing there was no chance of me and bump moving anywhere. She embraced me in her petite arms, my features feeling giant in her grasp.

'Oh Suzy, it's awful,' I moaned into her shoulder, smelling her familiar floral scent. 'She told me they've been seeing each other since I told Max I was pregnant.'

'I don't believe it! Have you spoken to Max?'

'I can't.'

'You can.'

'Suzy, I can't.' I pushed myself gently away from her, and leant against one of the cushions, resting my hands on my bump.

'He's still going to be there for the babies.'

'What twenty-four/seven?'

'You need to talk to him about the best way for him to support you.'

'I don't want his support.' Of course, I needed it but at this moment if I never saw him again, it would be too soon. But then, all I wanted was to see him. Turn back the clock. It was so confusing to be so angry one moment, so lost the next. 'Look at me, I'm a mess. I'm stuck here in this room where I grew up. I've lost my business. I've lost my home. I've lost him …'

'You don't need him. These babies are going to be the making of you.'

I gazed at her, hoping she was right.

Biting back the words: but what if they're not? What if I fail at being a mother too?

What do I do then?

28

June's rented cottage was cosy. It was filled with shabby chic furniture, traditional with a contemporary twist. She was dressed today in a perfectly ironed cream linen dress, and a gold knitted wrap. Three ornate necklaces hung elegantly around her neck, and five pearly bracelets clung tightly together around her thin wrist. I asked where she was going, but she was having a day in. I glanced down ruefully at what I was wearing: once again, black trousers and a plain black top. Maybe a wardrobe refurbishment would help me inwardly.

I'd called to see June on my way to Clare's. Her visit to the area seemed to be flowing by very fast, I was worried she'd leave before I'd had answers to all my questions. Yes, there was email, phone, skype and whatever else modern technology could throw at us, but it wasn't the same as talking face-to-face.

'Do you know that your father lost a business?' she said casually, pouring tea into the dainty china cups.

'Really? Marianne never said.'

'Don't suppose she would.' She handed me the hot cup, my hands appreciating the warmth. 'It was before her time.'

'I thought he was a site manager; or something like that, anyway.'

'He was, but before that.' June sipped her drink. 'He had his own electrical company, but he couldn't keep it going, so he had to close it down.'

'I can't remember him owning his own company.'

'Oh yes, for many years, you were probably too young to understand. His depression really started when he lost the company, although he had bouts of it beforehand, losing the company sent him over the edge, I think,' June said, confirming a question that had played on my mind for years. 'It got a lot worse when Lanie died.'

'Libby's going through a bad time at the moment,' I admitted. I'd not really told June too much about how Calvin had died, just that he'd taken something he shouldn't have. I had no idea whether she knew what I was talking about, but she didn't ask any further questions, which suited me. 'Since losing Calvin she's not herself. She doesn't come out of her room. I'm really worried about her.'

'I didn't want to say I'd not seen much of her, I wasn't sure if Marianne had put her off seeing me.'

'Why would Marianne do that?'

'Perhaps Libby is suffering like your dad did. Once they're in a bad place it can take a hell of lot to get them out.' June ignored my question.

'I don't think Dad ever came out of it.'

'Alcohol doesn't help.' June shook her head. I didn't ask if Dad was a drinker before Mum died; I just nodded in agreement, not wanting to analyse his troubled personality. 'Have you taken her to the doctor's?'

'She won't go. We can't really drag her by her hair.' I tried to smile, make light of the serious situation.

'You could call the doctor out,' June suggested.

'Suppose we could; but then yesterday she went out after lunch; not sure where, or what time she got back, or if she got back at all.'

'It doesn't mean she isn't suffering because she's going out.'

'I know.' She was right. I needed to address the situation, talk to Libby, and force her to talk to me. I'd thought that leaving her to sort this in her own head was the best way of helping her, but I think she was beyond helping herself. She needed one of us to hold her hand.

We talked about Mum for a while, how she coped with Dad's depression. Apparently, most of the time she could cope with it, but it wasn't much of a life for her. His down moments could last for months and months. I asked questions that would help me get to the truth, but part of me wanted to sew my mouth up and hang on to my fantasy family. The family that laughed, played and sang together, a bit like *The Brady Bunch*. I knew June was covering up heaps of information, lots of untold secrets and messy stories that I didn't need to know. The small part she was exposing me to, was putting me off asking further questions about Mum and Dad's relationship. I wanted to believe it had been a happy one. With my life falling apart around me at the moment, my perfect memories were all I had left. I didn't want them tarnished.

Before I left June's cosy cottage, she explained she would be travelling back on Christmas Eve. She only had the place until then. She had so much to get back for. I wondered what. Who would she spend Christmas Day with? I asked if she had good neighbours and good friends around her. She said she had, but she didn't mention any names. I wondered if she was lying, but I didn't probe.

Once I'd left, I drove along the country roads towards Hutton Rudby. Clare wanted to talk through some plans with me. Not that I was sure what it had to do with me, but still I willingly agreed, feeling as if I owed her something. I agreed to go after ensuring Max definitely wouldn't be there.

With the surface of the winding roads shimmering, I steered the car carefully in case there were patches of ice. I really should have stopped driving; there was little space between my bump and the steering wheel.

I felt a little apprehensive about the visit, as I hadn't seen Henry since Max's secret had been revealed. I was worried he'd blame me.

I'd tortured myself endlessly. Was *I* to blame? Little things kept popping into my head, especially about how we'd become distant. But then if Gina *was* telling the truth, we'd become distance because his mind (and body) had been with her.

We hadn't had any kind of love-making in months; no passion or pure uncomplicated sex. When I'd found out I was pregnant, we'd succumbed under the covers a few times, but when I'd started to show, Max had said he felt a little uncomfortable about it. I can see you thinking now: for God's sake, Kat, that must tell you something: but it didn't. I'm not naïve, well maybe a little, but I'd read in countless magazines, searched on the internet and confirmed with Suzy (the oracle) that this was quite common. Some men didn't think it appropriate. So, I'd accepted that Max didn't want to go there. Luckily, I wasn't one of those women who felt extremely horny all the way through pregnancy. It suited me to wait. Backache, pelvis ache, headache, feet ache: come on! Horny? I don't think so.

But if she was telling the truth, Max's lack of interest in me would make perfect sense. But it also meant he was sleeping with us both at the same time. The thought made my skin crawl.

I expected Max's car to be outside, assuming that Clare had fooled me, but the driveway was empty except for the black Land Rover and new silver Mercedes Benz, proudly owned by Clare and Henry. I'd thought that she would try to headlock me into talking to Max. Force a situation upon us. But then, she probably knew I'd drive off.

The bare vine that covered Clare's wall made me smile. I remembered how she'd corrected me about the *Clematis Montana* plant. How she'd seemed horrified that I lived in a flat: the idea that someone wouldn't have a garden was preposterous. And now here she was, offering me the flat rent-free. How things had changed in a year.

Clare greeted me at the door before I had the chance to knock. Her warm, welcoming smile was soothing. Henry was singing some tuneless song in the kitchen. My concerns about his hostility proved totally unwarranted as he hugged me.

'Sit down, dear.' Clare pulled a chair out for me, then switched on the kettle. I wasn't sure I could hold any more tea, I already felt as if I was going to burst.

Architectural plans were laid out in front of me, stretching the length of the kitchen table. Max's company logo was spread across each drawing. I'd seen plenty of his blueprints to know they were his without his symbol being displayed.

'I wanted your advice.' Clare came and sat beside me, her excitement apparent. 'I thought because you know the space, you could give some guidance on which design you think will work best.' I understood her reasoning, even if I knew nothing about hair salons.

We mused over numerous designs. Sinks were placed at the back, sides and more unusually in the middle. She'd even knocked walls down in one design, which I knew the landlord wouldn't be happy about. He'd only agreed to my original temporary wall idea, because it could easily be taken down. But still, I'd had to send him mounds of information about the designs before he agreed.

Max had actually done some great designs, but I didn't admit that aloud.

Two cups of tea later, after endless discussions about layouts and decor, my bladder was calling. I went to their downstairs toilet, which, like the rest of the house had character. A pottery figure of an old man stood smiling down as I peed. It reminded me of the Indian who'd stood watching over Dad. I wondered if this figurine from Clare's travels had any meaning. I'd never asked about the wooden Indian that I noticed back in Marianne's newly decorated bedroom. My thoughts confirmed that she'd missed out the hallway, but I didn't want to know why!

As I pulled up my maternity pants, adjusting the comfy elasticated waist that I wasn't planning on getting rid of once the babies were here, I heard the front door slam. Footsteps marched heavily across the wooden floor, making the toilet door vibrate.

'Where is she?' Max roared. I wanted to keep the door locked and not face him. My stomach churned, worried about the confrontation, but then suddenly rage rose within me: who the hell was he to be angry?

'I'm here, but I'm leaving,' I said curtly as I walked back into the kitchen, hoping I sounded more confident than I felt. Gina stood next to Max. I was gutted, her presence confirmed they'd all fallen back into their cosy family life.

'I've got to go.' I grabbed my bag, wishing I could do it with a sophisticated swing of the arm, and march confidently away. Max dribbling at what he was missing. But my ungainly waddle and my flat comfy boots (wishing I'd worn my *UGGs* for a more stylish exit) were far from the image I so wanted it to project.

'Kat, you have to talk to me.' Max demanded, as I left the kitchen. He was behind me. I was shaking as I walked out into the cold, brisk air, needing to feel its freshness on my burning face. Pressing my keys to unlock my car, wanting him away from me, I ignored his pleas. My hand was on the handle, when he pushed himself between me and the car.

'Please talk to me.'

'As I said to Gina, I have nothing to say.'

'To Gina?'

'Oh sorry, didn't you know she came to see me?' Vicious, I know. But I was pleased I'd stirred a bit of trouble into their relationship. No wonder she'd stayed quiet in the kitchen: she'd probably crapped herself when she realised I was here, not having told her lover that she'd been to see me and made things worse. 'Yes, she did, she told me all about your sordid affair. Oh, yes, and how I'd tricked you.'

'Kat, I'm sorry ...' He sighed loudly. He looked tired, thick lines appearing under his deep blue eyes. 'Things just happened, before I knew where I was it was too late.'

My lips were started to shake, as I fought back the urge to cry. 'I don't understand why you didn't tell me in the first place. Why you fought so much that we kept the babies, if you had no intention of staying.'

'I wanted the babies ...'

'But not me ... and because of that you tricked me.'

'No ... it wasn't like that.' Max ran his hand through his thick waves. 'I thought if I told you I was having feelings for Gina, you wouldn't keep the babies. I thought we could try and make things work between us.'

'It was because Joe had asked her to marry him, wasn't it?' I was torturing myself asking him these questions, but I needed to know. I knew *that night* there had been a spark between them, I should have followed my instinct. I'd known, and he'd denied it.

'I think so, yes …' he said quietly.

'I can't believe you …'

'I'm sorry …'

'Can I please get in my car,' I whispered, forcing back the tears.

'We need to talk about the babies.'

'What the fuck do you want me to say?' I suddenly lost it. I threw my hands in the air, desperate to be away from him. 'You can have them on Wednesdays and every other Friday? For fuck's sake Max.' I was shouting at him, knowing that Clare was probably standing behind the front door listening to every word. I would have died at one stage had she heard me say the 'F-word' let alone flinging it at her son. But I didn't care. I wanted to shout *fuck, fuck, fuck,* from the rooftops. I didn't care who heard, or judged me.

'We have to talk about the logistics.'

'The logistics? This isn't one of your business plans. We're not a project.'

'I'm not saying that, but you've got to let me in.'

'You've got a cheek … what do you want from me?'

'To talk properly about how this is going to work.'

'Jesus …' I shook my head. 'At the end of the day Max, you will be paying child maintenance, and yes, we'll sort visiting, but for fuck's sake, let the babies arrive first.'

'Right.' He nodded, and without hesitation stepped away from the car. I wondered which part had made him move. I didn't care. I was just relieved he was letting me go.

With my foot hard on the pedal, the gravel spinning from beneath the wheels, I could see him watching me leave; the tall, handsome figure that I'd fallen in love with, the man I was willing to share the rest of my life with. As he became a smaller figure in the distance, I knew that all of this had happened for a reason.

It hurt; God, it was tearing me apart.

But as he'd stood blocking my way, his masculine figure looming over me, I realised I felt sorry for him. I actually pitied him.

We didn't need him. We would be okay.

And the pain would eventually ease.

29

'I was thinking.' The question that had been on the tip of my tongue at last dared to come out. 'Maybe we could invite June over for Christmas dinner.'

'Isn't she going back home?'

'I think so, but she said she could stay a little longer, and I don't want her to be alone for Christmas.'

'Well, yes, we could do.' Marianne's response surprised me; but then she abruptly turned away.

'Great, I'll ask her then.' Although I didn't want Marianne to feel uneasy on Christmas Day, June being alone had been preying on my mind.

'Yes love, you do that.' Still she didn't turn to face me.

I wasn't sure whether to broach the feud between them or leave well alone. I decided on the latter. 'I'll let you know what she says.' I left the kitchen, not waiting for an answer. Not because I was being rude, but because I was torn between putting Marianne or Mum's sister first.

As I entered the hallway, Libby was coming in the front door, her features gaunt, her skin pale, her dark bob, usually sleek and glossy looking greasy, hanging grubbily around her black denim jacket. Her vacant gaze was focused on the stairs and not on me.

'Lib, are you okay?'

'I'm fine.' Her foot was on the bottom step as my hand grasped her arm. 'What?' Her aggression knocking me back. Her eyes met mine. She had a cold sore, red and raw, I'd not noticed it before. Hatred exuded from her as pushed me away.

'I just want to be sure you're okay. I wondered if you wanted to—'

'I said, I'm fine,' she interrupted, coldly.

I watched her disappear up the stairs. Her head was down; her dark clothes, emphasised her thinness. Her anger was expressed in each step. The bedroom door slammed, shutting us out from her existence.

I sat down on the stairs, my bump resting uncomfortably; debating whether to follow or leave her. I couldn't let her waste away upstairs. I had to help her. I knew how she was feeling. I, too, wanted to disappear; I wanted the world to understand how frustrated I was.

I was ready to battle with her by the time I reached the top of the rickety staircase; I wouldn't take no for an answer; she would listen to me and I would help her.

I didn't even bother to knock as I barged in, ready to have this fight, but the sight that met me, deflated me like a burst balloon. My breath catching in my throat. Libby was sitting on the floor, her back against her bed. Half a bottle of vodka was next to her, a large tin was open; foils, wrappers and an unidentifiable object protruded from it. I noticed instantly, on a small mirror, a line of white powder. Holding a plastic bottle that was filled with smoke, her mouth covering its opening, she held a lighter against a pipe that was inserted into the plastic as she breathed in the toxic fumes.

My body seemed to lift from reality. The little girl who had smiled at me from the family photos on the wall up the stairs seemed to disappear in an instant.

'Libby, what the—'

'Get out.' She coughed, choking on her words as smoke poured from her mouth.

'What are you—' I held the door handle, as she rose quickly. Her face was full of hate, disgust, a loathing I'd never seen before, as she pushed my shoulders. Losing my balance, I fell backwards against the bathroom door opposite, the pain shooting through my spine as Libby slammed me out of her world.

'Kat, what's going on?' Marianne shouted from below.

'Nothing,' I lied, trying not to sound too wounded. 'I've just bumped into the door.' It was the first thing I could think of. I didn't want to make the situation worse.

I knew I was going to go back into the bedroom, but I needed a few minutes to catch my breath. Stubborn, determined, or just plain interfering, I needed to talk to Libby. Shifting myself to a graceless position that allowed me to raise myself from my knees, with my backside bruised and my back throbbing from the fall, I held the door handle and forcefully pushed it down, expecting her to have blocked it with something. But she hadn't.

'What are you doing?' I demanded.

'For fuck's sake, leave me alone,' she screamed as she threw the bottle to her side, her rage mounting. She pushed herself up, came towards me and pushed me viciously from the room. 'Get out!' she shrieked, her face close to mine, her body taken over by whatever it was she was inserting into it.

Marianne was at my side, trying to help me to my feet as I struggled with the pain where my back had knocked against the doorframe.

'What on earth is happening?' Marianne's usual calm demeanour had switched to one of pure terror.

'It's Libby. Things have gone too far.'

'What do you mean?'

I was trembling as she led me to my bedroom.

'What is going on, Kat?'

'I don't know,' I lied, unsure whether Marianne's Christian heart could take such news. 'I don't think Libby is very well.'

'Does she need anything? Paracetamol? Medicine? Should I get her some water?' She walked towards her door. I stopped her.

'No, it's fine, she needs to be alone.'

'Right ...'

'I'm not sure how serious this is, Marianne,' I said hesitantly. Not wanting to tell her, but I didn't really feel I had a choice.

'Serious? What do you mean? What's wrong with her? Should I call a doctor?'

'No, no …' I shook my head, unsure how to explain. Was Libby a drug addict? Was she an alcoholic? The bottle of vodka flashing at me, the line of white powder, the bottle she was inhaling from: whatever it was she was doing in there, it looked lethal. 'I think Libby is taking drugs.'

'What kind of drugs?'

'I know she's been using cannabis, but I think she's taking something stronger.'

'Don't they use cannabis to help with illnesses?' Marianne quizzed me.

'She's not ill. Well, she wasn't. But look at the state of her now. She's taking something stronger. I think she's drinking, too.'

'Yes, she does drink a lot. Derek has noticed, actually.'

I grabbed my laptop which sat at the side of the bed. As I booted it up, Marianne sat beside me so she could see the screen. My bump made it uncomfortable to sit properly. I pulled my legs round to my side, placing the laptop on a pillow.

We sat silently waiting for the laptop to load, the atmosphere tense. My body was still shaking as adrenaline pumped furiously. At this rate, I'd be sending myself into labour. At that thought I tried to calm my mind, but to no avail.

As soon as the laptop was ready I typed in 'inhaling smoke from a bottle' into the search engine. I knew that the line of white powder was cocaine. I was concerned that the bottle included an unknown substance. I was surprised to see numerous websites showing people how to smoke cannabis. I searched around a few of the sites, searching for information that would help me, but all I found was video links that gave demonstrations by people who were high. At one stage, I clicked on a link to find a chat forum for people asking for help on 'where to shoot next,' I couldn't believe people were openly chatting about which veins were best to inject heroin into. I searched a few sites about cocaine, making a few notes and searching for which step to take next.

The internet convinced me that one thing Libby was using was cannabis. Cannabis is legal in some countries, so maybe I shouldn't be so worried about that. That sounds bad, doesn't it? But I'd never really thought it was a serious drug. As Marianne had pointed out, it helps with illnesses. Remember Mrs Garney? Between ourselves, she's been taking it for years; it helps her arthritis. She told me in confidence one day, when she was telling me about her aches and pains. Her son helps her, apparently. I'd been shocked, but had kept my face straight as I thought about Mrs Garney smoking her joint with her elderly friends. Some coffee morning that would be.

I scoured the internet endlessly. Marianne left me after a while, too upset, ordering me to tell her what I'd found. There were conflicting views, and arguments varied; *it can lead to stronger drugs* (which seemingly was the case with Libby). *It's better than drinking alcohol or smoking* (but there had been an empty bottle of Vodka too). *Mental health problems can occur.*

'Mental health problems' jumped out at me.

My fingers quickly typed the words 'cannabis and mental health'. It seemed there was a correlation. Much research showed that cannabis can relieve depression, but it can then become addictive, and the withdrawal leads to further depression. Had Libby been seriously depressed and I hadn't noticed? Bubbly, fearless Libby with her outgoing personality. I found it hard to believe.

Images of Calvin's body leaving the house had haunted me over the last few weeks. What had he really taken? I'd been convinced he'd tried something new. Something that didn't agree with his body; a dodgy drug, I'd been told. What if Libby took a dodgy drug? What if the drink killed her? How much was she drinking? Was she drinking the vodka neat? I remembered Dad used to drink vodka because it didn't smell; as if he thought we didn't know!

A rush of fear hit me, nausea swirling as thoughts of Libby ending up like Dad tormented me. I needed to know what the hell was going on. She was in deeper than I'd realised.

I hoped I wasn't too late to help.

30

The night passed in a haze of confused uncertainty. I couldn't sleep. I had tried, but knowing Libby had probably passed out in her room unnerved me. I couldn't settle. If I sat up my legs were restless. If I stood up, I couldn't stand still. If I lay down, I wasn't comfortable.

I had searched the internet to a point where I couldn't possibly take in any more information. I'd reached the conclusion that I couldn't help Libby unless she wanted to help herself.

Did she even want help? I knew there was no point bursting into her room demanding answers, demanding that she get some help. I thought I'd give her the night, then I'd approach her. I'd tell her I was here for her, I wanted to help her. I would have to see where that took us. I also felt I was somewhat to blame as I should have seen this coming. I should have been there for her, instead of throwing her out of my home. But I'd been so angry at the time, I hadn't known how to deal with her. Calvin throwing up all over the room hadn't helped.

I didn't want to go to the salon, mainly because of Libby but also because it was my last day. The few appointments I had scheduled I didn't have the heart to cancel, because they were loyal customers who had stayed with me in all this mess, and I felt as if I was letting them down by closing the business. But I knew the customers who had stayed loyal wouldn't sustain a healthy business, especially with the overheads that needed paying.

As I spruced up my customer's nails, she chatted about her friend who had recently had the most horrendous birth ever. (As if I needed to hear stories like that at the moment!) She described how her friend was in pain for two days, and they kept sending her home because the dilation was only two to three centimetres. 'They told her established labour was four centimetres. I tell you, it's a good job she has a good pain threshold' she'd told me. By the time the baby was arriving, he had become stuck and the mother had been rushed off to have an emergency C-section.

I really didn't need to hear all this. I had no energy to make myself a cup of tea lately, let alone pant around for two days. But my customer proceeded to tell me how her friend's scar had become infected, how they'd then found a blood clot and how she ended up back in hospital for over a week. Well, that was a great story!

The chime from the door interrupted our conversation. My next appointment wasn't due for another hour, so I knew whoever it was wanted something else from me. It could be Max, Gina, Clare, or even a customer wanting to make an appointment; which should be a good thing, but the fact that I would be turning them away saddened me.

I shouted for whoever it was to take a seat. They didn't answer. My stomach turned over in trepidation as I realised that this would be another confrontation of some sort. It wouldn't be Clare, because she wouldn't be polite enough to wait, and anyway I was meeting her tomorrow at the solicitor's to sign the final forms.

It was strange to think it would soon be over. I'd no longer be a business woman with my own identity. Everything I'd built up, everything I'd worked for was being taken away. It had all happened so quickly, I'd not had the chance to digest it all. My decision to get out was based on fear, but still I knew I was doing the right thing. I just wished it felt right, I wished the knot in my stomach would disappear, my shoulders would relax and the sickness that kept gushing over me like a tidal wave would stop.

My customer had moved from the subject of horrendous labours onto Christmas; how stressed she was becoming, how she had all her family coming to her. She would be catering for about twenty: her mum, her dad, his mum and dad, her two brothers, their wives and children, her husband's two sisters, their wives and children. I couldn't help but wish that I had that same stress, ensuring my perfect family were all okay for Christmas. As she talked about sibling rivalry and the stress of keeping two family members apart, I had to bite my tongue so I didn't mention the sibling stress I was dealing with at the moment.

I would willingly have changed lives with her.

Although I'd slowed down in performing her treatment, delaying the inevitable, it was over sooner than I wanted it to be.

I went to greet my visitor.

31

I waited for my customer to leave. She was obviously stalling in the hope she'd hear some gossip she could pass around the small community. Catfight at Kat's salon!

I couldn't look at Melanie as my customer paid; slowly, might I add, glancing from one of us to the other to see if she could be part of the bust-up that was about to happen.

The tension building around us was suffocating. My customer wrote her phone number down for me, (although, I had it stored in my files), announcing that as soon as I was up and running again I must call her. Melanie bowed her head, as if the knowledge of what she'd done embarrassed her. The customer left, but not without a glare at Melanie who turned away.

I didn't speak when my loyal customer had left; one of the loyal customers who'd made me feel not so worthless. I pretended to sort things on my desk, not wanting to acknowledge Melanie.

'Have you got two minutes?' she asked quietly, rising from the sofa.

'I'm really busy.' Do you not see all the customers lining up outside, the place brimming with appointments? I wanted to scream at her. The only place I was busy was in my own bloody head. It was like a motorway in there at the moment; thoughts rushing from one end of my brain to the other, overtaking each other, shooting off as other thoughts rammed together.

'Can I come back later?'

'I'd rather you didn't.'

'I understand,' Melanie nodded. 'But … I wanted to tell you how sorry I am.'

I couldn't answer her. All these people around me who had apparently cared for me, now wanted my forgiveness. I didn't have it in me to give.

'I've heard you're closing down.'

'And …'

'I know, it's all my fault and I didn't think this would happen.'

'What exactly did you think would happen?' I stopped pretending to mess around with papers and stared at her. 'You've contacted all my customers …'

'Mandy has—'

'Does it matter now?'

'It does to me,' she said. 'I thought you'd survive this, you're so strong. I really thought I was doing it at the best time, that we'd both have enough customers to survive.'

'What by undercutting me at every single opportunity?'

'That was Mandy …'

'And you've taken Sophie too.'

'That was Mandy too. I didn't know anything until I came to work and she was there.'

'What is it you want from me?' I sighed. The conversation was pointless.

'I want you to know I'm sorry. I made a mistake. Mandy is a nightmare. She's totally focused on making money rather than on the customers. It's not how I imagined it to be. I wish I hadn't left.' I shook my head at her, still at a loss as to what she wanted. My sympathy? My forgiveness? There was a silence between us. 'I've been thinking … why don't I come back here and help you rebuild things.'

'What!?' Was she crazy?

'It would be like old times.'

'Seriously … it could never be like old times.'

'I want to help. I want to make it better.'

'Not only is it too late as this is my last day, but I don't trust you.' I slung the words that I thought would pierce her.

She nodded slowly, I could see her swallow away a lump as she blinked away a tear.

'I want you to understand why I did it.' Her lip started to quiver. Her eyes filled with tears. I refused to feel sorry for her.

'I don't care.' My voice was hard and cold, trying not to let my insides soften. 'You have ruined what I built up over many years. This place was my life and when I needed you, you let me down. Everything is ruined, and you played a huge part in it all. So please forgive me if I find forgiving you a bit too much. And let's be honest, if things were working out for you over there, you wouldn't be here now. So, please leave me alone.' I had to tell her. She had to know what she'd done to me.

She backed away, and at the door, she turned to face me. Her whisper was barely audible. 'I truly am sorry, Kat, I wish I could turn back time.'

'So do I,' I muttered quietly. The cold wind from the open door disturbed the leaflets on the desk, the draught rushing through the salon like a force of doom.

I sat on the chair behind the reception desk, staring at the door. A darkness seemed to surround me as my throat burned and the tears began to sting my eyes. A loud sob suddenly escaped, startling me as I tried to swallow away the angst.

I was terrified of what life would bring next. Who would disappoint me, or let me down?

How could I keep smiling when so much crap was flying at me? I had to stay strong. I had to stay strong for my babies.

As I closed the door to my salon for the last time, the salty tears fell onto my lips. My tongue swiped them away. The noise of the shutters closing seemed louder than usual, echoing across the dark village as I locked up the last few years of my life.

I remembered the opening day. We'd had balloons, music, champagne, strawberries and much more. I'd invited everyone I'd met on the networking scene, asked them to bring two friends. The atmosphere had been amazing. I remembered how Melanie had hugged me, telling me how excited she was.

Sitting in my car, I stared at the place that had helped me grow, had given me a new life that I wished I could bring back.

I knew I had to get through this. I had to believe all of this was happening for a reason, that my life was being turned upside down, for a reason. If I didn't put this down to fate, I'd crash when I was needed the most by two little people.

I had to believe that the reason all this was happening was that I had better things to come. I had to believe.

32

'Libby, can I come in?' There was no answer.
When I'd arrived home, Marianne had explained that Libby hadn't ventured out of her room. I'd asked if she'd checked her. She'd said she hadn't wanted to disturb her. I'd nodded, but wanted to give Marianne a little shake. This wasn't Dad we were dealing with. Libby needed our help. The more isolated she was, the worse this would become.

My heart was pounding fiercely, flutters of anticipation rushing through me, as I made my way up the creaky staircase, fearful of what I might find behind her closed door.

I knocked again, but still no answer. Nerves mounted, my hands shaking as I pressed on the door handle. The door was ajar. I whispered her name. There was no sound. Opening the door fully I was surprised, or relieved, to see her bedroom empty.

Her curtains were closed, her bed unmade and the paraphernalia associated with her drug-taking was hidden. I entered, not turning on her light but guided by the hallway lighting. I walked across the room, checking that I wouldn't stand on anything that would injure me.

I opened the curtains, but the darkness of the night faced me. I wanted to open the window to clear the staleness from the room but the wind was too strong. It would have sent ornaments, pictures and other bits that could only be described as rubbish flying across the room. Not that Libby would have noticed.

I aired her quilt, smoothing it out flat. It was one of Max's pet hates; getting into an unmade bed. Not that it was ever unmade, but he had this habit of making the bed even if I was still in it, telling me that if I was to slide out of the bed in the mornings rather than ruffling the covers, it would still be perfect when we got in it later that night. Sometimes when he wasn't there, I'd pulled the quilt back, airing the sheets below. Generally, they didn't need airing, but it felt nice to be a little bit deviant. As thoughts of Max and bed-making flashed through my mind, I had the urge to push the covers back to the mess Libby had left them in.

I sat on her bed and scanned her room. The orange streetlamp threw shadows across the ceiling and walls. I wished for some miracle that would make this whole nightmare disappear.

I was supposed to be meeting June in an hour and some part of me had hoped Libby could come with me. As I sat staring at the wall, I wondered why I'd considered this a possibility. She'd not made any effort since June had arrived.

I wondered where Libby might be. How long she'd been gone. I hadn't checked on her before I'd left for work. I hadn't wanted to disturb her. I'd not slept, so I was sure she hadn't left in the middle of the night.

Marianne appeared in the doorway, breaking into my thoughts. She entered the room that felt as if it had a layer of dampening film hanging over it. 'Is she not here?' She seemed genuinely surprised.

'No. Have you been out today?'

'Just quickly this morning, to the shops.'

'She probably went out then.'

'Where do you think she's gone?'

'I have no idea.' I wasn't sure what Marianne wanted me to say, or what she wanted to hear. Libby could be with a dealer, her friends (who I know nothing about), or she could be wandering the streets. I had no clue, hence the reason I couldn't go out and start searching for her.

I'd read so much on the internet last night, but most of it came back to the fact that you can't help someone who doesn't want to be helped. I wanted to talk to Libby about it, but she'd been so full of aggression towards me, I was worried she'd harm the babies. Her eruption had been terrifying.

'Derek has offered to talk to her.'

'What does he know about drugs?'

'He's worked with lots of groups. He does lots in the community.'

'Does he?' I was surprised. But then, if I've learnt anything about myself over the past year, it's that my judge of character is shockingly bad.

'He might be able to help.'

'Maybe.' I raised myself from Libby's bed. 'But firstly, it would be nice to know where she is.'

'Do you think we should call the police?'

'No!' I was quick to stop her. Mainly because I didn't want Libby to get into trouble: while researching I'd found that people had been arrested for possession. I didn't want that happening to Libby. I imagined her wanting to go into teaching and having a criminal record stopping her from succeeding; that's if teaching was still an option for her. I didn't really know much about her life at the moment, her plans for the future, or if she even had any.

My head was reeling at the thought of where she could be and with who. Was she out of it somewhere? Was she safe? I assumed she'd been doing this for a long time without any of us realising. 'We'll wait to see what tonight brings.' I told Marianne, trying to sound more assertive than I felt.

I shut the curtains and turned on the bedside light, so that it looked welcoming if Libby did arrive home. I wondered how many nights she'd stayed out, without Marianne's knowledge. This was the place where I'd have thought Libby would be safe.

I didn't blame Marianne, though, I was to blame, more than anyone.

I checked that Marianne would feel okay if June came to see me here. I felt I needed to be here in case Libby came back. I wanted so much to go searching for her, but I had no idea where to start.

I applied blusher to my puffy, pale cheeks. The strokes slightly brightening my tired complexion. I thought it might make me feel better. But it didn't work. My dark dreary locks tied back off my face, I cared little for what I looked like.

I heard muffled noises from downstairs. Although I knew it was probably June I hoped it was Libby. I made my way downstairs, taking each squeaky step carefully. I stopped as I listened to their strained conversation.

'Are you going to be rude every time I come around?'

'You don't deserve my hospitality,' I heard Marianne say briskly.

'I'm not here to cause upset.'

'As long as that is the case. Kat has enough going on at the moment.'

'They are my family.'

'You should have thought about that before you did what you did.' The silence between them was cutting. There was nothing more said as I heard Marianne show her into the lounge.

Was Marianne really that angry with June for leaving? I was obviously missing something here. I would have to work on them both to find out what this secret was.

Marianne brought us a cup of tea, but didn't sit with us. She shut the door behind her as if closing out a world she didn't want to be part of.

'I don't think it's a good idea I come over on Christmas day.'

'Of course, it is; better than being on your own.'

'Marianne doesn't want me here.'

'What is going on between you two?'

'Nothing.' June was quick to answer. 'She has issues that should be forgotten.'

'It's strange, because Marianne's not really like that.'

'Maybe she's pulled the wool over your eyes for too long.'

I didn't answer. I sipped my tea, wondering if that could be the case. Could Marianne really be so vindictive? Everyone else around me seemed to be fooling me. I didn't believe it of Marianne, though.

I heard the front door open and I nearly fell off the chair with anticipation, but the sound of Derek's cheery voice sank the hope that was building inside me. His voice disappeared into the kitchen. I could hear the muffled tones, hidden behind walls of plasterboard and newly spread wallpaper.

June didn't seem to notice my torment as she asked me about the babies.

'Everything seems fine,' I told her.

'What about you and Max?'

'There is no me and Max …'

'But what will happen when these babies are born?'

'We'll deal with things ...'

'Your mum used to do that.' She smiled, picking up her tea, knowing that she'd caught my attention.

'What do you mean?'

'Block things out.'

'I'm not blocking things out.'

'But by being blasé about you and Max, what's that going to solve?' Her brusque attitude threw me slightly.

'I just … I don't …'

'Now, let's look at things logically here.' She put her tea on the coaster that was sitting on the new coffee table; another table that had replaced Dad's old table. (I'd like to call it Dad's antique or vintage table, but it was just old.) 'Excluding Max isn't going to solve a thing. Max needs to be part of the babies' lives. He is their father.'

'I understand that and he will be, but we're weeks away from them arriving.'

'You are just like your mother.' She smiled, shaking her head.

'I'll take that as a compliment,' I said, even though it didn't sound like she was giving one.

The front door opening again jolted me from my seat. I knew it had to be Libby; there was no other alternative. Derek and Marianne were in the kitchen. No-one else was permitted to just walk in. There was no knock, no doorbell. I heard the kitchen door open, Marianne obviously thinking the same as me.

'Are you okay?' June asked, confusion spreading across her face.

'I think so,' I whispered, but put my finger politely to my lips. I wanted to open my heart to her, ask for advice, but I found it hard to talk about.

The stifled voices from the hallway were barely audible, unlike the thuds that then echoed throughout the house, as Libby ran up the stairs. Her bedroom door slammed forcefully against its frame.

'What's going on?' June asked.

'Oh, nothing.' I didn't want June to know about all this upheaval.

'Depression can do that too,' she said, nodding towards the door. I assumed she meant the anger, but I decided to cover up for Libby.

'She's fine, I'm sure. Probably had a bad day.'

'Your mum would often close herself off. Sometimes it's needed.'

'Really?' I resisted the urge to tell her that Mum wasn't a drug addict, but to be fair that wasn't what she'd implied.

'When she was dealing with your dad, sometimes she would shut herself away. It would drive me mad. I'd want to try and get her to talk about it.' She smiled as if remembering a particular scene that had happened between them.

'I'd always thought she was laid-back.'

'She was, in some ways. She would hide any upset from you girls, but if she and I argued she wouldn't speak to me for days. She was one for stewing, was your mum, whereas I'd say what I wanted to say and then it was over with.'

'Did you argue lots?' I was surprised; I'd always remembered their relationship being solid.

'No, not really; a few sisterly spats.' As she finished her tea, she told me about when they were children, how they'd argued over the same boy. How Mum had won the fight; the boy had no interest in June.

We chatted for a while. I couldn't really focus but I tried to keep the conversation going. I asked questions, but all the while I was wondering what Libby was up to. I wasn't sure if June could tell I was distracted, but it only took about half an hour for her to make her excuses and get up to leave.

'You haven't been here that long,' I said. I felt as if I'd upset her, as her sudden exit startled me slightly. Had I been unintentionally rude? But then, as I thought about it, I realised I'd been asking thoughtless questions about Mum that maybe she didn't want to answer. After she'd opened up about this random boy, I'd asked her to tell me more about school. Had Mum been a goody-two-shoes, or had she been quite disobedient? Maybe when I'd starting asking questions about underage drinking and perhaps using things they shouldn't be using, she'd thought it was getting a little intense.

I thought about the times we'd met since she'd come back into my life, how she'd avoided telling me most of the things I wanted to know. She was quite happy telling me factual things, but when it came to how Mum felt about certain matters, her emotional outlook on life, she seemed to change the subject. She'd informed me about Mum and Dad's relationship, Dad's depression, how Mum had dealt with it; but she'd not really told me how Mum actually felt about it. She wanted to know about me and I'd found myself telling her things about my life, rather than finding out things about Mum that I longed to know. I thought about the times June and Mum had spent together, as images flashed through my mind: times they'd gone shopping, times they'd had their salon treatments together, times they'd had dinner. It occurred to me that maybe those times were few and far between.

I'd concocted an array of happy memories, bunching them together into an album of smiling faces, pretty backgrounds; a rosy world of happiness and laughter. But if I thought back hard enough, I remembered June actually wasn't around that much before Mum died. It could have been a week or a month or even a year before, I couldn't pinpoint a definite time. But what I knew was something major had happened between them before Mum died.

33

I went upstairs rather than face Derek and his slimy hands, the staircase creaking under my weight (which admittedly was huge). I half-expected Marianne to wander out of the kitchen to speak to me. I was pleased she didn't. She was probably caught up in her world of Derek. Pity I wasn't over-keen on him. I didn't dislike him, but I thought his overconfidence was a little intimidating. But Marianne was happy and that was all that mattered.

I stood at the top, contemplating entering Libby's room, wondering if she'd noticed the warmth of the lamplight, or the bed that I'd made for her. Would she think it a violation of her space? I'd not really thought of it like that when I was making it cosy for her. The prospect of her anger unsettled me slightly, so I went to my own room instead.

I sat on my bed, wondering whether I should have entered Libby's room, playing tennis in my own head;

It's a good idea. I'd stand and walk towards the door.

It's a crap idea. I'd sit back on the bed.

Back and forth the thoughts argued with each other.

My mobile rang, Suzy's childish face flashing at me. I'd already missed three of her calls, so I knew she was in panic mode, thinking I'd either gone into labour or murdered Max and Gina. I answered, trying my hardest to sound upbeat, seriously making an effort to sound cheerful.

'What's wrong?'

'Nothing, I'm fine.'

'I can tell you're not.'

'How?' I swallowed away the lump that was catching in my throat as my eyes pricked with unexpected tears.

'You sound like you've won the lottery. I don't believe this to be the case as I'm sure you would have rung me. I tried to meet you at the salon, but you'd already closed.'

'Sorry … I closed after my last customer.'

'How are you *really*?'

'I'm fine.' I smiled although she couldn't see me; I knew it would help the tears subside. 'I'm meeting Clare in the morning at the solicitors.' I felt sad but maybe also relieved that a chapter would be closing, making room for something new. I had to go with the feeling of relief, as it felt better than the alternative.

'Do you want me to come with you?'

'No, Clare will be there, she'll take care of me,' I said, smiling. I really appreciated Suzy's support.

'Well, I'm here if you need me.'

'Thanks, Suz.'

'So, have you spoken to Max yet?'

'Sort of.' I told her about our altercation at Clare's. 'Anyway, he's the least of my worries at the moment.'

'Why?' Suzy seemed surprised that anything more could be happening in my life.

I told her about Libby. Suzy was stunned into silence. Her quiet gasp of shock was the only reason I knew she was still there.

'What are you going to do?' She finally asked, her voice a whisper, barely audible.

'I don't know.' My voice as quiet as hers. 'She's in there now. I should go in, but I daren't.'

'But she needs your help.'

'I can't help her if she won't let me.'

'I have some clients who smoke it, you know?'

'Really?'

'Yeah, but it's not an everyday thing.'

'I think Libby's is. Plus the coke and the drink. I'm so worried she's taking Dad's path, and look what happened to Calvin. I have absolutely no idea what I'm dealing with.' Suzy was silent as I whispered, 'What if something happens to her?'

'It won't, I'm sure, but it really is best you go and speak to her.'

'I know, but it's no use talking unless she is willing to accept help. I've read so much stuff on the internet I think my next profession will be a drug counsellor.'

'Worth a thought,' Suzy said, encouraging my jesting, but the tears that had threatened earlier escaped, running in small streams down my cheeks. 'Oh, Kat, do you want me to come over?'

'No.' I sniffed, trying to control my tears. 'No, please, you've got Lawrence there. No, honestly, I'm fine. It's all these hormones.'

'It's all the bloody stress. I'm coming over now.'

'No, honestly, Suzy, I'm fine. I'm sorry. It's a rollercoaster of bloody events at the moment.'

'It wouldn't be your life if it wasn't like that.' Her humour, I knew, was an attempt to lighten my mood. 'I wish I could do something.'

'I wish you could too.' I sighed loudly, rubbing my hand across my forehead, pushing back a strand of lank dry hair.

'If I come over, we could handle Libby together.'

'I think it will make her kick off again. Honestly, I thought she was possessed. She'll probably think we're ganging up on her.'

'S'pose.'

'It's a nightmare,' I told her, before deciding to change the subject, just to get a bit of relief. 'Anyway, how's things at your end? Have you and Lawrence decided which sports event you're going to do?'

'Not yet,' she said, quickly. Not allowing any distraction from me. 'Kat, I'm worried about you.'

'Don't be.'

'I want to be there for you.'

'You are.'

'I wish I could pass some luck to you.'

'Do it in spirit. It might rub off.'

'I'm sorry I can't do more,' Suzy sighed, 'You should probably go and see if Libby is okay.'

'Yes. I probably should.'

'I'm here if you need me. I'll keep my phone on.'

'Thank you.' As we said our goodbyes, I felt thankful I had her to rely on. I didn't want to feel like a burden but it was nice to have her support. It was the tiny threads that had built our friendship over the years that kept us close. Anger suddenly boiled as I thought about how Gina had made me feel Suzy had deceived me. I may have interpreted it in my own way, but still, she hadn't helped.

Working in the salon I listened as customers talked about friendships dissolving, breaking, shattering over things that seemed so trivial compared to the trust and love gained from a friendship. I couldn't ever imagine losing Suzy. At that thought, I knew Gina was insignificant to me, I couldn't worry about her.

My phone in my hand, I rubbed the screen as if trying to connect with someone, anyone, rather than having to face Libby. Not because I didn't want to help her, but because the reality of the situation was petrifying. The weight of worry was hanging around me like a ball and chain. A release was needed but a feeling of helpless entrapment felt as if it was paralysing me.

I took a deep breath, wishing I could banish the nausea that was swimming over me as I pulled myself from the bed and headed for Libby's room.

34

The door opened with a slight creak and for some reason my thoughts diverted to putting washing-up liquid on the hinges, one of Mum's helpful tips that had stayed filed away in my brain.

The room was in darkness. She'd turned out my welcoming light; because she couldn't bear it, or the welcome? I'd knocked several times; they were feeble knocks, though, which I hoped would win her trust.

She lay in the blackness, underneath the covers. The back of her dark head was towards me, her body was turned away from the door as if trying to shut out all her torment. My heart ached for her, knowing how that felt.

My optimistic side hoped that she was fine. My realistic side knew that she wasn't.

I tried to tiptoe across the room so as not to disturb her, but my bump made it difficult. I walked slowly towards her dark form, my heart pounding and butterflies in my stomach.

Her smooth tranquil face lay peacefully, unperturbed by the anxiety around her. Stepping closer, I saw her as the delicate child I'd always seen her as. My younger sister, who needed so much love, care and affection, wrapped in her covers, protecting herself from the world.

I wanted to pull her from the covers, shake her senseless, shout in her face and tell her the drugs had to stop. Scream until I was blue in the face, make her understand what she was doing to her body. But I knew that wouldn't help. It wouldn't make any sense to her.

So, I tried to sit down as quietly as possible next to her bed. Kneeling, I let my hand stroke her thin cheek. Her dry, chapped lips parted slightly. I found myself kissing her cheek, as if I was a prince in a fairy tale, waking the princess from her nightmare. She didn't move. I knew there was no such thing as a fairy tale; princes didn't come and save princesses on white stallions, and knights didn't recuse dames from horrendous situations.

It was all a myth. Although how many of us hoped it wasn't?

'What should I do?' I whispered into the darkness. I wanted Mum to call out, tell me which step to take next.

Libby stirred slightly, her body moved as her arm stretched out in front of her, her head rolled away from me as it melted into the softness of the pillow. I noticed the tiny bruises, the defined marks that were etched on her thin arms. I lifted her loose sleeves to get a closer look. Slashes, bruises and grazes were everywhere on her arms, defacing her fragile skin.

My heart was pounding loudly, feeling slightly dizzy, I struggled to breathe. I wanted to turn away, run from the bedroom, pretend this wasn't happening. If I'd not seen the damage she'd done to her frail body, I wouldn't have believed it. But, I knew I had to face this, as my little sister had been caught in a plague.

She had started to cover herself up more, with baggy tops and longer sleeves. But, I'd put this down to it being winter and the weather was freezing. But, as I thought back to the summer months, when she'd normally be in the skimpiest outfits ever (she had no reservations when it came to showing off her body,) her sleeves had been longer, her legs barely on show.

She was living with Marianne: how could this have happened in the house of a woman who prayed to God every five minutes?

I'd been so wrapped up with moving in with Max, organising my life for the babies that I'd not really taken much notice of Libby. I really thought things were going well for her.

How the hell I had missed this?

I moved away from the bed, letting my tears fall.

'Oh, Libby, please let me help you.' I stared at the ceiling, my hands together, begging Mum for her help, pleading with her to show me how to help my sister; the sister I'd failed.

35

I sat in the small waiting room, the space allowing for four chairs, a square table and a water dispenser. A plant stood brightly in the corner, its leaves were shiny, and I wondered if it was real. A neat pile of magazines stood next to the plant, as if they were on display, not to be used as reading material. A window let in the winter sun through the horizontal slats of the blinds, making the room unusually warm for the time of year. I undid my cardigan that was shielding me and my bump, rubbing my hands over my stomach, my black top tight to my skin, telling myself this was all worth it.

I was doing it for my babies and it would be worth it.

The door opened and Clare entered, smiling. She was perky and cheerful. I wished I shared her joy, her enthusiasm for the new lease of life she had. I remembered signing the contract for the salon, how nervous but how excited I'd felt.

'How are you feeling?' Clare asked, sitting down next to me on the rigid blue chairs.

'I'm fine.' I smiled, trying to put on a brave face.

'We don't have to do this if you've changed your mind.'

'No, I want to.' I suppressed the lump in my throat. 'It's just the end of an era.' I shrugged, trying to sound nonchalant.

Clare, however, had come to know me well, and she placed a hand on my knee and smiled, 'Thank you.'

'I think it's really brave of you,' I told her and she smiled at me.

We both knew that this was an amazing, life-changing break for Clare. I'd finally accepted she wasn't having some kind of mid-life crisis; this was a positive, inspiring step for her to take and should be applauded. Clare, who'd never fulfilled her dreams, who'd lived her life for her husband and son, was grabbing an opportunity with both hands and making it work for her. Her age, her lack of knowledge, her lack of experience didn't matter to her; it would be her drive and tenacity that would make this work.

A young man appeared at the door, calling us through. Clare helped me from my seat as if I was an elderly lady. I waddled inelegantly, my bump pushed forward and my jeans, although maternity, straining against the lower part of my stomach, pressing on my abdomen, making me feel as if I constantly needed a wee.

We followed the man through the array of offices. Everyone was dressed in dark suits. There was the odd bright shirt or colourful blouse but the scene was set for serious business. We were taken to a desk, where a woman with dazzling blue eyeshadow, rosy cheeks and red lips was typing on her computer, telling us she wouldn't be a second. Her smile revealed red lipstick on her teeth. I tried not to glare at her: I had this habit of wanting to 'redo' people, especially when it came to make-up. I think anyone who has a specialism does it. Max was forever judging buildings; constantly making comments about structures and improvements he'd make.

I pushed Max from my thoughts, as the woman explained she was my landlord's solicitor and then she quickly highlighted different parts of several agreements that we both had to sign.

As my hand moved across the dotted lines, I felt sadness overwhelm me. I felt as if I was signing away my life. My salon had been my world, it was all I knew and here I was scrolling my autograph to end it all.

I thought I'd feel some kind of relief, but all I felt was loss. I felt a part of me had been removed, a part I needed, like an organ that kept my body ticking over healthily.

Suddenly, it was all over.

Clare could have the keys. It was now Clare's salon.

I made my excuses to leave, to be alone. To just be. I didn't know what I needed: water, air, help … I had to get out. I could hear Clare following quickly behind me, calling my name, workers staring at us as we caused a mini-drama in this sombre setting.

I headed towards the sign that said, 'Ladies'. My stomach swirling, I just made it to the loo in time before I threw up.

'Oh God, Kathryn, are you alright?' I hadn't had time to close the cubicle door.

I put my hands up to stop Clare coming any closer. 'Please, Clare, give me two minutes.' Give me my dignity.

'Okay, dear,' she said softly, then, mercifully, left me alone.

I lay with my head on my arm, hoping Clare was guarding the outside, not allowing anyone else to come in and see me in this state.

Breathing deeply, I slowly began to feel better.

'Oh, Kathryn, you don't look well,' Clare said, when I walked weakly towards her. Her look of concern made me feel a bit guilty I'd shunned her away.

'I'm fine.'

'It's all this stress, and I know Maxwell hasn't helped.'

I couldn't do this now. I'd throw up again. I didn't want to talk about Max. 'Honestly, I'm fine. Have you got the keys?' I purposely changed the subject.

Clare realised she hadn't, so left me as she headed back to the solicitor's desk. I'd signed all I needed to. I couldn't head back in there; I was far too embarrassed by my exit.

We left the solicitors in separate cars, but we were meeting at the salon as I had to show her how to use the boiler, where the gas and electric metres were and anything else a landlord should do. It seemed unreasonable to ask the landlord to come back into the country for a five-minute training session. Although, I'd wanted to.

We pulled up outside. It felt strange knowing this was no longer mine. I would be living in the flat again soon, but this place that I'd filled with culture and style was no longer my shelter. The place where I'd always come to feel safe had been ripped from me. Clare unlocked the door, and I wondered if this feeling of misery would ever lift.

She wandered around the salon, her mind obviously ticking over, as she wiped her hands gently along the white-washed walls. She studied the windswept woman which adorned the back wall. The woman that had caught Max's attention when he'd first walked into the salon. If I'd been staying here I'd have painted over her, as every time I met her dreamy eyes, she reminded me of Max. I wondered if Clare would keep her. I hoped not.

I could see her thinking through the layout, the style; how she would make my haven her own. I appreciated that she didn't say it aloud. Yes, I'd seen the plans, given my opinion; but actually, being here was worlds apart from drawings and sketches.

Although I knew this was the best thing to do, the only thing to do before I landed myself in masses of debt, I still watched Clare and wished I was her. I wished I could turn back time, before Max was ever on the scene, or push it forward so the babies were older, wiser, living their own little lives. I had a long way to go before that day arrived.

Three years ago, I'd excitedly taken the keys, I was a fresh-faced girl who'd had the world at her feet, who'd felt her soul belonged in this tiny village.

But, I was a completely different person now, older and most definitely wiser.

36

'You didn't have to take me out for lunch,' June said as she studied the menu.

'I wanted to,' I smiled. 'It's Christmas Eve, I didn't want you spending the whole day on your own.'

'Thank you.' She seemed sad for a fleeting second. It would be her first Christmas on her own, but I thought it best not to bring that into the conversation. I suddenly felt sorry for her. She gave off an air of confidence, but I wondered how self-assured she really was.

'Will you be okay tonight?' I asked.

'Of course.'

'I could stay with you,' I offered, but I didn't want to. I wanted to keep an eye on Libby, but was torn that June would be sitting alone, reminiscing, lost in old memories.

'Don't be silly,' she said, waving her hand dismissively at me. 'I'm a big girl.'

'It's such a shame that Marianne doesn't have room for you to stay with us.'

'I doubt she'd want me there.' She continued to study the menu, not meeting my eye. 'What are you having?' she asked causally, changing the subject before I had the chance to ask what had happened between them.

I browsed the menu, debating whether I should go for a jacket potato, a sandwich or a panini. None of which I particularly fancied, but knew I would force it down. I'd had a few rumbling twinges since waking up; nothing too strong, but enough to make me uncomfortable. It was probably wind, I'd told myself.

June ordered our food at the counter, not allowing me to pay; which annoyed me slightly as I'd asked to take her out. But she insisted, so I told her that next time it was on me. As she'd walked away from the table, she'd told me, 'You need to keep an eye on your finances, not throw your money away on me.'

She was right. Things were manageable at the moment while I was living with Marianne. I gave her some money for food, or bought bits myself, and I'd offered to pay board and lodging but she wouldn't take it. I'd had to push money into her hand or purse. 'Libby doesn't pay anything, so, why should you?' she said.

'I'm not Libby, and I want to pay my way,' I'd told her firmly.

I was trying not to worry about the future and how I would support the babies on my own. Obviously, Max would have to contribute and I knew I would have no problem in that area. But still, once I moved back to the flat I would have to think about my next step forward: maybe have a table in Clare's salon, or I could become mobile. It was just too much to comprehend at the moment. I was trying to get through each day, without thinking about where I would be in six months.

'It'll be about five minutes,' June said, as she sat back in her chair.

'I've brought you a little something,' I said, delving into my handbag. 'I thought it was best to give it to you now, instead of in front of everyone tomorrow.'

'Oh, Kat, you shouldn't have.' She seemed surprised. 'I've left yours at home. I'll bring it with me tomorrow.'

'Here we are.' I handed her a neatly wrapped gift. A red ribbon surrounded the silver wrapping paper. I'd run scissors along the edge of the ribbon to create a refined finish.

'Oh, Kat, you've wrapped it perfectly,' she smiled. 'It looks too good to open.'

I loved that she'd noticed the effort I'd taken. It was amazing, though, how simply wrapping a present could bring back a host of memories. Every year, we'd design a raffle in which a customer would win a range of expensive beauty products and the money raised would go to charity. I'd always taken my time to wrap the prize: three ribbons in different colours would embellish the clear cellophane that bounded the products.

'I hope you like it,' I said, as her fingers slowly released the present. 'It's only small.'

'It's beautiful.' She took the embroidered, jewelled photo album from its box, holding it delicately as if it was glass; worried she would drop the precious gift and it would smash into smithereens.

'I thought we could start some new memories.'

'It's stunning.' Her eyes filled with tears as she grabbed a tissue from her bag. Dabbing the tissue under her eyes, and then blowing her nose, she smiled gratefully, 'Thank you.'

She lifted the cardboard pages gently, the tissue paper that accompanied each page wrinkling as a waft of air got hold of it. She flattened down one of the cream sheets before it became crumpled, her hand slowly caressing the smoothness of the pages.

'You're welcome,' I smiled. 'I was thinking you must have lots of photos of Mum when she was a child.'

'I have a few but not many.' June blew her nose again. 'They're back home though.'

'Could you bring them with you next time you visit?'

'Of course,' she nodded. 'If I can find them.'

She placed the album back in the crêpe paper that was inside the box. I hadn't thought it would affect her so much. I was secretly pleased that it had.

Blowing her nose once again, she shook her head. 'That was really thoughtful. Thank you,' she said, getting up from her seat, cuddling me close.

'I'm glad you like it.'

'We can start with building some memories tomorrow,' she smiled.

'Sounds great.' Wondering what her plans were after Christmas, I asked, 'Are you staying for New Year?'

'No. I'm going to go in a few days. I was thinking of coming back when the babies are born. I know you have Clare and Marianne, but I'd love to help where I can.'

'Yes, great. When I'm back in the flat, you could stay with me.'

'I'd like that.'

'What happened between you and Marianne?' I asked suddenly, surprising myself. The question, though, was on the tip of my tongue and if I'd thought about it, I wouldn't have asked.

'It was a long time ago.' June peered down at her cup of coffee. 'We never got along. I wanted to help your father, she stepped in and …'

'And …?'

'It was hard to watch her in your home,' she admitted. I nodded, totally understanding. 'But I wanted to help, and I was pushed away.'

'Panini?' The waitress interrupted us as she placed our food down.

'This looks nice.' June changed the subject as she unwrapped the knife and fork from the paper napkin.

I watched her; her laughter lines, the age lines, and her pale skin reminded me of Mum. 'Why do you think they pushed you away?' I needed some answers.

'I think I interfered too much and Marianne didn't like it,' June said, loading potato onto her fork as she glanced at me, though she wasn't meeting my eye.

'But what about Dad?'

'He listened to Marianne.'

'But what about us? Me and Libby.'

'Your dad thought I was meddling, intruding into your life, so it was best that I left.'

'Dad asked you to leave?'

'He did, but it's all in the past. I'm back and we can start afresh,' she said adamantly.

I didn't dare argue. It felt rude to probe her any more. But I knew she was missing out vital parts of her past: my past.

Marianne's words: *you should have thought about that before you did what you did*, were constantly flashing at me. It was all very messy. There wasn't enough depth to any of their stories; Marianne was dismissive and June was too minimal.

As we chatted throughout lunch, I wondered if I was looking for something that wasn't there. Maybe it *was* that simple; June had upset them and she was asked to leave. I found it hard to believe that Marianne wouldn't allow Mum's sister in our lives. She'd been a significant part of our family. Dad wouldn't have banished her because of Marianne, and Marianne wouldn't have wanted him to.

It didn't make any sense.

Maybe if I queried them further tomorrow, something would be revealed. It would just be nice for June to accept Marianne the way I had, although, it wasn't June putting up a barrier, which surprised me.

I would find out their past haunts and help them build a relationship. They were both in my life. I'd come this far. I needed to help them move past whatever was stopping them from being friends, or at least, allowing them to be amicable.

37

'Why don't you come with me?'

'Honestly, I'm fine here.'

'What about these pains?' Marianne was desperate not to leave me, but her call from God, and Derek, was fighting against her loyalty to me. 'I'd feel better if you were with me.'

'Marianne it's a few Braxton Hicks, it's expected.' I'd had a few niggles in the night, feeling slightly uncomfortable throughout the morning, I'd not even mentioned it to June earlier, and wished I'd not mentioned it to Marianne either. I knew it wasn't the real thing. I wasn't ready; the babies couldn't possibly arrive yet. Plus, they weren't the double-over-in-pain stabs that I was expecting. A bit of tightness, a pain that was similar to having wind; bit of flatulence. I'd be fine. I imagined being shipped off to the hospital. 'Oh no, false alarm: she's just got the farts,' and they'd send me home, but then I'd be too embarrassed to go back.

'What if it's not?'

'Then I'll call you.'

'It will do you good to be around people.'

'I'm worried Libby will come home to an empty house.' Admitting the real reason I didn't want to go out.

'She won't even notice if we're here or not.' Marianne's words were true but still the sting they produced dug deep. She was standing over me, her black coat wrapped tight around her plump body, her hands covered by black leather gloves that held her hand-bag in front of her. Her fair curls were in their traditional style as always; her make-up was flawless. I was pleased to see she was using some of the tips I'd given her. She looked poised and sophisticated. I often wondered how she had ended up with the life she had. Such a generous person, always smiling as all around her caused mayhem and disruption.

'It's Christmas Eve, Kat. Please come with me.'

'But I'm fine here, honestly.'

'I won't settle, so if you don't come, I'll have to come home early and I don't really want to.' She smiled warmly.

'Are you forcing me?'

'Maybe a little.' She laughed. It was obvious she'd had a few glasses of sherry. It was the only thing she drank, but it was few and far between, so it went straight to her head.

'I'm worried about Libby.'

'Whether you're here or with me, it won't make a difference. Libby is doing what she needs to do and hopefully she'll join us tomorrow and we can connect with her. God moves in mysterious ways; he'll take care of Libby.'

What, in the way he took care of Calvin? I wanted to say, but thought it would be cruel.

'Okay,' I sighed, giving in to her persuasion. I could at least go and pray. Pray to the Lord to help Libby. And help *me*. Although, I wasn't even sure if there was a God … I believed in some form of afterlife, because this made it easier to cope with Mum's death; knowing she was watching over me. And, at least by going with Marianne I wouldn't be sitting staring at four walls, driving myself crazy with my cluttered thoughts.

I'd heard Libby leave earlier. I'd shouted her name, but she'd slammed the door in my face. Riled by her rudeness I'd followed her out of the door, the cold air making me shiver. But she was quickly making her getaway in an old red car, her hood shielding her face. I couldn't see the driver either.

I contemplated phoning the police: I'd had time to memorise the number plate. But that wasn't how I wanted this to end. I felt as if I was living a soap opera lifestyle. Kat, pregnant with twins, loses her business, her sister's a drug addict, her partner leaves her for his former lover – it would be a great part to play, if it wasn't so bloody real.

I'd been reading more on the internet about her condition. I'd decided to call it a condition: it didn't feel as raw as referring to her drug or alcohol problem. I'd read that drug addiction started in many ways, but the one that I couldn't get out of my mind was depression. I'd blamed her peers, I'd blamed Calvin, the people she used to live with. I'd blamed everyone but Libby. I'd blamed myself.

But had Libby started the drink and drugs because she was depressed? I'd assumed she was so low at the moment because of Calvin's death. I thought the drugs were making her miserable. But maybe it was the other way around; she'd used them because she was down.

I'd not really noticed. She'd always been funny, easy-going; she would be the one that would make us laugh with her crude ways. She didn't care about things in the way others did. Her laid-back attitude had seen her through many stupid situations.

Had it been a cover? A façade? Was she like many of us? Presenting an image to the world when inside we were dying? The state of her arms, where she'd purposely hurt herself, told me: yes.

Why hadn't I seen it? Why the hell hadn't I noticed? I wanted to shake her and ask, 'Why are you doing this to yourself? Why, Lib?' I was so angry with her, but at the same time so worried, so lost in this state of agonising apprehension.

I felt sick all the time. My body felt weighed down, not by the babies – well yes, they did contribute – but by my worries. My mind wouldn't rest, my stomach churned. I wished I could make it all stop.

The church was only five minutes away, but we took my car. Marianne was adamant that my twinges could be the real thing, and if things started to happen we wouldn't want to be running back to the house. I wouldn't be running anywhere, I'd thought.

Not only was the church car park full, but the small country road leading up to the church was lined neatly with parked cars. I was surprised to see so many people; so many people wanting to embrace this special night. People were smiling, talking, welcoming each other. Children's little hands were securely held by their parents, protection and warmth surrounding them. Couples walked arm in arm. Although everyone was wearing their winter attire, beating off the cold, the affection that shone from everyone was enough to light a flame.

As I walked with Marianne, I could feel the love all around me. I felt as if I was in a place where I belonged. For the first time, I understood why Marianne came here, why she had focused so much of her life on the church. It didn't matter what was happening in her world, she had this safe haven, this place that accepted her for who she was.

Just how I used to feel in my salon.

Derek was greeting people as they entered the church, his face alight when he noticed me with Marianne. 'Oh, Kathryn dear, how lovely of you to come.' His hands were on mine. I tried to ignore the fact that I hated his touchy-feely tendencies. He was a kind man, I told myself as I felt his breath on my cheek, as his wet lips planted a kiss. 'Oh, the Lord will be happy to see you.'

'Thank you,' I managed. He exchanged a few words with Marianne, then we moved slowly into the church, leaving the others behind to suffer his slimy greetings. I was being unkind, I know, but it was the whole personal space thing; I wished he understood it.

The church opened up to us, a picture of beauty and serenity. The immense Christmas tree stood at the front of the church, lights sparkling and baubles perfectly aligned. Grand and opulent it looked more likely to be exhibited in Harrods than the local church. Candles surrounded the altar, the choir pews and the front rows, welcoming people to take their seats, encouraging them to come forward and embrace this wonderful night. I suddenly felt proud to be part of it, as Marianne chatted to people, introducing me as her stepdaughter. I felt proud to be with her.

It was as if a whole different world was going on inside this building. A place full of so much love and affection could easily become addictive. At the thought of addiction, images of Libby passed through my mind. Where was she spending this evening?

Libby and I used to be so excited on Christmas Eve. We were always allowed to open one Christmas present, which generally consisted of new pyjamas and slippers, but just the unwrapping was enough. I used to feel so sick with excitement, about Santa Claus. Even when Hannah Johnson had revealed the truth, and the magic had disappeared for me, it had still been enchanting for Libby. It had still made the whole evening mystic for her.

After Mum died, I'd tried to keep the fairy tale going, entrancing Libby with Santa and fairy stories in the way Mum had. The first Christmas without Mum, Libby had woken me at 3 a.m., tears rolling down her cheeks. 'He's not coming,' she'd sobbed quietly. There was no present on the end of her bed, as there always had been. 'Do you think he's forgotten us because Mum's not here?' It broke my heart to see how devastated she was. She'd climbed into my bed, and I'd cuddled her as if she were my own child. Stroking her forehead and running my hands along her long dark hair, as I told her that Santa was a very busy man and he only left presents in bedrooms for younger children. She accepted this; luckily, at the age of six she didn't wonder why I'd been getting presents up to the age of twelve.

It was hard, though, to keep Christmas special when Dad was at such a low ebb. It wasn't so much the lack of presents, but the absence of Dad: not physically but emotionally. He'd switch off, wallowing in a state of self-pity for most of the Christmas period. Marianne would try to compensate for his lack of effort, but we didn't appreciate it at the time.

I watched Marianne work her way through her friends and acquaintances, then introduce herself to others that she'd not met before, and welcome them to the church as if it were her own home. To be honest, she was more at home here than she was in the house in which she lived.

I thought of Suzy, who was having a cosy night in with Lawrence. She'd asked if I wanted to join them, 'We want you to come. Honestly, Lawrence doesn't mind, he'd love it if you were here.' I loved Suzy for making the effort, for considering me and insisting I be with her; but this was her time to be happy.

I wondered where Max was; how he was celebrating his Christmas Eve. I imagined him and Gina snuggling together as we used to before I fell pregnant. What gifts had they delighted in buying for each other? Had she considered his hobbies like I had? Had she thought about his favourite movies, books, interests, clothes, excursions, adventures? I blinked back a tear. I'd become an expert in choking back my sadness, holding onto my pride.

'Are you alright?' Marianne was at my side, her hand on my arm.

'I'm fine,' I smiled, wiping away the stray tear from my cheek. 'It's just being here, it's so ...' I couldn't find the words to describe the emotion that was flowing through me.

'I know.' She placed her arm around my shoulder. She understood.

The muffled voices of people chatting fell silent, people strengthened their vocal chords with a cough or a clearing of their throats, and a sneeze rattled through the high ceilings. The vicar was standing at the front, the figure of Jesus on a cross stretched high above him as if watching over us all, protecting us from any evil. I felt that if I stayed in this place for ever, I'd never have to deal with any more hurt or disappointment.

A few words were spoken by the vicar. I could see Derek nodding vigorously in agreement. The vicar focused more on love than on Jesus, God, Mary and how Christmas started. I felt as if he was talking to me. I felt as if every word was targeted at me, as if he knew my situation. I was starting to think about forgiveness (could I ever forgive Max?) when we went into a rendition of *Come, All Ye Faithful*.

The choir sang perfectly, the church filling with cheerful voices, the passionate vibes reaching the heavens.

It was the vibration from my pocket that distracted me. Discreetly bringing my phone into view, I saw that Libby had left me a text. The joyous singing around me became suddenly distant, as I read her call for help.

'Where r u Kat, I need u.'

38

I'd lied to Marianne, told her I wasn't feeling too good. After insisting quite forcefully that I stay by her side, she finally agreed to let me go, and I convinced her that Derek could take her home later. How pleased I was that she hadn't accompanied me. I was trying to protect both her and Libby.

Pulling up outside the house felt like the days when Dad was alive. The same dread I used to feel was with me. Under the orange streetlight the house looked grey and damp, as it always had whenever I'd come to visit Dad.

The front door was unlocked. My voice echoed as I shouted Libby's name. There was no response as I shut the door behind me, closing out the chill of the freezing night air. I thought about all the children who would be wrapped up in their new pyjamas, snuggling close to their parents as they watched a Christmas film, leaving out their mince pie, brandy and milk for Santa and his reindeer. I wished for a second I was that small child again.

I could feel myself shaking. The twinges I'd felt earlier were becoming gradually more intense, but I blamed the text from Libby. The babies were three weeks away; there was no way they'd be coming so soon. It was all this stress. The living room door was ajar, the small lamp that Marianne had left on was beckoning me forward. I went in to find Libby sitting with her head in her hands.

'Oh God, Libby, what's happened?' I knelt beside her, relief filling me that she hadn't passed out, or worse. She looked up at me, her pale, tired face pleading silently for help, her eyes red from crying. Her dark hair was tied in a short ponytail, but greasy strands fell aimlessly around her gaunt features.

'I'm sorry, Kat.' Her chapped lips shook as she tried to form the words.

'It's fine.' On my knees by her side, I rubbed her leg, as she rocked herself backwards and forwards. 'I'm here, Libby. I'm here to help you.'

Falteringly, she told me that she was desperate; she had no idea what to do next. 'It's become so much harder now Calvin's not here,' she told me. Her nose was running she wiped it listlessly with a tissue.

'I know.' I tried to show her I was here for her.

'He went too far ... he'd started with coke, then played with heroin.'

'Have you done that too?'

She didn't answer my question, as her breath seemed to catch in her throat, 'I need the pain to go away. I miss him so much.' She let her sobs escape as my colossal body hugged her tiny frame. 'A bloody heart attack at his age, it's not fair ...'

'What? I thought it was drugs.'

'The coke caused it.' I sat silently, unsure how to respond. 'I really want this to stop ... I need help.'

She started to cry again, and the whole story came out slowly between bouts of sobbing. I listened as she explained how she'd tried coke when she'd moved out of my flat. It had been fun, it wasn't anything serious and they were all doing it. I resisted the urge to shout, 'Would you jump off a bloody cliff, if they had?' sounding like the parent to her that I wasn't. As I absorbed each word, I realised that my failure to be a good sister, let alone a substitute parent, had been catastrophic.

She'd loved the buzz, the freedom, the ability not to have to worry. Libby worried? She'd been my chilled little sister who didn't worry about anything. She was the easy-going one out of the two of us. I was the one that worried for us both. She admitted she'd been hoping one of us would find her in her drugged-up state; she'd planned to confess everything had we walked in on her, as I had. But she told me the need for the drugs had been greater than the need to admit to me that she needed help. She apologised for pushing me over, breathlessly trying to tell me she'd never forgive herself if anything happened to the babies.

I took in all that she told me. Her deceit. Her lies. And the stealing; she told me about that, too. As the truth about her world unfolded, mine seemed to crash around me. She'd practically stripped Marianne of her possessions, and Marianne had no clue. Or if she did, she hadn't mentioned anything to me. Libby had sold jewellery, pawned expensive items, her laptop, and anything else she could find. I tried not to show my disappointment, my anger, my utter frustration when she told me there was no teaching course. She'd not enrolled. She'd taken Marianne's money and spent it on her and Calvin. She sobbed as she told me, she thought it would make him love her. Finally, she'd no longer had anything left to sell, as she confessed that the one thing she did have, she'd given away that evening: her body.

'What you've slept with someone for money?' I asked, trying not to sound aghast. I didn't want to use the word prostitution.

'I had sex with someone for drugs,' she said, obviously disgusted with herself as she didn't look at me. I couldn't speak. 'I know him, but still …' Her head in her hands.

I listened, as she reminded me of what had happened one night outside the house she'd shared with Calvin: two men fighting over her. I'd been disgusted that she was messing around with married men, but she admitted to me that one of them had supplied her with cannabis and helped Calvin find the stronger drugs which she, too, had often used. The man I remembered had looked far too 'normal' to be a dealer; not that I was aware of what they should look like. However, she and Calvin had found another source so she'd moved on from him.

I tried not to judge my sister as she begged for my help, hanging onto me like I was a length of rope, knowing that if I let her go she'd fall into a bottomless pit.

She told me that she knew things had got out of control, but she didn't know how to stop it. She'd talked to Calvin about stopping, but they always went straight back to it. They couldn't help each other. 'It was like we were trapped,' she said. She also told me how much she loved Calvin. How he'd never wanted her, but she'd held onto a glimmer of hope that she could change his sexuality. She knew she was dreaming, but being so close to someone, loving someone so deeply, had stopped her from leaving him and the circle of friends they'd built. The circle of friends I didn't even know existed.

As the tears tumbled down her face, my own worries and concerns that were keeping me awake on a night felt small by comparison. Libby's world had stopped; her main focus was on her drugs and her drink.

She'd betrayed not only Marianne and me, but herself.

Her life had become a living nightmare: a day-by-day effort to acquire the substances her body needed.

The only thing I could hold onto on this cold Christmas Eve, while parents rushed around to fill their living rooms with gifts from Santa, while choirs sang their hearts out to the heavens, while children forced their eyes shut as they lay in bed, was that Libby was finally holding out her hands for help. She had aired her soul, stripped herself bare, laid it all out for me to see. And I had to be thankful that she'd reached that point before it was too late.

The hours passed, the night moving into Christmas Day as exhaustion claimed Libby's thin, frail body. I helped her to the sofa, covering her with the soft red velvet blanket that was a new addition to the freshly decorated room. I didn't want to let her out of my sight, not knowing if she'd actually taken anything before she confessed all. I stroked her face as her eyes stared vacantly into the distance, hopefully into a world of indulgent dreams, away from this reality that was a nightmare.

The pains I'd been feeling all evening had jolted me slightly as Libby had told me about her life. I sat next to her, rubbing my hands across my bump, wanting to shield my babies from this horrendous world. My mouth felt dry, my heavy eyelids longing to close, but the nagging pains were not allowing me to be comfortable. There was no pattern to the random twinges. It wasn't as if I could time them: they weren't five or ten, or even fifteen minutes apart. The pain didn't clamp my body like a vice, or render me breathless as it ripped at my insides; it was random waves of aching soreness that ached, a throbbing which made me yearn to rest.

I could hear the sound of a car pull up outside. I assumed it was Derek, dropping off Marianne. I imagined them deciding how it wouldn't be convenient for him to come in this evening; as if Libby and I were the parents. Marianne had always respected our space since we'd lived with her. I heard the car door closing quietly, Marianne trying to be considerate to the neighbours. Derek's engine ticked over until Marianne was safely inside the house. Then he drove away, unaware of the mess she was about to face.

I knew I had to tell Marianne everything. It would be unfair to ask for her help with Libby, but not allow her the whole truth. She entered the living room cautiously, with the same expression I used to have when I came to visit Dad. I noticed for the first time that the door had been glossed; her decorating had been thorough. An odd thing to notice, but the shiny white paint underneath her fingers seemed out of place when such dull darkness was surrounding us.

'How is she?' she whispered, nodding at Libby, but still holding onto the door, as if not knowing whether she should enter or keep her distance, unsure of her boundaries. It was moments like this where the definition of her being our mother were defined. Our mother, any mother, would have barged through the door, demanding to know what was happening.

'We have to talk.' I told her. I was still seated next to Libby, worried that if I took my eye off her, she might slip from my sight.

39

Marianne and I sat for hours talking, long into Christmas morning. She was all that I expected her to be. Her kind nature reaching out to Libby. I tried to imagine how I would feel if I was her. Would I have been so compassionate? I doubt it.

I was aching to help Libby. I wouldn't turn my back on her – but she hadn't stolen from *me*. She'd lied about going to college, yes. She'd actually made up a life that didn't exist, but that was to protect herself; I understood that. But Marianne had been cheated and stolen from; not that I used those words or encouraged Marianne to think like this, because I wanted her help. I *needed* her help. She was calm, understanding, and forgiving, explaining that she would do what she could to help.

As I cried and blamed myself, she told me that under no circumstances must I blame myself. 'It's about choices. Libby had a choice.' She was twenty-three. She was a grown woman, an adult who'd had numerous roads she could have taken. This didn't help to take away the guilt, though.

There was no shouting, no screaming; Marianne was calm and kind. Her stillness was settling. She told me Derek had many contacts on different help programmes. I felt a little guilty that I'd judged him badly when he was actually well-respected in the community. Not only the church community, but the charities he was involved in. He'd told Marianne that the best thing to do would be to see the doctor, who would refer Libby to the most appropriate programme. Unfortunately, with Christmas Day upon us, popping to the surgery wasn't an option. Should we have called out an emergency doctor, or should we take her to A&E?

Who knows these things? It wasn't like deciding which medicine was best to take for a cold.

I was reluctant to do anything without Libby's consent. We had to help her, but it had to be in a way that was comfortable for her, as more than likely she wasn't going to stick to it. But she'd made the first move. She was begging for help. This was progress in itself and I would hold onto that fact.

At last, Marianne left me downstairs with Libby. I couldn't leave her. I was worried that she'd wake up, remember our conversation and flee. She had nothing left to give but her body, 'Please, Kat, don't let me do it again.' Her words still echoed. If she did have sex for drugs again, she would blame me. *I* would blame me. I felt guilty enough that it had gone this far, that I hadn't grasped how serious it all was. Now I knew, I couldn't let her fall back into the trap. She had taken the first step out of her dark pit. She was reaching for me. I had the rope and I had to keep pulling. No matter how tiring, exhausting or painful it was, I could not let the rope go.

I angled myself on one of the chairs throughout the night. I kept dozing off for five-minute intervals, being constantly woken again by the throbbing that seemed to be surrounding my stomach. It couldn't possibly be contractions. It wasn't a tightness or a pain that increased intensely then died off, like everyone had told me. It was an ache, an urgent sign that if I didn't need to fart, then something major was going on. But it wasn't what I was expecting. Customers had given me in-depth descriptions of their labours; painful, excruciating labours. It was as if I'd pulled a muscle, a constant ache with fleeting stabs, especially if I moved in the wrong direction. I needed to settle myself down; body and mind.

Marianne's tapping on the door interrupted my thoughts. I'd say dreams but I wasn't asleep long enough to embrace any. Libby was still sleeping on the sofa.

'Did you get any sleep?' Marianne asked, wrapping her quilted dressing gown around her body.

'Not really,' I said, sitting myself up, rubbing my hands across my tired face, which felt dry and dirty. I didn't want to tell her about the pain, I didn't want her fussing and worrying. I knew it was nothing. We had Libby to focus on, plus we had Christmas Day to get through.

'I have a few presents for you girls, but it would be lovely if we could open them when Libby is awake; if she wants to join us, of course.'

'That would be nice.'

'You look tired. Now I'm down here, why don't you go and have a proper lie-down before June and Derek arrive?'

'Do you need any help with anything?'

'It's all done.'

'Really? You don't need me to help with the vegetables, or anything?'

'I did it all yesterday.' She smiled. 'Go and get some rest.'

'I might go and have a bath …'

'You do that.'

'Are you sure?'

'Absolutely,' she said adamantly. 'I'm aiming for a relaxing and calm day today.' Marianne told me as I passed her. A relaxing and calm day watching Libby like a hawk, Marianne and June at each other's throats, Derek with his touchy-feeling ways and my bump ready to burst. Relaxing and calm didn't sound likely.

With my pale bump protruding from the water, I could feel the babies moving around next to each other, fighting for space like they'd probably fight for my attention when they arrived. I'd been told that the babies would quieten down just before labour, so if that was the case they wouldn't be coming soon, as there was no quiet going on. You'd think they were preparing for an Olympic event. The bath helped to ease the pain slightly, the aching still hanging on, throbbing at the lower part of my bump.

I splashed the water around my skin. I'd used the Bio-Oil after Suzy suggested that stretch marks weren't so picturesque. I know they weren't her words, but I knew that's what she'd meant.

Plus, many customers had agreed it was the best thing for stretch marks. Vain, I know, but if there was a way to prevent them I was up for trying it. Some of my customers were adamant it didn't work for them. 'If you're going to get them, nothing will stop them coming.' I did have a few, but I wondered if I'd have had more if I'd not used the oil.

I'd also been told by a customer about rubbing vegetable oil on my perineal area. Yes: I too, wondered what on earth that was. 'It helps with tearing,' she'd whispered loudly, and nodded to my lady's bits. The word *tearing* had me searching for my perineum. It wasn't the easiest thing to massage and I hadn't done it as often as I apparently should. Plus, I felt a bit naughty. Many women may have found it pleasurable, but the thought of ripping apart down below soon diminished any sexual urges. I'd have been embarrassed if Max had caught me. Doesn't that say something? I wanted to be with someone who I could have discussed these massaging techniques with. In fact, I wanted to be with someone who I was so comfortable with, they could have massaged my nether regions for me. Not that, might I add, there'd be any need to massage the perineal area once these babies had arrived. I'll be getting sewn up. I'll never be touched again.

The pain eased slightly. I forced myself from the warmth of the bath, following my usual method; onto my knees, stand up and climb out. I could hear muffled voices below. I hadn't heard anyone else enter the house, so I assumed it was Libby. I quickly dried myself and threw on my fleece dressing gown, feeling the dampness as my body stuck uncomfortably to the fluffy material. As I left the bathroom the humidity had steamed up the mirrors so I had no idea what I looked like. I suddenly felt hot all over and dizzy, I held onto the doorframe.

As I went slowly down the stairs, feeling my temperature rising even further, I had to stop to allow a sharp pain to pass. I didn't scream, but I felt the intensity of something that could easily escalate. Once I'd caught my breath, I stepped cautiously down the rest of the stairs, holding onto my bump as if the babies might pop out at any moment (I wished it would be that easy).

Libby was sitting at the kitchen table holding a cup of tea close to her, her feet resting on another chair.

'Merry Christmas,' she managed.

'And to you,' I replied, expressing a cheerfulness I didn't feel. I walked towards her, moving awkwardly, and hugged her close. She responded. I didn't want to let her go: I was holding the rope.

'How are you feeling this morning?'

'Fine.' She was lying. I knew it; she was crumbling inside, she was hurting and I wasn't sure how this worked but I knew she wouldn't be able to simply stop. I might be naïve about the whole drug world, but there was one thing I knew: an addiction was just that. I didn't know if any withdrawal had set in, or what the time frame would be. But I knew this wasn't the end. If anything, this was just the beginning.

'Do you want a cup of tea, love?' Marianne asked. 'There's some fresh in the pot.'

'Yes, please.' The pains were slightly worse, and I thought a warm drink might help to get rid of them. I rubbed my bump, my face obviously showing my concern because Marianne asked if I was okay.

'Just a few twinges,' I said.

'Still?' She looked worried. 'Are you sure we don't need to go to the hospital?'

'I'm fine, honest.' I sat down at the table. Libby was watching me, probably trying to figure my thoughts and wondering if I was going to grill her more. But as we sat there, we decided we would see a doctor after the bank holiday; we would sort this before the New Year. She'd agreed, but from the things I'd read, she could easily go back on her word. But I didn't discourage her with my research.

'Shall we open our presents?' Marianne's face was lively with enthusiasm and my heart reached out towards her.

'I haven't ...' Libby's voice choked, her eyes brimming with tears.

'We didn't expect anything,' Marianne said, reassuringly. 'I want to *give* to you girls. I don't expect anything back.'

'I feel ...' she started again.

'Libby, it's fine,' I smiled. 'You're coming back to us and that's all that matters.' She swallowed away her misery, smiling although her eyes filled.

'Come on.' I stood up steadily and put my arms around her. She felt weak and tiny. Her strong, self-assured character was hidden beneath this scared, timid girl. Although sometimes Libby's arrogant personality would drive me mad, I couldn't wait to get her back.

We followed Marianne into the living room, where an array of presents had appeared that weren't there earlier. Sheepishly Marianne handed each of us one of the twenty-odd presents she'd bought us. My small gifts to them seemed feeble, but I couldn't say anything as I didn't want to make Libby feel worse.

We unwrapped our gifts: perfume, underwear, nightwear, slippers and other knick knacks that had been meticulously thought about. I couldn't believe the effort Marianne had made. How she'd spoilt us as if we were children again.

We enjoyed each other's company, relished the love between us, the unbreakable bond forged by the journey of life that we'd experienced together. There had been roads that were smooth, bumpy or damaged. We'd driven down the winding paths, circled the roundabouts and experienced more than one dead end, but still we'd kept going. The three of us, somehow, always made it through to our final destination.

The love that passed between us that morning was also passionate determination to protect each other. We were closer than we'd ever been before.

Silently I thanked Mum once again for bringing Marianne into our lives, regretting that I'd not allowed her in sooner, repentant that I'd missed years of her generous, tender heart. Warmth surrounded me as I imagined what we would look like to the outside world: a normal family (if there was such a thing), a happy, contented, worry-free family. How many other families looked this way on Christmas morning? The merriness of the festive season often concealed many cracks: problems consciously ignored. But it didn't feel as if we were hiding anything anymore. There was nothing to cover up. We'd accepted each other for who we were.

I felt lucky as I sat with two women whom I was proud to have in my life. Proud to say I loved them both deeply.

40

I didn't really want to alarm anyone, but the pains had increased and the intensity kept taking my breath away. June had arrived and I was saddened to see how the atmosphere was suddenly dampened by her presence. She said she would help Marianne in the kitchen, which I thought kind of her. Marianne had insisted she could manage, but I'd practically pushed June in there. I felt mean, as if I was locking them in a cage to fight out their differences. But it needed to be done. Whatever their issues it was time they sorted them out. I hoped we wouldn't find pieces of them in our Christmas dinner.

'Do you fancy going for a walk?' I asked Libby, who had cocooned herself on the sofa. I'd allowed her a shower and five minutes to get dressed, not wanting her out of my sight. She'd not argued, which I appreciated.

I'd read, or heard from one of my customers, that walking was good when in labour. If I was in labour (which I really didn't think I was; this was just a few Braxton Hicks) then a walk would help. 'You'll know when you're in labour,' was another comment that had been made to me several times. I didn't know if I was; so, did that mean I wasn't?

After we'd told Marianne and June we wouldn't be long, (Marianne eyes seemed to beg us not to go) we walked into the freezing cold air, our bodies protected by our thick winter coats. It was nice. I wrapped my arm in Libby's, my chunky robust limbs were huge compared to the thin bones Libby had become. I felt that if I squeezed too hard I would snap her arm in two.

'Do you miss Mum, Kat?' She asked.

'Every single day.' We'd not talked about Mum in a while, not like the way we used to, the way I'd tell Libby the stories I could remember. How we'd laugh at the way we were so similar to Mum: or in some aspects so different.

'I've let her down,' Libby said in a small voice.

'Don't you be silly, you absolutely have not. Mum would be so proud of you.'

'Proud of what?'

'She'd be proud that you're trying to do something about your life now.'

'I'm really sorry.'

'There's no need to be sorry. We will sort this out together.'

There was a silence between us as the wind gently blew across our faces. Her pale skin looked fragile. She'd washed her hair, allowing her long bob to hang around her thin face. She appeared to be fresher than she was last night, but still tiredness covered her frail features. But then I knew I also looked as if I could sleep for a week. I also felt it, and hoped these pains would back off; as I had no energy to give birth at the moment.

'I miss Mum,' Libby said. 'I know I don't remember much, but I miss her.'

'I know,' I said softly. 'I'm sorry she's not here with us.'

'I miss Dad too, do you?' Our walk had slowed to a stroll. Part of me wanted to set off into a run, so I could be as far away from that question as possible.

'In a small way,' I admitted, glancing away from her. But I could feel her eyes upon me as she waited for me to expand. 'He was hard work. Things were never the same once Mum left. I don't really think that the Dad I remember ever came back.'

'He was all I can remember,' Libby said. I wondered if it had been Dad's fault she'd gone down the drugs route. But I pushed the thought from my mind, not wanting to play the blame game.

'Don't you remember Lampford Hall?'

'Vaguely.' Libby shrugged. 'I remember bits but to be honest, most of it was a blur.'

'Marianne's been great though, hasn't she?' I changed the subject away from Dad.

'I'm so pleased you two are getting along now,' Libby admitted, smiling slightly.

'Me too.'

'I feel as if people keep leaving me.'

'I haven't left you.'

'No ... I mean, now that Calvin isn't here, it's like people I've truly loved get taken from me. I'm scared it's going to happen to you or Marianne. You're all I have.'

'I'm not going anywhere.'

'Calvin would have been disgusted with what I did last night,' she said, shaking her head. 'When I was seeing Alan, we were in a relationship, it didn't feel as bad. But last night was just sex. Calvin always said if we get to the point where we would sell our bodies ...' she shivered, as if remembering what she'd done, 'we must tell someone ... we must get help.'

'But you have done that.' I tried to encourage her not to go over bad memories.

'I was meant to shout for help before I slept about.'

'Lib, we're here now, so let's move on.'

'That's what Marianne said. She was so lovely this morning. Part of me wishes you would both be horrible then I wouldn't have to feel so guilty.'

'You need to stop worrying about the past. We are where we are,' I said, noting I should really take some of my own advice.

'Thank you,' she whispered.

'Thank you for coming to me.' Suddenly, pain grabbed at my stomach, stuck its teeth in and refused to let go. Abruptly I stopped walking and gripped at Libby's arms.

She glared at me, horrified. 'What's wrong?'

'I really don't want you to panic,' I said between gritted teeth, 'I think I'm in labour.'

'Oh shit,' Libby squealed. She was totally panicking. 'Oh, shit! Shit! Should I run back? Shit! Are the babies coming now?'

'Stay calm,' I mumbled, as I held her arm tight.

Once the pain had lessened, I made Libby walk a little further with me, although she'd gone a degree paler than she already was, if that was possible. She begged that we turn around. 'A few more steps won't do us any harm,' I told her, but she looked as if she might pass out. I tried to explain that I'd read walking is good, it helps the babies come along.

'But, they're coming?' Libby practically shrieked, clearly terrified. 'But you're early, we really need to get back. What if they pop out now? What if your waters break?'

She forced me to turn around, I was staying calm because I knew they wouldn't just pop out. I didn't want to sit in a hospital for hours (or days) on end; I wanted to be in and out. The twelve-minute walk back to the house (I can be precise because we were timing) allowed us to ensure I'd had three definite contractions. Four minutes apart. The pain was awful, overwhelming. I knew this could go on for days, or could suddenly stop. But the fact that the babies were trying to make an appearance three weeks early was particularly scary.

Libby ran upstairs to grab my maternity bag, which had been ready for weeks; well since week thirty-two, to be honest. I walked towards the kitchen but the raised voices from inside stopped me. The angry women were going at each other like dogs, snarling, sniping and whirling abuse. I was about to walk through the door to stop them, when I heard something that explained everything about their long-standing feud.

'I needed to see if Brian still wanted me.'

'He's no longer here and neither should you be.' Marianne's bitter tones were worlds away from her usual gentleness.

'You're jealous because you know Brian would have chosen me.'

'Jealous?' Marianne let out a laugh. 'If he was going to choose you, he'd have done it a long time ago. Your sister will be turning in her grave if she can see you now.'

'Don't you talk about—' June's voice was rising and my pain was increasing again, so I opened the door and went in. I saw the fear seizing them both, their quarrel forgotten as they rushed towards me. 'Come on, I'll take you to hospital,' June said.

I held up my hand, 'Were you having an affair with my dad?'

41

The midwife was an older lady, her quiet voice with its soft Scottish accent instantly making me feel at ease. 'We're going to check you,' she told me as I lay down, my body in a position that would allow her to examine me.

With my legs apart, her hands roaming somewhere below, I knew she'd done this many times before, but still she'd not done it to *me*. I tried to relax, tried to appreciate this was her job. I pushed my thoughts to something simple; the dinner I could have been having. All other thoughts seemed far too stressful. But, then I realised I was focusing on the tubes and other equipment that hung from the white walls. I thought about Dad when he was in ICU, how much technical paraphernalia had surrounded him, how little there was in this room compared to the number of machines that had been needed to help him.

'You're well on your way, dear; six centimetres. So, we'll get you comfortable and see how we get on.'

'Okay.' My poor response seemed pathetic and weak, but I couldn't say anything else. I wanted to ask her what that meant. I knew I had to reach ten centimetres, but how long would that take? She asked if I'd like some pain relief. 'Can't you knock me out?' I cried.

I tried not to panic. The pains had all merged into one: every inch of my stomach was in agony.

Yes, now I knew I was in labour.

My back felt bruised, as if my spine had been jumped on for hours. I had no idea where it started or where it ended. I breathed deeply as I'd seen people do on *One Born Every Minute* and other baby programmes I'd been glued too. The only thing I could keep in my head was, 'Don't panic'. If I was to panic the pain would rocket, apparently, but it couldn't get much worse than this … oh, no, I think I spoke too soon. The gas and air helped, slightly. It helped to mask the pain, the contractions increasing, reaching a peak then easing back off.

Marianne was at my side, holding my hand and softly giving me encouragement. When I'd interrupted her row with June, she'd not allowed June to answer my question, not allowed her to crush the blissful memories I'd had of Mum and Dad.

June and Libby were waiting outside. They'd been told to go home, but apparently, they'd not wanted to. I was secretly pleased, that Libby had somebody with her: I did have a slight thought that she'd try and break into a medical room to steal some unknown substances.

'She was seeing Dad, wasn't she?' I asked Marianne, as I squatted on my hands and knees, my head against the pillow. I couldn't get myself comfortable in any other way. My backside in the air can't have been a pretty sight, but little did I care.

'Let's worry about that later.' Marianne rubbed my hand.

I didn't want to worry about it later, I wanted to know all about it now. I let the next contraction take over my body, focusing on the breathing, gulping in the gas and air, tying to allow my body to naturally do as it needed to do.

'That's why she moved away, isn't it?'

'You need to concentrate.' Marianne was still rubbing my hand. 'Let's focus on the matter at hand here.'

I understood it probably wasn't the best time to dig up our family history, but it was giving me something else to think about other than the pain. I realised Marianne was right, though, I was only going to get angry which wouldn't help me at the moment.

The next hour or two – it could have been three or four to be honest – seemed to last for ever. I could hear screams from another room, a baby crying as it entered the world. Midwives rushed in and out of the room, my world becoming smaller as I focused on nothing else but allowing my babies to travel safely from my body.

It was happening. It was really happening.

'Push!' The encouragement came from the voices around me as I forced my lower body down through the pain, held onto the scream inside of me, my energy focused on getting the babies out. They needed to come out, I wanted them out.

I tried not to panic as we waited for the next contraction to take my body, guiding me to push my way through the agony, naturally following my body's lead. At one point I shouted, 'I can't!' wanting someone to make it stop. I told myself to focus: 'Look at everything you've been through. You can do this. Switch off. Focus.' I breathed deeply, listening to the voices around me:

'Come on – you can do this.'

'Gently push.'

'Good girl, Kat.'

'Nearly there, keep going.'

I followed the instructions, my body taking over, taking me through each stage, until a burning sensation below ripped through my body and a small cry echoed across the room.

'A baby girl,' the midwife announced, smiling. Marianne clapped, tears springing to her eyes. Another midwife carried the baby to me, allowing me to see her petite, screwed-up face. She was then whisked away from me and I wished I didn't have to do this again.

Six minutes later, the pain ripped through my body, taking me through the final push. The silence from my baby sent fear through my exhausted body. 'Another baby girl,' a voice said.

'Why's she not crying?' I heard my own voice say. Suddenly, I heard whimpers. The relief overwhelmed me. I was amazed at the impact those tiny cries already had on me; how much I wanted to hear them.

'She's fine. She was just having a good old nosey,' the midwife smiled.

'Oh, Kat, two gorgeous baby girls. Born on Christmas Day.' Marianne was holding one of my tiny babies, tears streaming down her face. 'Well done, sweetheart.' She kissed my forehead.

My fear, my anguish, all those other self-doubts seemed to vanish as the midwife placed one of my baby girls into my arms. Her tiny, squashed face was close to mine, her watery blue eyes trying to focus, blinking at the light as her tiny hands rested on her face. Marianne placed the other baby into my arms. Her little face was screwed into a frown, her tiny eyes were shut, not wanting to see this new world.

My heart felt as if it had exploded as I held them close to me, wrapped in white blankets, their lives in my hands. I kissed their tiny foreheads, breathing in their fragility.

'Welcome to the world, Poppy and Rosie.'

42

'Can I come in?' June was already halfway through the door when she asked me. I wanted to tell her, 'No'. No, it wasn't possible for me to see her.

Before Marianne had left late last night, I'd begged that she tell me what was going on. I could have left it until I was out of the hospital, but the desperate urge to find out the truth was tearing at me. I'd forced her to sit and tell me, or I would only ask June, and what lies might *she* tell me? Marianne had reluctantly taken a seat, saying, 'This isn't the time or place.' My babies snuggled next to me in their plastic cot, sleeping soundly after their first feed.

I told her, 'There's no better time.' Marianne had talked me through an enduring affair, between Dad and June. Apparently, Mum had found out about six months before her accident.

'He'd planned to leave your mum for her. He'd invested money into a business for them to start afresh down south.'

'In Devon?'

'Yes.' Marianne nodded. 'Anyway, when they were about to leave, June decided she didn't want to move, she didn't want that life. She wanted to make things work with Ernest.'

'I don't understand. I thought she and Ernest were really close.'

'From what your dad told me, Ernest couldn't have children so that caused a lot of problems for them. I think June thought she was going to step into your mum's shoes, but when your dad had arranged for them to move away, she'd panicked, because that would mean she wouldn't have been near you and Libby. Your dad explained there was no way your mum would have allowed you two to live with them. But that had obviously been June's intention.'

'I still don't understand why she moved away.'

'When your mum died, your dad blamed himself because your mum knew about the affair.'

'How did she know?'

'Your dad had an electrical company but he had to let it go. He'd financed another house—'

'In Devon?'

'In Devon.' Marianne nodded. 'Your mum looked through his business bank statements when she realised the business was in trouble. She could see he'd spent a fortune and obviously questioned him about it.'

'What did he say?'

'He tried to make excuses, but your mum knew.'

'Oh my God, poor Mum.'

'I know.' Marianne nodded. 'Apparently, your dad and June had planned on running a café together.'

'Dad running a cafe?'

'He said he was doing it for June.'

'So, when Mum died, why didn't they get together then?'

'Well, after the affair had stopped, your mum and dad decided they would try and work on their marriage. Your dad had to close the business. He did get another job, but the pressure of paying off all the debt caused them lots of problems. He tried to sell the business in Devon but he couldn't. Your mum was involved in the accident months later and your dad blamed himself. He thought this was God's way of punishing him. But believe me Kat, God doesn't punish in such harsh ways.'

'So where was June when this was going on?'

'Obviously she and your mum fell out. Your mum wanted nothing more to do with her.'

'Understandably!'

'Once your mum died, your dad couldn't move on. June was forcing herself into your home, but he didn't want to be with her any longer.'

'Do you think he felt guilty?'

'Yes, but I also think he realised that June didn't want him. She wanted you and Libby.' I shook my head as Marianne explained, unable to take this in. 'I think she thought your mum dying would allow her to have the best of both worlds. She could live her life with Ernest without him knowing anything about her life with your dad. Obviously when I came on the scene she didn't like it. She tried to push me out, but your dad told her that if she didn't move away and out of his life he would tell Ernest everything.'

'So that's why she moved to Devon?'

'Yes, because if you're dad had told Ernest, she'd have been left with nothing.'

'What a nightmare.' I shook my head, thinking my own life seemed a bed of roses compared to the mess June had caused. At least, Max hadn't slept with Libby.

'Yes, and that's the reason your dad went bankrupt. He'd used all his money on their project, so he transferred the contract into June's name so she could run it, but he'd lost everything here.'

'But it meant she would leave him alone.'

'Exactly.'

'He was struggling, he couldn't cope. He'd lost his job and the house. It was a huge mess.'

'But he would have left me and Libby?'

'I don't think they thought about it properly.'

'What?' I shook my head. 'They thought about it enough to set-up in Devon.'

'Your dad wasn't looking at the bigger picture. He loved June. He loved you girls. He thought you'd have the school breaks with him.' I didn't answer, not really wanting to confirm whether she'd made this up to make me feel better, or whether Dad had shared that information. 'He loved your mum, though. Very much.'

'Poor Mum,' I said again. 'I know I've said this before, but I really don't understand why you stayed with him.'

'When all this was going on, he needed me more than I can tell you. I couldn't walk away. Plus, I've told you I also needed you all.'

'Thank you.'

'Don't be silly. Now, you need to get some rest.' She was out of her chair before I could argue. She hugged me, kissed the babies and then left me to my own thoughts.

The last day we'd all been together at Lampford Hall, the way they'd hugged each other: to a child's eye it had been the perfect scene, but it had been Dad trying, desperately, to save his marriage.

***

As June sat on the chair next to my bed, her face pale and tired, her short, cropped hair slightly messy as if she'd not really sorted herself out, I waited for her to speak. She avoided my eyes as she stroked the babies' faces, asking me if they'd slept well. I nodded, not really wanting to get into a conversation with her about my babies.

'Marianne told me last night that she'd told you everything.' She seemed ashamed, embarrassed, her cheeks a darker shade of pink. I didn't answer her. 'I'm sorry, Kat, truly I am.'

'What did my mum think of it all?' I couldn't take the edge of bitterness off my voice.

'What do you mean?'

'Had you two sorted it out before she died?'

'No.' She shook her head regretfully. 'Every day I wish it had never happened.'

'I don't understand why you're back now. Did you think that now Ernest was dead you could come back into Dad's life?'

'No, not at all. I came back for you girls. I came back to see you—'

'That's not what you said to Marianne in the kitchen.'

'I was angry, she's been rude to me since I've arrived, I—'

'You're surprised?'

'No, but …' she stuttered. There was a tense silence between us, as she stared at my babies. 'Having cancer has changed my life. I realise what is important now. I thought about you every day, I wished so much I could turn back time.' She peered at me waiting for me to answer. Although I knew exactly what she meant, I didn't speak. 'All I ever wanted was my own children. Lanie allowed me to play a huge part as your aunty, but it wasn't enough. I wanted so much more.'

'So, you stole her husband?'

'It just happened between me and your dad. We were young. I was horrible, I was so focused on having my own little family. I'd made them both think they weren't right for each other.'

'How?'

'I don't know ... I'd say things to your mum about your dad and vice versa,' she shook her head, staring at her hands. 'I tried to make them not love each other.'

'That's awful.'

'I know. All I can say is I was young ... so young. If I could change things I would. I *so* would,' she said desperately, as she twisted her hands together. Another uncomfortable silence fell, which she clearly felt the need to fill. 'Once your dad purchased the house and business in Devon I panicked. The fantasy I'd made up in my head wasn't the reality. I've regretted the whole thing since.' A stray tear ran down her tired face. 'Your mum hated me so much. She banned me from seeing both of you girls. She knew it had all been about you two.'

'It all seems a bit dramatic just because Uncle Ernest couldn't have children. There are ways and means.'

'It wasn't that simple in those days. And Ernest didn't want to go down the adoption route. I became so focused on you both I wasn't thinking straight. When your mum died – I mean this from the bottom of my heart – I was devastated. I'd not had my chance to say sorry, or a chance to explain. I thought the best way forward would be to help your dad, but then Marianne came on the scene and he didn't want to know.'

'I can't believe you would be so vindictive,' I said, but for some reason I felt sorry for her, for this woman who'd made so many mistakes, whose life had been one long unhappy journey. She was shouting out for me to help. I could imagine Marianne telling me to be careful. I could hear my mum telling me not to waste my time.

'I've changed,' she sobbed.

'Really?'

'Yes. Marianne and I never really got along.'

'But you can understand why?'

'I totally understand why and she's right: I shouldn't have come back. I'm going to travel home tomorrow.'

There was a silence before I said, 'Maybe we can work through this.' It was as if my body was possessed; someone else was speaking for me.

'We can?' June's face brightened. 'I would really like that.'

'Would Mum, though?'

'I was very young and very stupid.'

I was unsure why it felt like the right thing to do. But it felt so wrong to send her packing, back to a place on her own. A place where she had no family. Although part of me thought I was probably letting Mum down, the other part knew she would understand.

As I thought about June's actions, I couldn't help but see that Libby too would have put her own needs first in a similar situation. June being the younger sister had looked up to Mum, wanting what she had, jealously propelling her to choose the wrong road. She was back for a reason. I couldn't turn her away. Something was telling me to allow her in.

June had been gone ten minutes when Clare and Henry arrived. I initially waited for Max to follow behind them, Gina hot on his heels, but luckily there was no sign of them. I was trying to sort myself out; I'd been told I'd be moving to the ward for the night. They'd told me they wanted me to stay for at least one night, maybe two, with the babies coming early – although they were perfectly healthy – but with there being two of them, they wanted to make sure I was okay. I wondered if they'd have said this if Max had been here with me, but I didn't ask. I was pleased I still had the privacy of my own room for now; but it was still stifling. The noises, the smell, the restrictions; I wanted to be at home. Or, at Marianne's home. I was secretly pleased I was staying there. The thought of travelling back to the flat on my own was scarier than I'd imagined.

Clare and Henry hugged both Poppy and Rosie, as they studied their little faces and comparing their noses, eyes, and bodies to Max's. I knew it was natural for them to do this, but it highlighted the fact that he wasn't here. It saddened me that I'd be raising them alone. But I fought my sadness of becoming a single mother when I hadn't wanted to become one at all, because the babies were perfect. They were small bundles that would bring so much pleasure to my life, I had to focus on this. They were my gift and I had to be thankful that they were here.

They were Mum's Christmas present to me, I'd thought, as I'd watched them sleep last night.

'So, I've scheduled all the work in the salon to be done in the first week of the New Year,' Clare told me, but she was still staring at Poppy. 'I was hoping to get it all done before you moved back into the flat.'

'That's fine,' I said, not wanting to talk about dates as if I had to officially sort out my life, right now, this minute.

'I'm hoping it will only take a week or so,' she continued. I nodded, again not committing to anything, or allowing myself to let her know I was apprehensive about bringing up the babies on my own.

I tried to make conversation, but there wasn't much I could say. I was tired; actually, I was exhausted. Henry didn't really say much, but he stared at both the babies as if he'd never actually seen one before. He was so in awe.

I felt sad that Max had chosen the path he had, not only for our lives but for his parents' lives too. I would never stop Max or his parents seeing the girls, but the whole family unit had been rocked before we'd even started, before we'd even had the chance to see if it would work. I had been planning on sitting down properly and talking to Max in the New Year before the babies arrived, but best-laid plans never seemed to work with me.

'We're really proud of you,' Clare told me, hugging me close. 'It will all be fine.' For some reason, I knew she was right. 'Please don't shout,' she said suddenly. 'But I felt he had to be here.'

They left the room – and Max entered.

43

Although I wanted to shout, 'Please leave,' I didn't. I held my tongue. I blinked back the salty tears and swallowed the lump that was blocking my throat.

He looked tired, his thick blond hair longer and unkempt, his weary face unshaven. If I didn't know any better I'd think he'd just completed one of the triathlons he so used to enjoy, but with the extra pounds he seemed to have gained I knew he'd not even stepped inside a gym lately.

'Hi,' he said, his hands uneasily clasped together. The confident, self-assured man I'd fallen in love with, stood like a small boy needing my reassurance.

'Hi,' was all I could say. What did he want from me? An open-armed welcome? Here's the champers? I sat down on the bed, which he seemed to take as permission to walk forward.

'So, how was it?'

'Awful.' I forced a smile.

'But you're okay?' He asked. I nodded.

'It's like King's Cross in here today.' A nurse entered the room, breaking the awkward tension. She busied herself with some sheets and towels, not even acknowledging Max; which pleased me. They sort-of knew my situation, because I'd told the midwife angrily mid-labour, when she'd asked where the father was. But her shift had finished hours ago. I hoped it wasn't the staffroom gossip. Surely there were more interesting patients than me.

'They are beautiful, aren't they?' she said to Max as she gazed at the babies. She then whisked around the room like a small whirlwind before leaving.

'She's right, they are beautiful,' Max said. 'Can I?' He held out his arms. 'Feel free, they *are* yours,' I wanted to say; but not only would that have sounded childish, it would also have sounded as if I were treating our babies like objects. So, I just nodded.

He was obviously unsure of what to do next. So, I lifted Rosie out for him to hold. Her tiny body rested in his arms. She was minute, a petite doll curled into a cosy position. She snuggled down and sighed loudly as if she knew that Max was her daddy. A tear rolled down his face, sliding down his masculine features; and my heart went out to him.

'I'm sorry, Kat. Really I'm sorry.'

I shrugged. Maybe I was still slightly high from the gas and air, but my anger for him had softened in this intense moment. As our daughter slept soundly in his arms, the turmoil that had been going on between us was diminished. I'm not saying forever. Explanations were needed. I needed some form of closure, but right now, I wanted to savour this time.

As I watched him stroke Rosie's soft skin, I realised I hadn't actually missed him. Maybe it was everything else going on around me: losing the salon and Libby's drama. But even that being the case, I hadn't needed him. It was only now as he cradled our daughter, as the reality of our situation was upon us, I knew we weren't meant to be, but the babies were.

I had enjoyed the first six months of our relationship, just as he had. I didn't want to take that away from us. I loved him. I wish we'd been able to make it work. But I was ready to accept that it wasn't going to happen.

The only thing that mattered at the moment, was the two little girls who had now come into our world.

The two little girls who were meant to be here.

44

We walked out into the cold air, Libby holding one baby's car seat, Marianne the other. My thick black coat was wrapped around my saggy body; a 'deflated balloon', was the only way I could describe my empty bump. Apparently, that would go in a few days. I hoped so. I thought about the celebrities who walked away from hospital looking fresh-faced and stick-thin. I'm a beauty therapist, obviously not practising at the moment, but it was still embedded in me to try and look my best at all times. It wasn't happening as we left the hospital. I was knackered, scruffy and I had dirty hair. I could have washed it in the hospital, but I was worried the babies would wake up. Then what would I do? I was trying to stay calm, knowing that women had babies every day, and they all had clean hair (or most of them did). I needed to figure out how to do all of this, without panicking.

There were all these other little worries flying through my mind. How would I know what they were crying for? Apparently, they had different cries for hunger, tiredness and wanting their nappies changing. How would I know which cry was for what? How often did I change their nappies? Again, I'd only just figured how to put the nappy on; yesterday, actually! It was quite scary to think of myself as a grown woman, a responsible adult who had no idea what she was doing.

We climbed into the car. I watched Libby's face. She was relishing her nieces. Marianne busied herself with the two car seats. Libby had to squeeze in and sit between them, as there was no way my backside would fit there.

As all this went on around me, I had to smile.

The year's events had once again turned my world upside down, but I knew and believed that everything happened for a reason. If this year meant that some relationships were broken, some could be mended and others were as solid as rock, then so be it.

My tiny girls were sleeping soundly in their car seats, dressed in snowsuits that were far too big for them, their faces relaxed, I knew that everything would be fine.

We would all be fine. We were all on a journey. We had to accept that life would throw obstacles at us to see if we could cope, to see how we would handle the barriers and walls that blocked us from moving forward.

As I watched Libby smiling, I knew we would knock down those barriers, climb those walls, we would keep going. We wouldn't stop, we would fight to survive. More than ever I would fight now; I had two little reasons that would not allow me to give up.

So, as we drove away from the hospital, our new family ready to jump those hurdles, I knew I was still in the midst of the chaos. I wondered if it would end; but if it didn't, I felt ready to swim, run and fly with whatever was thrown at me.

-THE END-

Acknowledgments

As always, a huge thank-you to Simon, Alexia and Gabriella for being my biggest fans and encouraging me to be the best I can be.

My family and friends who give me constant support and encouragement, you are the best.

Immense thanks to the late, Jenny Drewery, a wonderful editor, who I loved working with.

A massive thank-you to all my readers and to everyone who has sent me encouraging messages, I'm eternally grateful for your support.

To Betsy and the team at Bombshell Books, I can't even begin to thank you for your belief in me. You have changed my world.